CHAINED SOUL

EVA CHASE

BOUND TO THE FAE

Chained Soul

Book 8 in the Bound to the Fae series

First Digital Edition, 2021

Cover design: Yocla Book Cover Design

Ebook ISBN: 978-1-990338-18-2

Paperback ISBN: 978-1-990338-17-5

1

Talia

The Unseelie woman stands stooped in front of me, her stance rigid and her skin tinged blue. She's the seventh winter fae I've healed in the week and a half since I escaped the Murk and made it back to the Mists, but somehow the process still feels different.

Not every part of that difference is necessarily bad. My tears well up faster these days, taking almost no effort at all. But that's because I can't help thinking about the several cursed fae I *couldn't* save while I was trapped by the rat shifters in the human world. The Unseelie men and women who waited, hoping for my return, while the curse's icy claws gripped them tighter and tighter until their bodies shut down completely.

As I brush my tear-damp fingers over the woman's cheek, her wan face lights up with relief. I wish I could feel the same thing. Even knowing that I'm saving her life, that no more lives need to be lost right now, I can't help remembering the worst of the things I learned while the Murk held me.

This curse is their doing. Their king, Orion, has managed to infect all of the Mists with the horrible magic of the false Heart he created. And every bit of the fear and distress his curse provokes has been flowing out of the Mists to add to the Murk Heart's power. The thought of its erratic orange glow sends a shudder down my spine.

I know how I'm connected to the curse and the Murk now. I escaped them in some ways, but in others, I'm still tied to Orion and his magic. I can't let the curse overcome the fae around me—that would only add to the distress that fuels his Heart—but with every healing I carry out, they rely on me more. Which means if Orion manages to tear me away from them again, they'd *hurt* even more.

The woman beams at me, the frost fading from her hair, and I manage to smile back at her. I can't think about all those things now. Orion *won't* tear me away from my home again—my mates are taking every step to ensure that's not possible.

Whether he brings his Murk forces here to attempt to tear all of us to pieces is a totally different consideration.

Which is why, when I step back from the woman and her mate helps her walk back to their carriage with the few flock folk who came along to witness the healing, I have to brace myself for a different sort of confrontation. When the cursed woman arrived, we'd already been preparing for a meeting of all the arch-lords in the border castle that's become my real home between the winter and summer realms.

They'll have delayed, waiting for me to return, but I'm not looking forward to another of these conversations that involve at least as much arguing as planning.

Corwin and a couple of his coterie members accompanied me to the spot by the Heart of the Mists where I always offer my cure. They stand poised in a half-circle around me like a protective detail. It seems unlikely that the Murk would spring at me right here, with the rhythmic pulse of the Heart's energy washing over me from just a few feet away, but the rat shifters did kidnap me from one of the domains by the Heart before. No one's taking the slightest chance with my safety now.

I turn to face the Heart for a moment, soaking in the brilliant glow that feels like the warmest beams of sunlight. My hand reaches automatically to my opposite arm, where a new bronze bracelet grips my wrist. August tied the magic in it to the matching bracelet he gave my brother when we made a quick trip to check in on him after my return. Jamie's okay. I'm okay. How can I ask for more?

I made it through Orion's cruel treatment. I have the tools to defend myself as well as I can. And the true Heart shines on me in ways he never guessed. Weirdly, I feel closer to it now that I know it didn't give me all my powers.

The bits of magic I can wield used to seem like they might be random chance, a fluke of nature. But really, Orion arranged for my power to cure and my ability to form a soul-twined bond. And even though I have the Murk's horrible influence twisted all through me, the Heart of the Mists welcomed me and offered me some of its own power. Without the true names I can call on in some small way, I might not have made it this far.

When I set off for the castle, Corwin comes up beside me, Zelpha and Olander keeping their positions ahead and behind us. My soul-twined mate slips his hand around mine.

It will get easier again, he says through our inner connection. *Healing the curse, I mean. You're still recovering.*

My mouth twists. *I don't think I'll ever be able to stop thinking about how the Murk have used me until the threat is over and the curse is ended. At least your colleagues decided to trust me enough to let me keep curing people instead of leaving them to die.*

That was one of the earlier arguments after I got back, out of concern that the Murk might have worked some surreptitious evil into the cure itself. But the winter arch-lords quickly decided that some unknown harm was less of a problem than their people literally dying in front of them.

I suspect their decision was helped along by the fact that the arch-lord who's been most opposed to my involvement with her people, Laoni, is going to need a second cure herself any day now.

As we come up on the winter entrance to the castle, a wave of weariness sweeps through me. I stop for a moment to gather myself and restrain a yawn.

Are you all right, my soul? Corwin asks, worry

furrowing his brow. *You've seemed more tired than usual today. Was your sleep interrupted?*

A little, I admit. I rarely have dreams of my initial captivity among the summer fae anymore, but since my return, images of the things I saw among the Murk have haunted my sleep. The steel cage Orion tossed me into. The pain that seared through my mind when he forced me to respond to his interrogation.

And also violence dealt to the Murk by the fae I consider my own. Every few nights, I find myself back in the sewer orphanage, watching several wolfish warriors tear apart Murk toddlers like bloody dolls.

Not all the crimes committed have been on the Murk's side.

I *have* been feeling especially worn down the past few days, for no reason I can point to. Maybe it's just taken some time for the weight of everything I've discovered to catch up with me after the initial relief of being home. I've hidden it from Corwin's awareness of me as well as I can because he has enough other things to worry about, and me being a bit tired is hardly comparable to an impending war. Today I just want to crawl back into bed and sleep for the rest of the day, though.

I'll take a nap after this meeting, I tell Corwin, rolling my shoulders to gather my strength, and limp on into our castle.

The rest of the arch-lords, both the four others of winter and the three of summer, are already gathered around the long meeting table in a room in the center of the castle. Several cadre and coterie members stand poised along the walls. I take a seat with Corwin at my left at the head of the table and Sylas at my right. Whitt, who's poised with August behind his lord, reaches to give my hair a playfully affectionate tug, as if just to remind me that they're all here for me.

"All right," Laoni says briskly, as if she's more in charge here than anyone else. "Now we can get on with things. The first order of business…" She fixes her piercing gaze on me. "Have you sensed any sign of the Murk's influence acting on you since our last meeting?"

Of course that's her first priority. "No," I say, keeping my voice even. "If I had, you'd already know about it."

Celia, the most senior of the summer arch-lords, clears her throat. "Well, then, let's discuss the progress we've made in our efforts at locating this 'refuge' where their king is hiding as well as the other Murk colonies. The scouting parties under my cadre's supervision haven't discovered any larger habitations of the vermin yet, although they did come across a building in Oslo that appeared recently vacated of rats. What about the rest of you?"

I'm tired enough that I can't stop my mind from drifting as the other arch-lords give their reports, snapping back to attention when one or another asks for my opinion on a specific observation they've made. That's why I'm joining this meeting at all when no one else's mates are present—I'm the only one with direct knowledge of the Murk's current status and habits. But no one seems to have encountered much of the enemy at all.

"They must realize that I'll have told you everything I

learned as soon as I got back to you," I say after all of the arch-lords are finished. "They're laying low because they know how thoroughly you'll be searching." But that doesn't mean the Murk aren't working just as hard on their war efforts as before. Orion's people were accomplishing plenty just within their underground home of abandoned subway stations.

"They're still attempting to spy on us," Uzziah mutters. The dour winter arch-lord scowls. "One of the patrols reporting to me caught a rat near the fringes last night and dealt with it as appropriate."

He means they killed it. My stomach knots, and I sit up in my chair a little straighter. My mind darts to the story Madoc told me about his parents, brutally slaughtered simply for daring to try to make a life for themselves and their son on the fringes of the Unseelie realm.

A protest rises in my throat, but I'm not sure what to say. I've already appealed to the fae around me that they shouldn't assume every rat shifter they come across is out to harm us, but at the first suggestion that I had sympathy for any of the Murk, even my mates tensed. Laoni accused me of being brainwashed by them.

It took another few days and several spells and conversations before they let me rejoin the meetings afterward, and even now, only Corwin and Sylas seem to understand my concerns. If I'm going to get the agreement of enough of the others to swing the balance toward a different policy, I know I have to approach it from a more practical rather than emotional angle.

Madoc, the Murk man who helped me escape his king, hoped that by helping me he'd give me the opportunity to push back against the fae of the seasons' hatred of the Murk, to encourage them to open some kind of dialogue so that the conflict might not come to outright war. So far, I've failed in that. But then, even Madoc made it clear he knew it was a long shot.

Mostly he helped me escape because he believed saving me from a fate worse than death was more important than his loyalty to his king. And that right there is how I know not all the Murk are spiteful villains.

"Did the patrol try to question the Murk they found?" I ask.

Uzziah turns his scowl toward me. "What do you mean?"

"What I said. Did they try to question the Murk and see if they could find out anything about what the rats are planning now, or did they go straight to killing? We need to learn everything we can, don't we? And they'll know more about what their own people are up to than anyone here does, including me."

Uzziah's scowl deepens. He probably suspects I'm concerned about more than just uncovering the Murk's schemes, but he can suspect all he wants. He can't argue with what I've actually said.

Not much, anyway. Celia gives it a shot. "We've already seen how quick the Murk are to end their own lives rather than risk giving anything away—and how much magic they can wield if they're given a chance to. When it isn't likely we'd get anything out of them anyway, it seems safer to simply dispose of them before they have a chance to attack our own people."

"Everyone should be prepared for their magic now," I say. "And when it's a patrol of several of you against one or two of them, I can't see how they'd get away with much. When we're not having much success with our own searches, shouldn't we at least *try* to get some information from them?"

Or to make sure they're even part of the enemy forces and not just random fae passing by, I think but don't say.

Sylas leans forward. "I agree with Talia. It's worth the risk for the chance that they'll give away something useful. We can't win a war by avoiding all danger to ourselves."

"Even if they told us something, we couldn't trust it to be true," Laoni says. "That false Heart of theirs obviously doesn't take issue with lying."

"Then we discuss what they do say and decide for ourselves how to proceed," Donovan speaks up. "We can't discuss it at all if we don't have the information."

Corwin nods. "Agreed. I've already instructed my own patrols to question any intruders as well as they can."

Terisse, who seems to have come around to Corwin's side somewhat after long supporting Laoni, inclines her head too. "I think that's reasonable. We've been acting in anger, wanting to destroy them, when we must keep our heads cool and handle the problem rationally. They've been counting on manipulating us through our emotions all along."

"All right," Laoni grumbles, and Uzziah sighs but nods. Celia grimaces a bit but offers her own acceptance.

I wouldn't be surprised if the orders they give still encourage the patrols under their watch to switch to violence with little provocation, but maybe I've managed to soften the viciousness a little.

The rest of the conversation doesn't have much to do with me. When we all get up at the end of the meeting, I have to suppress another yawn. I definitely need that nap. But first I hang back with my mates as our guests head out of the room in the directions of their own realms.

August tugs me against him from behind and presses a kiss to the top of my head. "You spoke well," he says.

"Only because I didn't say half of what I wanted to," I mutter, and pause. "Do you think there's any real chance that we could work toward finding some sort of common ground with the Murk?"

I catch a flicker of skepticism through my bond with Corwin that echoes the expressions on my other mates' faces.

"I'm still not convinced there *is* much of a common ground to be found," Whitt says, leaning against the table. "Yes, that one rat helped you get free, but there was plenty of self-interest in that gesture in the grand scheme of things. He's expecting you to help the Murk in return—as you are."

"He knew it might not work, and he was risking his life going against Orion," I protest.

Corwin rests his hand on my shoulder. "What I've seen in your mind of your interactions with Madoc appear genuine, but he's an admitted expert at illusions. I don't think it's wise to trust any of the Murk without further proof, especially when we have plenty of proof that so many of them want to destroy us all."

My mind feels too bleary for me to come up with a coherent argument to that point. Maybe there isn't one; maybe he's right. I just can't shake off the horror of the scenes I saw, the ways the Seelie and Unseelie have fanned the flames of the Murk's hatred by treating them like, well, vermin.

"We'll attempt to talk rather than do battle where we can," Sylas says in his reassuringly steady baritone. "We simply have to be more wary than ever of the threat they pose."

"I know." I exhale slowly, and a yawn finally stretches my jaw before I can hold it back.

August nudges me toward the doorway. "Get some rest. You've been spreading yourself thin."

"I'm all right," I say, but as I take the first few uneven steps past the table, a rush of dizziness washes over me. I sway, snatching at the nearest chair for balance, and my stomach flips over with a twinge of queasiness.

Corwin is at my side in an instant. As he peers into my eyes, a quiver of anxiety pierces my heart. What if I'm not just tired—what if something's wrong with me?

But he leans a little closer with an intake of breath, and when he pulls back so I can see his face clearly again, the smile that's appeared there is nothing short of dazzling.

"My soul," he says in a voice soft with awe, "it's no wonder you're feeling out of sorts. It must have only just taken root—you're with child."

2

Madoc

he sentry reaches me just as I've emerged from my private room. "Orion wants you," she says, her tail twitching nervously, and darts on down the shadowed tunnel.

I was heading to the throne room to check in with my king anyway, but the fact that he's specifically called for me, and this early in the day, sends a ripple of tension through my body. Willing my muscles to loosen, I set off to find out what news he has to share.

The everyday work of the Refuge carries on around me. I don't catch any excited murmurs or notice any unusual movement in the same direction I'm heading.

If Orion had somehow gotten Talia back into his clutches, *that* news would already be buzzing through the Refuge, wouldn't it?

I tell myself as much, but I can't help bracing for the worst as I step through the throne room's broad doorway, controlling my reaction in case I come face to face with the woman Orion considers his "pet" back in a cage. When I see only my king pacing the dais, no one else around other than a couple of his other knights lounging nearby and a few petitioners lingering by the walls waiting to be heard, relief washes over me. It doesn't wipe away all of my apprehension, though.

There are other horrible developments I could encounter here. For example, Orion might have discovered proof that I'm the one who allowed Talia to flee the Refuge in the first place.

As I approach the dais, Orion keeps pacing, his tail lashing from side to side and a manic gleam in his yellow eyes that puts me even more on the alert. The other knights are keeping casual poses, but they watch our king with subtle wariness.

In the two weeks since Talia's disappearance, with what he's rightly assumed was the help of at least one of his subjects, Orion's temper has been even more unpredictable than usual. To reach him, I have to walk over fresh blood stains on the floor from the servant he dispatched yesterday for not having quite a fast enough answer when questioned about Talia's escape.

So far not just that one but five others of my fellow Murk have died instead of me for my crime. With a lot of blood spilled in the process too, although Orion's torture didn't convince any of them to own up to opening Talia's cage or offering her tools. I didn't point at any of them, but the guilt weighs on me almost as heavily as if I had.

I'd have owned up to my part and accepted my punishment if I didn't think life would be so much worse for all the rest of our people without me here to be a voice of reason if Talia convinces the fae of the seasons to make overtures of peace.

Of course, that *if* is seeming increasingly unlikely. As far as I know, we haven't received any sort of message from the Mists in those two weeks. The Seelie and Unseelie squadrons we've observed prowling through the human world have looked much more menacing than friendly.

Maybe it's overly optimistic to expect Talia to sway any of the fae of the seasons out of millennia of prejudice and animosity. Maybe she never intended to speak up for us at all. It could be that all her claims of caring about the atrocities the other fae have carried out against us were a trick of her own, designed to win my sympathies so that I'd end up helping her.

My experience with the world has left me jaded enough that I've entertained the thought for a few minutes here and there. My sense of the woman who convinced me to take her side against my king has faded over the days without her presence. Can I really be so sure she was as genuine as I thought at the time?

But then I remember her retching as she came out of the vaulted memory of the orphanage slaughter, the defiant tremor in her voice when she told me she was willing to give the Murk the benefit of the doubt—but I should extend the same to the fae of the Mists in turn. She didn't think she was winning me over. She thought I'd be angry that she was daring to speak honestly about her feelings.

And even if she had been manipulating me, would she really have deserved the torment Orion had planned for her?

No. I did what was right, even if my king wouldn't see it that way. She'll have needed time to recover and to persuade the other fae. Even her mates will probably find the idea of associating with any of the Murk a difficult pill to swallow. I can't criticize her for not making it happen faster. How much progress have *I* made toward preparing my people for the possibility of negotiating a truce rather than waging war?

None at all.

I come to a halt at the base of the dais near the throne, peering up at Orion. "I was already on my way here when I heard your call. What do you need?"

Orion continues his restless trek back and forth across the platform for a few more iterations before he finally stops and turns toward me. He runs his thumb over his lips. His claws are out, and he draws a thin line that beads with blood along his mouth without seeming to notice it. Or maybe he does, and he enjoys the sensation. It's hard to tell with Orion at the best of times, which are definitely not now.

"That Bren," he says in his coolly offhand way. "I've been thinking. He made quite the disruption while we were settling my pet in. Could there have been an ulterior motive? Have you seen any reason to be suspicious of him?"

I carefully avoid mentioning that Bren didn't cause the disruption he was involved in anywhere near as much as a couple of Orion's lackeys set it in motion and Orion himself fanned the flames. I doubt that the young fae wanted to end up fighting to the death with one of his colleagues, even if he's happy with the reward he earned.

A memory flickers through my mind—harsh breaths rushing from my lungs, limbs striking out to claw and snap, a fist hitting me in the throat so hard a hint of that ache remains now, even decades later. I resist the urge to touch the spot. Orion will know what I'm thinking about.

"Nothing I've seen from him has made me suspect he was helping her," I say. "Do you think more of our people were involved than those you've already dealt with? I'd imagine by now the problem is solved."

And you can stop slaughtering your own people out of nothing but paranoia and the sadistic enjoyment of watching them beg.

How had it taken me so long to see just how toxic Orion's leadership is? How he breaks us as often as he builds us up? And what he's building is a community in his image, far too close to the vicious vermin the other fae make us out to be for my comfort.

After I went through so much to earn my place in his inner circle, I never let myself look at the reality all that closely. I let myself believe this was the only way and that it would be better once we'd won back our home.

Now, with Talia's words in the back of my head and clearer eyes, I can see that's not true. Orion will always be as he is: a man who could gather enough power to take on the fae of the Mists and who delights in the suffering that power can bring as much as he does the hope. Possibly more in the suffering.

My king lets out a huff of breath. "I haven't gotten concrete acknowledgement from any of the traitors. Maybe I've got the bastard—or bastards—that the girl twisted around her finger somehow, but maybe I haven't. We all need to stay on guard." He shakes a bony finger at me.

I dip my head. "Of course. I've been keeping my eyes peeled for any sign of rebellion. If I catch any, I'll obviously bring the perpetrator straight to you. So far, from what I've seen, everyone's hard at work preparing for the next steps in the war."

I was hoping that statement might prompt Orion to comment on what those next steps will be now that his original plan of using Talia in our initial offense has been foiled. Instead, he wanders away from me, his gaze going distant. His Heart's orange glow dances on the white spikes of his hair, turning them into flames.

"We'll have the Mists," he mutters. "We'll crush all of them, even the little girl who'd rather be among those monsters than with us."

I decide to prompt a little more overtly. "How soon do you expect we'll move on the Mists? Are there any other supplies you'd like me to have our people and the other colonies gathering or making?"

Orion shakes his head. "Everything can proceed as it is. My pet's escape changes things a little, but that only means we'll have to wait a short while longer before the time is ripe for our attack."

He spins abruptly toward me with another wave of his finger. "I've set that in motion—I've just sent someone to press the trigger. It should start to kick in soon. I want you to go back to your former duties, watching over the girl and the fae around her in the Mists. You may need to be there for some time, so take a day or two to prepare accordingly. You can report back as the situation evolves. We want to be ready to strike as soon as they're at their most vulnerable."

A chill creeps through my chest. What has he triggered? "Have you launched some early attack already?" I venture.

A sharp chuckle tumbles out of Orion. "In a way. You will need to be more cautious than ever before. They're patrolling the fringelands much more avidly these days. There've already been a couple of men who haven't made it back. But with your skills, I'm sure you can manage."

"I've always been able to dodge the wolves and ravens before, even coming into the arch-lords' domains," I say. "I'm not worried about that. But what exactly do you want me to be watching for? Is there some sign I should anticipate?"

Orion laughs again and goes back to his pacing. "I want those pricks totally wrecked before we attack. Carved up on the inside before we slice into them from the outside. Carving *her* up in front of them would have done the job nice and quick, but this way should be equally effective, if slower." He swings around toward me, his eyes even brighter than before. "The best word of advice I can give you, Madoc, is always have at least one backup plan."

3

Talia

I hadn't thought my mates could get more protective than they already were. It turns out I was wrong.

"You really didn't need to do this," I tell August as he sets a tray with a full, extravagant lunch on my lap where I'm sitting up in bed. "I'm already feeling better. I could have walked down to the dining room no problem."

August tucks himself next to me against the pillows propped along the headboard and kisses the side of my forehead. "But it was even easier for me to bring the food up to you. There's no reason you shouldn't get to relax."

I'm a little afraid he's going to start trying to spoon-feed me next. I grab the spoon before he can attempt to and dig it into the thick stew, which gives off a meaty smell laced with cinnamon and cloves. It makes my mouth water even though my stomach is still a bit queasy.

The little chunks of meat and vegetables practically melt in my mouth. I close my eyes, enjoying the flavor, but then open them again to give August a pointed look. "It's very sweet of you, but I don't think it'll be good for me if I do nothing except lie in bed for the next nine months."

"I know." He nuzzles my hair and slips his hand across my waist to give my belly a gentle stroke. "But you're only just getting used to the physical changes. You can give yourself a break and let me look after you for a little while."

I'm so early on that there's no outward sign of the life that's growing inside me. It's definitely had an impact internally. For the past few days, waves of fatigue have continued to hit me at random moments, and I've been sleeping more than usual in general. The nausea comes and goes. It's never gotten too bad, other than yesterday when the smell of frying eggs had me running out of the kitchen on the verge of vomiting.

I'm pretty sure August has since scoured every trace of egg from the entire castle.

But even in my frequently tired state, there's a giddy energy to my spirits. I haven't given much thought to having children with my mates before, other than avoiding it happening by abstaining when I'm fertile. There's been so much going on in our lives that's put all of us in danger, it's hardly seemed like the right time to consider starting a larger family. Now that it's happened, though, a smile immediately springs to my mouth every time I imagine bringing a baby into the world that's partly me and partly one of my men.

I was with all four of them during our urgent interlude right after I escaped the Murk. There'll be no way of knowing which is the father until the baby's born, although my mates have said they might be able to tell whether it'll be Seelie or Unseelie by my scent as it grows. None of them seems particularly bothered by the fact that the child might not be genetically theirs. I can already tell that whoever this baby owes its heritage to most closely, it'll have not one but four devoted fathers watching over it.

Just like I have all four of those men watching over me right now.

As I cuddle next to August's brawny frame and get on with devouring the stew as well as the buttered roll, sugared berries, and lemon tart he's brought me, Sylas strides into the room. A soft gleam comes into his mismatched eyes as soon as they settle on me, sparking a flutter of warmth in my chest. The Seelie lord has always been kind to me, and I've never doubted how much he loves me from the first moment he told me he did, but there's a new quality to his affection that gives me an even cozier sensation.

Is it like this in human families too? I was only four years old when Jamie was born, so I don't have any clear memories of how Dad might have treated Mom differently when she was pregnant. And maybe it'd be different with a first child compared to the second.

The fae don't have children easily. I know it's

particularly special to them to have one on the way, more than I can fully understand even with the direct access I have to Corwin's joyful reactions.

Sylas comes over and leans past August to give me a quick kiss. "You're well?" he asks as he draws back.

"I'd have a hard time not being well with all the coddling I'm getting," I say, raising my eyebrows.

He chuckles, but a hint of a shadow crosses his expression. "Have you felt anything unusual at all— different today from the other days?"

I shake my head, frowning. "No, not that I've noticed. Why?"

Sylas exhales with relief, and his smile returns. "One of our patrols caught a Murk spy last night. She'd made it past the fringelands—we're not sure exactly how long she's been lurking around. They managed to subdue her and have brought her to Hearth-by-the-Heart for questioning, but so far we haven't gotten anything out of her. I just wanted to be sure, knowing one of them has been on the loose within the Mists."

A twinge of my own protectiveness runs through my gut, and my hand moves to my belly automatically. I was ready to do whatever I could to stop the war and defend the place I call home as it was, but now—now I feel like I could knock aside trees and blast down walls if that's what it takes to make sure the new life inside me stays safe.

From here on, it's not just about my mates and the rest of the fae. We're growing our family. I *can't* let this war touch that.

Sylas catches my defensive response. "We aren't

holding the woman anywhere near this castle—or Hearth-by-the-Heart's castle either. She'll be kept at a careful distance from the entire pack and especially you."

"Okay." I let out my breath, but my appetite has faded. It's an uncomfortable feeling, both being glad that Sylas's warriors held themselves back from outright slaughtering the Murk woman on sight and unnerved by the thought of her existing anywhere near me. "Are you sure she's working with Orion?"

Sylas nods. "She's made no attempt to deny it, and she was using the same sorts of illusion spells we've seen from the others."

The illusion spells Madoc might very well have taught them, or at least helped perfect their strategies for. My stomach twists a little more. "I'll let you know if anything changes, but I really am totally fine right now."

"Then I'll leave you to your meal." The Seelie arch-lord gives me one last tender glance and heads out.

I eat a little more of the stew and some berries, but I find I'm too unsettled now to gulp down the entire feast. Thankfully, August doesn't take offense.

"The tart will be just as enjoyable later on if you want it then," he says, leaving its small plate on the side table. "And let me know as soon as you're at all hungry again."

I'd ask him if next he's going to set up a bell so I can ring for him, but I suspect he might actually do that if I gave him the idea. I stretch my arms over my head and wiggle my legs beneath the covers. "I think I've done enough resting. You can't argue with me getting some fresh air, can you?"

"You do whatever makes you happy, Sweetness," August says. "Just don't leave the castle unless you've got company."

"I know, I know." I don't actually mind *that* precaution, considering I have been kidnapped from under my mates' noses once.

August bustles out to return the dishes to the kitchen. I'm just sliding off the bed when Corwin's and Whitt's voices reach me from the hall outside. Corwin has been keeping a wall partly raised against our connection so I'm not bombarded with impressions from his often stressful preparations for war, but a flicker of his apprehension touches me now as their words become clearer.

"—don't think this is the best time for that kind of experiment," he's saying.

"It's the perfect time," Whitt retorts. "Anything we can do to improve our chances, we have to jump on as quickly as possible. It isn't as if it'll hurt her." He sounds offended that Corwin would even imply that anything he'd suggest might harm me.

"Even involving her in any of this..." Corwin trails off as they come up on the doorway. They both come in with an air that's both tense and vaguely sheepish, as if they're embarrassed to realize I must have heard them arguing.

"What's going on?" I ask. "What am I maybe getting involved in?"

Corwin catches my eye with a tendril of fondness mixed with resignation. He knows that I'm not going to back away from the opportunity to help, no matter how much he'd like to shield me from the harsher parts of the conflict.

Whitt gives me one of his typical crooked grins, but the good humor in it doesn't quite reach his ocean-blue eyes. No matter what he said to Corwin, he's hesitant about asking anything of me too.

"I had an idea," he says. "A way we might be able to more easily track down the Murk or be alerted if they come into the Mists."

I perk up immediately. Searching for Murk presence by scanning for traces of their magic hasn't been easy—the fact that the woman Sylas's patrol caught made it out of the fringelands can attest to that. Finding their colonies in the human world has been even harder. If we had a way to locate Orion and his Refuge, deal with him directly... that would end the war right there, wouldn't it?

"That's wonderful," I say. "What's the idea?"

Whitt and Corwin exchange a glance. Whitt goes on, his voice softening. "I got the idea after Corwin noticed your... current state the other day." His eyes twinkle at the mention of my pregnancy. "We can scent the new life energy forming inside you through its presence in your blood. But that isn't the *only* energy you have running through you. The Murk king used a lot of magic to shape you, to make it so that your blood and tears could heal our curse and your soul could bind with Corwin's."

I resist the urge to hug myself at the reminder. "I know. How does that fit in to your plan, though?"

"Like can call to like. I suspect that with a tiny sample of your blood—or perhaps even something as small as a bit of skin or hair—we could create a tracking spell by having the Murk influence in your blood reach out to any of the rats present within the spell's range."

The thought that my body contains so much Murk "influence" that a spell like that would work makes my skin crawl. But I can understand what Whitt's saying. And it *wouldn't* hurt me at all. Corwin was only trying to spare me the pressure of thinking about it.

I might be more tired than usual, but I'm not going to fall apart, I say to him gently through our bond. *I still want to contribute everything I can.*

Of course you do. I just—

A wordless surge of emotion passes to me, but I know him well enough to understand his uneasiness. He thought he was going to have a child once before, only to discover the woman he'd been with was lying to him. He has no fears that I've deceived him in any way, but as far as I know, he's the only one of my mates who's previously had the possibility of a child and then lost it. Even when he's aware the baby might not be his, genetically speaking, it makes sense that he'd have the most trouble reining in his protective impulses.

It's okay, I say, sending him the impression of an embrace. *Just remember that I'll feel worse if I'm left in the dark or if something bad happens that I could have helped prevent but didn't get the chance to.*

As he inclines his head with an apologetic grimace, I focus back on Whitt. "I don't see why we shouldn't at least try it. What do you need from me right now?"

"We have the means for an easy test," the strategist

says. "I believe Sylas told you about the Murk woman we captured? She's being held on the outskirts of the domain. With a drop of your blood, I can cast the spell and we can see if it'll lead us to her."

That sounds simple enough. I hold out my hand, and Whitt takes it, dipping his head to brush a kiss to my knuckles in thank you.

He produces a small glass disc from his pocket and murmurs a quick word to split the skin of my forefinger. The second a drop of blood wells up, he presses it to the middle of the disc. Then he closes the tiny cut with another intoned true name. I barely feel the slight sting before it's over.

"All right." Whitt studies the blotch of blood on the disc with obvious concentration. Gathering himself, he closes his eyes and mutters several more syllables under his breath that are beyond my comprehension. When he looks at me again, his expression has lit with hope. "I obviously haven't had the opportunity to try the spell out yet, but I think that should work."

I guess he's been working on the idea for the past few days, not wanting to disturb me with the request until he had an easy way to perform a trial run. Now that the trial is underway, an unexpectedly eager sense of anticipation shivers through me.

When my mates turn toward the door, I move to pull on my boots, the brace fitting snuggly around my warped foot. "I want to come with you—I want to see if it works."

Corwin stiffens. "We can't be sure the rat won't attack you if she gets you in her sights."

I give him a baleful look. "Haven't Sylas's warriors restrained her better than that? If she could attack *anyone*, I have to think she'd be doing it already."

Whitt rubs his mouth, his gaze flicking from me to the disc and back. "I can't say I love the idea of you getting all that close to her, but I don't see how it'd hurt for you to come at least far enough to be sure the spell is effective. The two of us will be there to defend you if need be."

We both look at Corwin, who sighs and grazes his fingers over my cheek. "If you must, my soul. I suppose I should know better than to try to rein you in."

"I'm just barely starting to be pregnant, not a total invalid," I remind him, and peer at the ruddy blotch. "Is it supposed to do anything?"

A smile curls Whitt's lips. "It already is. Look there." He points to the edge of the smear. It's vaguely circular and fairly even all around—but that one edge protrudes just a little farther. As I watch closely, it creeps a tiny bit more toward the edge of the disc.

Even after all the fae magic I've seen before, it's kind of amazing. A little laugh spills out of me. "Wow. Is that the *right* direction?"

"I don't actually know," Whitt says with obvious amusement. "I asked Sylas not to tell me where they set up the holding cell so that I'd be able to run this experiment if you agreed. If I know where we're supposed to be heading, I might accidentally steer the spell. Why don't we go find out?"

The three of us hurry through the castle, our pace only slowed by my limp. Once we've come out the front door,

Whitt studies the disc again and motions to the right, toward the field that leads to the northern forests.

As we walk on, I take peeks at the bloody blotch. The edge that protruded before is pointing even more obviously in the direction we're going. Whitt tests it by turning the disc in his hand, and the original bulge contracts while another forms, aimed at the path we were already following.

In the shadows between the trees, Corwin's apprehension wavers from him into me through our bond. He eyes the terrain in front of us pensively. "I'll go ahead," he suggests. "If the holding cell is over here, I'll confirm and meet you a safe distance away."

Whitt waves him away, and Corwin springs into the air in his raven form. He flies off through the woods.

The spymaster contemplates the disc and adjusts our path just a smidge to the left. "It can't be too much farther. Sylas said he was keeping her within the boundaries of the domain. How's your foot?"

I'm not limping any worse than normal, but I guess the question is part of the increased attentiveness I can expect from now on. "The same as usual," I say. "Don't you start worrying about me too. If I need help, I'll say so."

Whitt shoots me a slyly affectionate glance. "I know how stoic you like to be. It can't hurt to check."

We tramp farther through the brush, following a trail few people have traveled before, judging by the natural debris that's scattered across the forest floor there. Twigs crackle under our feet, and bushes tug at our clothes.

The ground veers downward as we reach the slope of the hill.

We've been walking a few minutes longer when Corwin appears in a spot of sunlight up ahead. His expression is still tensed, but there's a hint of satisfaction in the set of his lips. "Your trick worked. They're holding her just at the base of the hill—if you kept going this way, you'd run right into her."

We have a solid way of tracking down the Murk. Whitt and I exchange a grin, and then Whitt strides ahead. "I'd like to see how it responds when I'm closer."

When I move to follow him, Corwin steps to intercept me. "I think you'd better not— As restrained as she is, it wouldn't be pleasant for you."

I'm about to protest when a ragged voice filters through the trees from farther down the hill. "You're all cunts and bastards. I look forward to seeing the bunch of you filleted and dumped in a pit."

I wince, drawing up short. The fury in the Murk woman's tone doesn't leave any room for talk of negotiation. I can't imagine how anyone could even raise the subject with her.

She only wants to hurt us… like so many of the fae who follow Orion still do. What if Madoc is a rare exception?

But at the same time I can't help wondering just what she went through to fuel her hatred toward the fae of the seasons.

I doubt she'd tell me if I asked. And seeing me might incite her anger even more.

I hesitate and then reach to take Corwin's hand. "Let's go back to the palace."

And hope that the war won't end up following us there no matter what we do.

4

August

The portals out of the Mists always point to the most peaceful parts of the human world. I've led my assorted group of fae warriors out onto the shore of a small, gleaming lake, this section sheltered from the rest of the shoreline by a thick stand of trees. The sounds—and smells—of occasional nearby traffic carry on the cool breeze, and with just a couple of steps, I can see the buildings along the city streets a short walk away.

Dawn light is only just creeping across the sky, the shadows still long and the sunlight dim around us. We timed this venture as well as we could in the hopes of finding more Murk activity while most humans are still sleeping—and reducing the chances that any humans might be caught in the fray if we get the opportunity to attack.

As we pause to confirm that our concealing spells have held solid during the trip through the portal, Kesral comes up beside me. Sylas asked the winter arch-lords to contribute some of their people to this mission so that we'd have a full range of skills to draw on. If this goes well, we might find ourselves tangling with more rats than we ever have before, and closer to their home turf than our own.

The Unseelie warrior peers at the glass disc I'm holding. "That little thing is going to find the Murk for us when nothing else did?"

I can't blame him for being skeptical. I gave Whitt an odd look of my own when he started explaining his new tool to me.

"I've seen it in action," I tell him. "Only on a much smaller scale than this, though. And we'll need to keep all our senses on the alert the whole time for any other sign of the rats. Our goal is to see if we can locate any sort of colony here, and if we have the upper hand in numbers, we'll take as many rats back for questioning as we can. It'll be easier if we notice them before they notice us."

Kesral nods, and I study the smudge of Talia's blood that marks the disc. We have every reason to believe there should be some Murk presence in this city. The rat shifter who helped Talia escape let her out onto these streets from their main colony, the one she said they call the King's Refuge. Even if the Refuge itself isn't here, because of the magical tricks they use to warp the paths between it and the world above ground, this is a location that's tied to it at least some of the time. We've caught hints of the Murk here and there during our past expeditions.

If we can find even one who could take us to the Refuge itself, we'll be within reach of a much bigger victory.

The urge grips me to tear straight through the city, savaging any of the vermin I stumble on—the horrible creatures that stole my mate away and tormented her. To protect both her and the child growing in her in the most immediate and thorough way I can. Just the thought of the pain they caused her brings up a fresh flare of defensive anger into my chest, alongside a twinge of affection even headier than any I've felt before.

We haven't spoken about it, and I don't see any need to, but it's most likely the child is mine. The one benefit to having much less fae in my blood than my true-blooded and nearly true-blooded brothers and Unseelie counterpart is that I won't suffer as much trouble having children as they will. My seed would have taken root more easily than any of theirs.

As happy as the knowledge makes me, Talia's current state makes *her* more vulnerable. I will not let her meet the same fate as so many humans caught up in fae passions. She deserves much better. And right now, the Murk are by far the greatest threat to her safety and happiness.

But as much as my fangs tingle in my gums, I know Talia is right about holding back our violence. I might not trust one hair on a rat's ass, but they're planning something bigger than what a single rampage of wolves could prevent. We need to find out more to be fully prepared, to hit them where it'll really hurt.

And that means keeping the bastards alive long enough to drag some information out of them.

My entire squadron knows the drill. As I set off toward the city streets, they fall into a loose formation behind me. The smear of blood offers an increasingly definite point to the south.

I keep my attention focused on it, knowing my companions will be scanning for any other signs of Murk presence while I can't. Every minute or two, I stop and give the smear a chance to shift. When the angle changes slightly, I head down a different street and then cross a broad courtyard.

A few human early-risers meander down the streets past us obliviously, our spells nudging them to avoid us without them even realizing they're being influenced. The smell of fresh bread with a rich nuttiness tickles into my nose from a nearby bakery just getting started for the day, and my mouth waters. If we weren't on such an urgent mission, I'd stop to steal a little for sampling. Instead, I walk on.

At my next stop, the pointed part of the blood doesn't adjust at all. The Murk must be close ahead.

One of my pack-kin sniffs the air and grins sharply. "I catch a whiff of rat. We're almost on them."

"Proceed slowly, watching for any hint of their presence," I remind the others. "We don't want them to know we're coming until we're ready to strike."

We murmur our concealing spells thicker around us

and tread onward, eyes sharpening and ears pricking. I shift more of my concentration to our surroundings, already knowing where Talia's blood is directing us.

Up ahead lies a narrow street lined with buildings three and four stories tall. With the sun so low, the shadows they cast cover the entire road. The windows are dark, all the inhabitants no doubt still in bed.

At the far end of the street, I can make out a larger structure that has a grand look to it—maybe a government building or a museum of some sort? Have the Murk managed to take over some part of that as their own?

My hackles rise. We're protecting not just ourselves and my mate but all the humans the rats would play their vicious tricks on too. Both worlds will be a better place if we can clear out the worst of the vermin.

Talia says they're not all horrible, but the sweetness in her that always sees the best in people is part of the reason I fell in love with her. *I've* never encountered a rat worth spitting on if it were on fire. But I guess once we've captured a few to talk with, we'll find out whether any will prove themselves worthy of her compassion.

My warriors spread out across the streets in a wider formation, checking doorways and the few tight alleys between the buildings. Talia's blood still points straight ahead. I don't think we're close enough to discover the rats yet, but I don't see how it'll hurt anything to make a quick inspection here regardless. We don't have to be fully braced for battle until we're nearly on top of them. How could they know we'd be tracking them so easily now?

But maybe I should have considered all I know about the Murk and their tricks a little more.

We're nearly at the end of the street when I glance down at the glass disc again and jerk to a halt, frowning at it. The most obvious point is aimed forward like before, but… has the entire smear gotten *larger*?

My squadron stops around me, waiting for my instructions. I stare at the disc and then press my thumb against the other side, framing the splotch of blood. At least, framing it at first. Now that I have another shape for comparison, I can see how the ruddy mark is expanding, creeping ever so slowly to match the width of my thumb. And the original point is starting to contract—

Understanding hits me with a chilling smack, a moment too late. "Back-to-back!" I shout. "They're surrounding us!"

But even as the words burst from my lips, a flurry of bodies spring at us from the thickest shadows along the edge of the buildings, all around us. The Murk tackle several of the warriors closest to them to the ground, blades flashing in their hands, needle-sharp claws glinting.

My own claws erupt along with my fangs. I lunge at the nearest flailing bodies, snatching my sword from its hilt as I go.

The Murk attackers managed to surround us—so quickly and discreetly we didn't pick up any trace of them even in our search. As I wrench a rat shifter away from one of my comrades and ram my sword into his gut before he can stab his knife at my throat, the pieces click together somewhere in the back of my mind.

We thought we knew what we were up against. We thought we'd prepared for the Murk to be stronger and slyer than we'd ever have anticipated before. But we underestimated them all the same.

They must have had a scout watching the portal where we came through who ran ahead to warn the others nearby. Either that one observed my new tool, or they've been able to spy on us so closely in our own world that they found out about our new use for Talia's blood ahead of time. They grouped together so that we'd be drawn on a clear course, and then surrounded us at just the right pace so that the movement didn't show up clearly on the disc. And they concealed themselves even more cleverly than I thought they could manage with us right here next to them.

The Murk aren't just the worst of the current threats we're facing. They might now be the worst threat we've *ever* faced.

It's not just their stealth and cunning that's allowed them to momentarily overwhelm us either. As well as the slash of blades and claws, the fae who've launched themselves at us are snapping out words of magic. One opens a deep cut in a Seelie warrior's arm without even touching her. Another makes an Unseelie fighter's feet fly out from under him so she can leap onto him and stab him in the back.

As I slam and slice through one rat shifter and then another, I register that there are more of us than them. The Murk probably didn't expect to completely overpower us, only to take down as many of us as they could before they were cut down themselves. My warriors are rallying, but the surprise of the attack got the better of some. Several of my comrades are sprawled in the street between the fallen rat shifters, a few struggling with their wounds, others gone limp, possibly dead.

I don't have the chance to help any of them right now. Yet another Murk dives at me from an unexpected angle, and his claws dig deep into my shoulder before I manage to drive my sword through his heart. As he crumples, a pained grunt catches in my ears. I spin to see two of the rat shifters lunging at Kesral from both sides.

The Unseelie warrior who's joined Talia and me on past trips to the human world is no slouch. He batters one of the desperate attackers away with the flat of his sword and then plunges the blade into the Murk woman's chest. But the smack of his other arm isn't enough to deflect the second attacker. The Murk man rams his knife right into the side of Kesral's neck.

I'm already dashing toward him. As he crumples, a roar of rage rips from my lungs. My wolf surges free automatically, my furred frame crashing into the vermin. My fangs sink into his own neck to tear open his throat.

The sickly metallic flavor of the Murk man's blood floods my mouth. There's nothing appetizing about it. I shove his slackening body away, sputtering, and shift back into the form of a man.

When I drop at Kesral's side, his eyes are already staring blankly at the sky. The blood spurting from the severed artery is slowing into a fainter pulse as the last shreds of his life drain out of him. There's nothing I can do for him.

Looking up at the scene around me, anguish squeezes my heart. The fighting is over. The last of the Murk are dead. But too many of my own people lie slumped between them. A few of the warriors who have particular skill at healing are leaning over those who haven't succumbed to their wounds yet, but I can tell at least a couple of them are fading.

Kesral is gone. I have to help those there's still hope for.

With a lump in my throat, I leave him and hurry to an Unseelie man who's intoning panicked words over one of my pack-kin who has a gash across her stomach. I join him, adding my own true names to the chorus.

We manage to bind her flesh to seal her wound, but the blood she's already lost drenches her clothes. Her eyes flutter shut, and her head lolls. I can't tell whether she'll survive the trauma she's been through.

None of the Murk have. I should be able to take some grim satisfaction from their dead bodies. But as I rush to the next injured warrior, the knowledge drags on my spirits instead.

The Murk have already discovered our new strategy against them and used it against *us*. We've lost several of our people in a horrible way. And we didn't even manage to take *one* of the blasted vermin captive for questioning like we'd planned. In every way, this mission was a failure.

When I've done what I can for those who are gravely injured, I straighten up and catch the eyes of my comrades who are still relatively unharmed. I will the roughness of grief and frustration out of my voice, but only barely.

"Carry the dead and those who can't walk with whatever magic you can most easily use. We'll bring them home."

And then I'll face the judgment I deserve.

5

Talia

As the sky darkens to shades of purple with the deepening evening, the pack steps back from where they've gathered around their two fallen kin. I slip through the gathering to where I can watch Sylas begin the funeral ceremony I first saw him carry out for his brother-in-law, Kellan.

For both of the murdered fae, a couple of family members or friends join the arch-lord in chanting the magic-laced words and moving through the gestures. The herbal scent that rises off the leafy fronds placed around the shrouded bodies takes me back to that past ceremony more vividly than I like.

Kellan was the first fae I ever saw die. There've been so many more since then. I've found a lot of happiness here in the Mists, but there's no way to deny that it's come with a lot of danger and violence as well.

I didn't know either of my pack-kin being honored tonight well. As part of the pack's contingent of warriors, they were often out on patrols, not hanging out around the pack village for the more domestic tasks I've helped with. But I can tell from the words Sylas and their loved ones say in their honor that they were well-respected and will be missed a great deal.

As Sylas raises the goblet with its shimmering liquid and asks that the summer sun embrace the dead woman at his feet "with all its warmth," a shiver runs through me. How much more will the Murk steal from all of us before they're finished?

Sylas pours the liquid over the body, and the shroud glimmers for a few moments before absorbing it. The other fae ease back as he falls into a more intent chant, the one that will transform the woman into her soulstone, a sparkling representation of the being she once was.

He finishes with a stretch of his hands over her body, and the flare of light washes over us all. I know to expect it this time, but it takes my breath away all the same.

When he's completed her ritual, Sylas moves on to the shrouded man next to her. Whitt brings him a fresh goblet of the ceremonial liquid. Even the spymaster with his normally impervious good humor looks grim this evening.

He thought he'd given us a huge advantage with the new tracking strategy he came up with. Instead it led to several deaths across the arch-lords' domains. I didn't see the body, but August said Kesral was killed too.

My gaze flicks toward the glinting haze along the border between the realms. How is Laoni coping with his loss, when she fought so hard against admitting she cared about him while he was alive?

Kesral might have supported his lady over me, but I can't blame him for that. He was kind to me and willing to open up the few times we traveled to the human world together. I might have liked to attend his funeral too, to honor him in my own small way, but I doubt Laoni would approve of my presence.

I didn't even ask Corwin. He's kept himself partly shielded from me as he carries out a funeral for one of his flock folk, the impressions that do seep through tinged with so much sorrow and fury that I can understand why he's trying to shelter me from them even though he doesn't need to.

August shifts his weight where he's standing at the front of the gathering just a few steps from Sylas, his head bowed low. I haven't managed to talk to him much either since he returned this afternoon, bearing the dead. The anguish I can read in his posture and his expression jerks at my heart. Knowing him, he's taking the full weight of the blame for himself. As if the rat shifters haven't taken so many of us by surprise so many times.

When Sylas has completed the second ritual, the families step forward to collect the soulstones. Then the pack drifts away, many of them gathering by the houses to grieve together.

Sylas nods to me and turns toward the castle of Hearth-by-the-Heart with Whitt flanking him. I'll stay with them there until everything's settled on both sides of the border. Both they and Corwin are worried about keeping our joint castle well-protected while everyone's distracted by the funerals.

August turns on his heel, stretches out into wolf form, and lopes toward the woods, his ruddy fur sparking with the last bits of sunlight before the shadows between the trees swallow him up.

I know sometimes he goes for a run on his own when he's grappling with his emotions. I hope he'll come back soon.

In the castle, I find myself drifting down to the basement. The leather sofa in the entertainment room holds a hint of August's musky scent from his many stints on the video game console. Maybe he'll come down here or to the gym once he's back to work off some tension in other ways.

I nestle against the arm of the sofa and wait, keeping my ears pricked. When footsteps rasp over the stairs, I raise my head in anticipation. But they stop just after they hit the smooth floor of the hall. I wait for several seconds and then limp over to the doorway.

It is August. He's standing motionless in the middle of the hallway at the base of the steps, the brighter light that streams down the staircase deepening the contrast of shadows on his brawny body. He seems to be staring at the wall, or at nothing—or maybe at something he can only see in his mind, drawn from his memories.

It isn't hard to guess what he might be remembering that has him looking so upset.

I walk over to him. He shakes himself out of his daze and turns toward me as I reach him, and I wrap my arms around his solid chest. He hugs me back, but something about his embrace feels more hesitant than I'm used to.

"It isn't your fault," I tell him, my words partly muffled against his shirt. "I know I've said we need to give some of the Murk the benefit of the doubt… but a lot of them do hate the other fae and are willing to be totally vicious to hurt you. And there's still so much we don't understand about their new kind of magic or how organized they are."

August sighs, his chin coming to rest on the top of my head. "I let down my squad. I led them into a trap, even if it was accidentally. I didn't respond quickly enough to prevent all those deaths. And I let *you* down by killing all the Murk too. I didn't even think about trying to capture them in the thick of it—I just ripped into them."

I hug him tighter. "You were defending yourself and your people. I'm not upset at you for that. If you'd tried to go easier on the ones attacking you, maybe more fae on our side would have died. It wasn't like you had much choice."

"I just…" He pauses, and his voice dips lower, as if he's not totally sure he wants me to hear what he's going to say. "I call you Sweetness because that's what you are— you're strong, but you're always caring and compassionate; you'd never hurt anyone unless you absolutely had to. And I have this beast inside me. There's a part of me that thinks of violence *first* when my temper sparks. How can you ever really be safe…"

He trails off again.

I ease back and touch his face with a noise of

consternation. "Do you honestly think I have any worries at all about you hurting *me*? Because I don't. Nothing about you scares me; it's been a long time since it has."

"You haven't had to see me fight, not really, not all that much," August says. "If I came toward you like Aerik and his cadre did that night, you'd still panic."

"You *wouldn't* come at me like they did," I point out. "And if you just mean your wolf, I'm not scared of that either. I've been up close to it and others before. I know the difference."

"I'm just saying it might not be so different if you saw me in certain states."

The determination to show him just how much I trust him swells inside me. I step back, toward the longer end of the hall that leads to the gym. "Why don't we find out? Let me see your wolf now."

August gives me a questioning look, but because he's August, he drops down at my request, shifting into wolfish form with the motion. There's a grace to the transformation that I appreciate more every time I see it.

He stands before me on all fours, golden eyes glinting within his ruddy fur, his tail swishing from side to side. His head comes all the way to my shoulder. A prickle runs through the scars embedded in my skin there, but it doesn't reach any deeper. I know the man in front of me, even when he's in the shape of an animal. All I feel for him is love.

At the thought of what I'm going to do next, my heart does skip a beat. But I gaze at my mate a few moments longer, letting the emotion settle. Then I turn on my heel. "Come catch me!"

I say the words lightly and with a dare in my voice, and then I start jogging down the hall as quickly as my warped foot allows.

August's wolf lets out a huff of confusion, and for a second I think he won't play the game I've instigated. But then his paws thump against the floor behind me at a slow lope, not really chasing me yet but following.

The sound provokes a quiver of panic that just as quickly turns into an excited jolt. "Is that the best you can do?" I call over my shoulder with a breathless laugh. "You're never going to claim your mate like that."

With a sound almost like a chuckle, August picks up his pace. He charges after me. I glance behind me, seeing his furred form closing in, and everything about his muscular stride echoes the man I love. The man I know would never run after me like this in anything *other* than a game.

Another giggle slips from my mouth. I push myself a little faster and manage to dive through the gym doorway with August at my heels. As I spin around, he pounces on me, shifting back into a man in time to brace his arm beneath me before I hit the padded mats that cushion the ground.

His expression is still a bit tense, but his eyes dance with exhilaration. The same giddiness lights up in me all the way to my core. Before he can say anything, I run my fingers into his hair and yank his mouth to mine.

August kisses me deeply, his pulse thrumming in his

chest even faster than mine. But it's a good energy, a sense of scoffing in the face of danger together, which sets my nerves even more alight.

I trust this man, and I love him, and right now I *want* him more than I know how to express.

August tears his mouth away for just an instant, his voice rasping. "You're sure you're okay?"

I tug at him insistently. "I'll be more okay if you keep kissing me."

The remaining tension finally melts from his stance. He meets my lips with a laugh that spills his breath hot across my mouth.

I haven't come together this urgently with any of my men in days. They've all been treating me so delicately since they found out I'm pregnant. But I don't feel at all tired or sick while the adrenaline hums through my body. With every kiss and caress, August wakes me up into sharper alertness—and desire.

I want to be loved in *every* possible way, not just the gentler ones.

My fingers fumble with the hem of his shirt. With a groan, August helps me pull it off him. He looms over me, his eyes darkening as I trail my hands over the muscular planes from his shoulders down across his torso. His abs flex as I graze the top of his slacks.

He kisses me again and finds the zipper on the side of my dress. With a few hasty jerks and a little squirming, I'm tossing it aside. My mate gazes down at me, nothing but hungry adoration in his eyes.

He claims my mouth once more, and then the corner

of my jaw, and then my neck, sucking hard enough that I gasp. As he charts that path downward, he cups my breast, swiveling his thumb closer and closer to the peak until I'm pressing into his touch. With an approving growl, he sucks the other nipple into his mouth at the same time as he pinches the first.

I arch into him, reveling in the pleasure that's quivering through my chest and throbbing between my legs for more. Thankfully, August picks up on my impatience, and he's never been one to deny me for long. With a pleased grin, he dips lower, hooking his fingers around the sides of my panties at the same time.

He pauses over my belly, still flat at this early stage, and kisses around my belly button so tenderly my throat constricts with emotion. I tease my fingers into the short strands of his auburn hair, and he dips even lower with a yank of my panties.

The second he's bared my sex, he's pressing his mouth to it. His tongue flicks over my opening, his lip sliding over the sensitive nub above, and a rush of bliss floods me.

I grip his hair harder, and he laps at me even more eagerly. It's all I can do to ride the storm of passion he's summoning inside me with each swipe of his tongue. I whimper and buck toward him, and he groans.

"So sweet inside and out," he murmurs, and dives back in.

My body starts to tremble with the sensations racing through it. My hips sway up, August grazes his teeth over my nub, and I come with a violent quaking, possibly wrenching his scalp with my grip on his hair.

August doesn't show any sign of minding. As my limbs sag in the aftermath of my orgasm, he looms back over me with a beaming smile and captures my lips, passing my tart taste on to me.

My hips bow up to meet his again, seeking that even deeper pleasure. I pull at his trousers.

August's breath stutters out of him. He kicks his pants off, and I'm already wrapping my fingers around his thick erection. It twitches in my grasp, so hard I have to swallow a moan at the feel of it.

"I want you inside me," I say, meeting his eyes. "I love you tame and I also love you wild. I'm not going to break."

August growls eagerly and pushes into me, stealing another kiss as he does. I raise my knees to let him plunge in deeper, unable to stop the moan that reverberates up from my chest now. We rock to meet each other, urgent but still tender, his lips dappling kisses across my face and neck. He keeps one hand braced against me while the other strokes more pleasure across my curves.

As the feeling of fullness inside me drives me toward my second peak, I push myself toward him more forcefully. August slides his hand beneath my bottom and lifts me up. At the new angle, his thrusts spark a hotter blaze of bliss that sweeps through my whole body. I whimper, pressing into him once, twice, and then cry out as I tip over that ecstatic edge again.

August's pace turns more erratic. As I clench around him, his chest hitches. He burrows his face against my shoulder and grunts as his heat fills me.

He sinks down beside me, wrapping his arm around me to tuck me close. I nestle myself in his embrace. For a few minutes, we just lie there, coming down, enjoying the lingering heat we generated between us.

"No more worries," I say, turning my head so I can look at him straight on. "Not about how I feel about you. We've got plenty of other things to worry about without adding that to the list. You're my mate, and nothing can change that."

August sighs, but it's more a sound of release than of resignation. He kisses my hair just above my ear. "You do know how to make a point, Sweetness," he says with a fond glint in his eyes. "I'll try to remember this one."

"You'd better," I mutter teasingly, and snuggle against him again, wishing there *weren't* quite so many other worries to take up the space in both our heads.

6

Talia

When the thumping on my bedroom door jolts me out of sleep the following night, the darkness outside my window shows that it's barely morning yet. As I roll over next to Sylas, who stayed with me in the border castle tonight, the voice of one of the castle's many guards on duty filters through.

"My lord, there's news from Tumble-by-the-Heart that I think you should hear right away."

Tumble-by-the-Heart is Celia's domain. Sylas sits up immediately. "Just a moment." He brushes a quick kiss to my lips before grabbing his clothes. "You go back to sleep," he murmurs to me.

I'm feeling that extra weight of exhaustion again, so I let my head sink back into the pillow, but my mind has started buzzing too much for me to drift off. I try until after Sylas has strode out into the hall and finally grab my thin robe to pull over my nightgown and pad over to the door. I'll feel better if I know what's going on.

I've just eased the door open when my own name reaches my ears. My pulse stutters. I hurry out. At the sight of me, Sylas and the guard fall silent where they were talking farther down the hall.

"What about me?" I ask. "What's happened?"

Sylas opens his mouth and closes it again with a pained expression. He obviously doesn't want to get me involved. But then he sighs. He knows me well enough to realize I'm not going to let go of the subject until he explains.

"One of Celia's patrols caught a Murk man not far from her domain," he says. "He's saying he only came to pass on a message… to you."

My heart outright stops for a second. I limp over, hugging myself. "They didn't *kill* him, did they? It could be Madoc—he might really want to help us." I hate to think what the Murk man who arranged my escape would have had to find out that was bad enough for him to risk coming here to tell me about it. Somehow I can't imagine he's bringing news that Orion's agreed to negotiate a peace treaty.

No, whatever it is, it's almost definitely awful.

The guard gives me an odd look, but says, "He's still alive, as far as I know. Arch-Lord Celia is holding him at the base of the hill on her side, like we did with the woman we captured." He turns back to Sylas. "She wants to know how you'd like to proceed."

I draw my posture up straight and firm before Sylas

can answer. "I'll go see what he wants to tell me, of course."

Sylas frowns. "We don't know for sure it *is* the Murk who came to your aid before—and even if it is, we can't be sure of his intentions now. I don't want you coming within range of their magic. If he has something to say, he can pass the message on through me."

I cross my arms over my chest. "I think it's a little late to be worrying about me getting affected by Murk magic. If he was willing to pass on the message to anyone other than me, he'd probably have done it already. Madoc doesn't exactly trust the rest of you—I'm not sure how much he even trusts me." Enough to think I deserved not to be tortured, but that's a pretty low bar.

"That's assuming it's even him," Sylas reminds me. "A lot of Murk are aware of your name and the fact that you've come back to us, I'd imagine. This could be one of their tricks to lure you into a more vulnerable position."

I let out my breath in a huff, but he's right. We need to be careful. "Fine. I'll describe him to you and give you a couple of questions to ask that only Madoc should be able to answer. If you're convinced that it's him, then we have less to worry about." I pause. "But even if it isn't, I think we should give whoever it is some chance to show what they came for."

Sylas lets out a disconcerted growl, but he doesn't outright refuse. "We'll cross that bridge if we come to it." His gaze skims over my nightclothes. "Why don't you get yourself dressed, and I'll see who else I can rouse at this hour to accompany us? I'm going to take every precaution."

As I limp back to my bedroom, Corwin's voice emerges through our bond, slightly groggy with interrupted sleep. *What's all this commotion so early in the morning, my soul? Are you all right?*

Yes, other than a little tired, as you'd expect, I answer as I tug the first dress my hands fall on out of my wardrobe. *I'm sorry I woke you up. It seems one of the Murk has been captured near Celia's domain, and he claims he has a message to pass on to me. It might be Madoc. We're going to go confirm.*

My sense of my soul-twined mate snaps into sharper alertness in an instant. *I can be there too, if the Seelie won't object.*

I don't see what reason they'd have to complain. It'd probably be good for someone from the winter realm to witness what happens too.

I shed my nightclothes and pull on the dress, which is simple enough that it doesn't require much fussing to get it lying right but significantly more ladylike than my nightie. I am going to be presenting myself in front of a bunch of Celia's pack-kin and maybe the arch-lord herself as well as fae I'm more comfortable around.

And possibly this rat shifter, whoever he is.

By the time I make it downstairs to the summer entrance to the palace, Corwin has already joined Sylas there—and so has Sylas's entire cadre, though Whitt looks a bit bleary-eyed. August is already tensed in a defensive stance, and Astrid has her short sword in her hand. She muffles a yawn and then shakes herself.

"I don't think you *all* need to be there just to protect me," I say with a twinge of guilt at the thought of them being tugged out of their beds.

Whitt shoots me a breezy grin. "Who says it's for you?" he teases. "I want to hear what the rat has to say." He stretches his arms over his head, no longer favoring his injuries from Tristan's attack on Hearth-by-the-Heart weeks ago. "And more eyes and ears never hurt anyone. He won't touch one hair on your head."

I suspect if I wasn't coming with them, they'd have shifted to take the relatively short trip at a wolfish lope. Instead, we step out into the warm night air to a carriage that's already been conjured. I settle onto one of the benches, restraining a yawn of my own, and consider what Sylas could ask the Murk man. Something only Madoc and I would know.

"If he says he's Madoc, and he looks right"—I glance at Corwin—"you should be able to recognize him from my memories, although I guess it could be an illusion. Ask him about the three scenes I watched in the vault of memories. There was the burning house, the man who was caught by the Unseelie while he was looking for food for his mate, and… and the kids in the orphanage."

I've told my mates about what I saw before, and their faces all turn somber at the reminder. "Is there anything else we could check?" Sylas asks gently.

I can't think of why Madoc would have mentioned all

three of those memories from the vault to anyone else, but just in case… "You could ask him what he needed to reassure me about—a lie Orion told me—when we were leaving the Refuge. I thought Orion might have been able to read my thoughts, but Madoc said he was only pretending to."

Will he even remember that? I hope so. But if he doesn't, he can simply say so and I'll have to think of some other proof.

The carriage glides across the open plains around the Heart and between the smaller stands of trees. As we reach Celia's castle, a sentry is waiting there. He waves his arm to us and motions for us to follow him into the thicker forest on the slope of the hill.

I figure we're about halfway down when Sylas draws the carriage to a halt. "You'll wait here with Astrid and August," he tells me. "Corwin, Whitt, and I will see to the captive. We'll return as soon as we have a better idea who he is."

They spring out of the carriage, the Seelie men immediately taking on their wolf forms and Corwin soaring after them as a raven. The Unseelie arch-lord raises his mental barriers again, with a tendril of apology. He doesn't want me being disturbed by what the Murk man might say or do when we're still so unsure of what we're dealing with.

August tucks his arm around me, and I lean against him, letting my eyes slide shut for a little while. I'm too wound up to have any hope of sleeping deeply right now, but I do doze a bit.

The next thing I know, Whitt is standing at the side of the carriage with a wary expression.

"It's your man, as far as we can tell," he says. "This Madoc. He answered everything to our satisfaction. Celia has a dozen guards staked out maintaining the holding cell —apparently they were pretty concerned by the fact that he managed to get this close to the Heart before anyone caught him, so they suspect he's rather powerful. Which tracks with what you learned about his skill with illusions too."

"How *did* they catch him?" I ask as August helps me out of the carriage.

The corner of the spymaster's mouth quirks upward. "It was one of the blood trackers you helped me make. It seems the Murk haven't learned how to avoid them completely, or else this one didn't hear the news."

The thought that I was responsible in a roundabout way for bringing about Madoc's capture makes my stomach twist, but it's done now. I need to find out why he's come—and make sure Celia's guards don't hurt him.

August and Astrid flank me for the last short tramp through the thicker woods, where it'd have been difficult to navigate a carriage anyway. We emerge into a large clearing. A few magical globes cast an amber glow over the space. Sylas and Corwin are poised by the edge of the ring of trees. The guards Whitt mentioned stand at attention all around them.

And in the middle of the clearing, surrounded by a translucent wall of light that shifts and whirls like oil in water—

"Madoc!" His name jolts from my lips, and I'm darting forward before I can really think about it.

My impulse is to run right to him, to check him over and make sure he's okay, but August sweeps me up before I can make it even to the glowing barrier around him.

"Careful still, Sweetness," he murmurs.

I stare at the man within the shimmering cage. Madoc has straightened up from the crouched posture he had before, his heavy-lidded eyes fixed on me, the amber light turning his straight, straw-pale hair faintly orange. My gaze darts lower, automatically looking for the long, thinly furred tail I got used to seeing on him. It's strange to find it missing, even though I know the fae tend not to show their animal aspects unnecessarily. It was only a quirk of the way Orion ran the Refuge that he wanted everyone to display theirs.

An angry bruise marks Madoc's left cheekbone, and a cut that runs from his right temple almost to his jaw is still seeping blood. Now that he's moving, I notice that he's favoring one side, as if he's got some other, unseen injury as well. My gut lurches.

"What did you do to him?" I demand as August's grip loosens enough to put me back on my feet, though he keeps his hands on my shoulders. I glare around the clearing at the guards. "You didn't need to attack him."

The one who must be the squadron leader scowls at me. "It wasn't us. He arrived like this. And the patrol wouldn't have known how hard they needed to come down on him when they spotted him. Why would we give the vermin a chance to get the upper hand?"

I guess that makes sense, but it doesn't stop me from feeling sick. I yank my attention back to Madoc, who offers me a tight smile.

"I'll survive," he says in the lightly hoarse voice that guided me through so many of the horrors I faced in the Refuge. "You could say it's my fault for getting caught. I meant to pass on my message in some way not quite so hands-on, but I'll take what I can get. I'm glad to see your defiant spirit hasn't gone anywhere just because you found your freedom."

An ache forms around my heart that he's taking this setback so calmly, unshaken even with fae who wouldn't hesitate to kill him all around. As if all that matters is seeing through his mission. But that's how he's always been, isn't it? Dedicated and determined, sometimes to the point that it frustrated me.

The fact that he's here at all is proof that he's capable of adjusting his resolve, though. I doubt Orion approved of him reaching out to me like this. He hasn't let his commitment to his people blot out every other consideration of what's right.

"Of course it hasn't," I say to his remark about my spirit. "I'll have them bring a healer." I spin toward Sylas. "You can get Celia to agree to that, can't you?"

Sylas inclines his head, but his gaze remains on Madoc. "First I'd like to know what brought our unexpected visitor here at all. What's the message? What did you want to tell Talia?"

Madoc's eyes narrow as he takes in the fae men around me. Then he focuses on me instead of Sylas. "Your mates are very careful about ensuring your protection, I'll give you that. Let's hope they can continue to be."

"Is that a threat?" August growls before the Murk man can go on.

Madoc's gaze hardens into a glower. "No," he snaps. "It's a warning, one I risked a lot to come here to deliver, so maybe you can give me a chance to actually tell you." He drags in a breath and meets my eyes again. "With all the magic Orion cast on you, there was one spell lying dormant that he was keeping in reserve as a backup plan. From what I understand, he sent someone into the Mists to trigger it about two days ago."

Two days ago? A chill washes over my skin. I don't remember anything unusual happening then. It's been a bit of a blur since we realized I was pregnant, but that was almost a week ago.

My hand rises to my belly instinctively. Orion's spell doesn't have anything to do with *that*, does it?

"What exactly did he trigger?" I ask, hardly wanting the answer but knowing I need to hear it.

Madoc grimaces. "From what he told me, it's a curse on *you*. It'll start by simply weakening you and causing you some pain. But it'll get increasingly worse within a matter of days, until—until it kills you."

7

Sylas

I lean against the carriage's hull, gazing down at my sleeping mate. She refused to go any farther from the holding cell than this, even though her exhaustion was obviously catching up with her. We arranged as comfortable a bed as we could nestled between two of the carriage's benches, and she drifted off almost immediately.

The early dawn light that filters through the foliage overhead catches in her vibrant hair. I murmur a few words to create a sunshade so the rays won't wake her as they brighten. Then I look at my lead warrior—and chief healer.

"You haven't sensed any signs of illness in her?" I ask August. He didn't show any indication that Madoc's claims fit with his observations, but he might not have wanted to say anything in front of the company. He may not even have wanted to speak to Talia about it yet until we've discussed it ourselves, so as not to worry her unnecessarily.

My brother shakes his head with a smile much tighter than his usual. "Nothing—and I've checked her over for any reasons for concern every day since we discovered the pregnancy. Other than the child forming inside her, I haven't picked up on anything about her physical presence that's changed since before her kidnapping."

"You don't think the pregnancy could be related to the curse, do you?" The thought makes my gut sink.

August's smile disappears completely. A frown creeps into its place as he studies Talia's sleeping form. "We knew she was fertile when we were all with her after she escaped the Murk. The timing of Corwin first noticing the pregnancy and the energy she's giving off fit that as the date of conception. I've specifically searched for any hint of Murk influence tied to the new life, and there's none of that either. But I guess we can't know absolutely for sure. They've hidden a lot from us."

"Yes." I stifle a frown of my own. "We'll have to keep a close eye on her and the progress of the pregnancy. It might be best if you do a physical scan of her twice a day now so we can catch any new developments as early as possible."

"Maybe Madoc is wrong," August suggests. "Or maybe the trigger Orion told him about didn't work. Talia's foiled them in other ways before. The Heart of the Mists has supported her."

"I'd like to believe that, but we can't count on that

being true. Our own curse doesn't show itself except one night every month. The Unseelie's strikes at random. It wouldn't be all that unexpected for whatever the Murk king has placed in our mate to take some time showing itself."

With that grim statement hanging over us, I turn toward the slope that'll lead me back to Madoc's holding cell. "I need to question the rat more. You stay here and watch over her, and I'll send Astrid up to join you." After everything Talia's been through, I don't feel comfortable leaving her without at least two trusted guards, even this deep in our territory and so close to our Heart. Corwin has gone off to fly around the nearby lands, watching for any hint that Madoc didn't come alone.

August inclines his head in acceptance of my orders, and I stride on down the hill to the clearing where I left my other two cadre-chosen—and the Murk man who's supposedly looking out for Talia's best interests.

I wouldn't trust *him* to guard her from his own kind, but it was easy to see how his demeanor changed in her presence—the difference in his expression and posture when he was focused on her compared to the rest of us. She's won some sort of victory with him, as she's won over so many other fae. But is it enough to overcome his obvious contempt for Seelie and Unseelie alike?

I'm interested to see how he'll talk when he doesn't have her presence to keep his more hostile impulses in check. Perhaps I'll learn something he'd only let slip when it's just us fae.

Nuldar's words come back to me from the last time I

visited the sage, when I asked him about how we could end the curse. He said the answer was on its way to us... and that we needed a "snare" to catch that answer. *If it can capture a single heart, it will bring all you need to know back to you.*

Could Talia be that snare—and Madoc the heart she's captured? So far he hasn't told us anything that would help us eliminate the curse, nothing we hadn't already learned from Talia after her time in the hands of the Murk. But then, she might not have come back to us at all if she hadn't made an ally of him.

We'll have to wait and see how that plays out as well.

As I come up on the clearing where Celia's guards are maintaining their solemn vigil, Whitt and Astrid both move to rejoin me. "How's our mighty mate?" Whitt asks, the playful note in his voice unusually subdued.

"Getting her much needed rest," I say, and nod to Astrid. "You should join August in watching over her. Alert me of anything at all worrying."

"Of course, my lord," the wiry woman says, and springs into her wolf form nearly as nimbly as if she were several centuries younger. She was the most faithful and capable of my guards, and she's proven an excellent addition to my cadre. I should have thought of inviting her into it sooner.

Whitt walks with me back to the holding cell. He may have some questions to contribute to the interrogation too. Stopping closer than the guards are standing but still a few feet from the glowing walls, I peer at Madoc through the shifting barrier.

He isn't as musclebound as my own frame or August's, but he could just about match Whitt's physical build. And both the fact that he made it so close to our inner domains and Talia's reports have made it clear his magical talent is one to be reckoned with as well. He could be a formidable ally if he's willing to remain one—or a formidable enemy if he's not.

He gazes back at me, his expression wary. He's dropped down into a crouch, leaning slightly forward with his forearms resting on his knees, but I can tell he's ready to leap from that pose in an instant should he see an opening. He definitely isn't happy about staying among us in captivity.

"I have more questions for you," I say, crossing my arms over my chest.

"Of course you do." He straightens up so we're closer to the same level. I have a few inches on him, but no more than that. "What else is it you want to know, arch-lord?"

He says my title with a hint of a sneer, as if it's more an insult than an honor. I grit my teeth automatically but keep my mind focused on the interrogation. I can't let him distract *me* with his attempts to provoke my temper.

"This curse your king supposedly put on Talia—you said he mentioned having sent someone to trigger it just a couple of days ago. Did he give any indication of when the curse itself was laid?"

Madoc's eyes flicker, and I suspect he's debating whether he wants to tell me even that much. But after a moment, he draws in a breath. "I asked him a few questions as if out of curiosity. As far as I could tell from his answers, which aren't always all that concrete, it was part of the initial spell he worked on her when she was a newborn."

The thought of Talia as an infant brings up all my apprehension about her current state. "But he didn't offer any details about what the curse on her would entail?"

"I told you that already," Madoc says shortly. "All he said was that she'd suffer and waste away, and he expected to see you all panicking and distraught because there'd be nothing you could do to stop it. I couldn't press all that hard without making him wonder why I was so concerned about the specifics. Believe me, if I'd been able to find out anything that would help you—help *her*—prepare better, I wouldn't be keeping it to myself."

I can't say I'm convinced of that claim, but I let his answer stand. Whitt has obviously been thinking along similar lines, though. As I pause to consider my next question, he clears his throat. "Did he say anything at all that hinted at the curse involving her being with child?"

So many emotions dart across Madoc's face, it's almost impressive to behold. From the shadow that crosses his eyes and the twitch of his muscles that's almost a flinch, the only thing I'm sure of is that the idea comes as a complete surprise—and he doesn't like it at all. Which might be enough of an answer in itself.

"No," he says, the hoarseness of his voice thickening a little. "I can't think of anything he said that would suggest... *Is* she? With child?" There's an oddly hesitant note in his voice, as if he isn't sure he wants to know after all.

"I'm simply covering every eventuality," Whitt says smoothly. "It seems a reasonable potential ploy."

Madoc regards him suspiciously but says nothing.

"Why *did* you come to pass on this warning to Talia?" I ask, bringing his attention back to me. "You pointed out that you've put your life at risk doing so. What made it important enough to take that risk?"

His gaze turns into a glower. "I already risked my life once getting her away from Orion in the hopes of saving hers. Obviously there wouldn't have been much point in that if I was just going to let her die anyway."

"I think the question still stands," Whitt says breezily, cocking his head. "Why help her at all?"

Madoc flexes his fingers, and for a second I think I catch a glint of claws emerging. But they vanish just as quickly. He scowls at both of us. "I wouldn't think I'd need to tell either of you that she's a pretty extraordinary woman. She managed to convince me that there might be some hope of this conflict ending in ways other than a bloody war. And regardless of that, no matter what you think of the Murk, I don't happen to enjoy watching someone who doesn't deserve it suffer."

I have the feeling he doesn't count us among those who don't deserve to suffer. I focus on the other part of his answer. "Is that what you'd want—an end to this conflict that doesn't include war? It was your people who started the war. It seems you've been waging it against us for decades without us even knowing."

"*We* started it?" Madoc sputters in disbelief, but then he shakes his head. "It doesn't matter. I don't think it'd be good for *my* people if we have to resort to that kind of combat. Talia sees something worthwhile in the lot of you, so maybe there are a few of you it'd be better to have sticking around too." He doesn't bother to hide his skepticism.

My eyebrows rise just slightly. "You value my mate's input quite a lot."

I purposefully referred to Talia by her relationship to me to check his reaction. Madoc doesn't show any additional animosity, but then, there's plenty between us already. His lips curl back just slightly. "I hope you do too."

I can't see any point in continuing to badger him. Other than being a little more open in his dislike of us, he hasn't given away anything useful, and the only things he's been able to tell us overtly, we already knew. I'm no closer to being sure of what we should do with him.

"You know the way to your Refuge where your king has his false Heart," I say carefully. "If we dealt with that—"

Madoc's gaze sharpens into a glare. "I'm not leading you back there to carry out what I have to assume would be a slaughter. *That* wouldn't do my people any good either. I came in the hopes of sparing Talia some pain, not to bring down heaps more on the Murk."

I'd expected it was a long-shot anyway. "I can understand that." Easing back, I dip my head to him— nothing like a bow, but a brief indication of respect. Regardless of how I feel about his people or him about mine, he's sacrificed a lot on behalf of my mate. I can recognize that generosity.

"That's enough for now," I say. "I'll leave you be."

As I head toward the trees, there's a rustle as Madoc steps forward. His voice drops. "Is she—is she all right? The curse really hasn't affected her at all yet?"

I glance over my shoulder at him. The anguish that seeped into his tone and the consternation on his face, as if he hates asking me for reassurance but can't help himself anyway, disarm my wariness in a way nothing else he's said before has.

He does care about her, not just about the role she might play in getting the Murk to their goals.

I still don't have much faith in anything else he's said, but the realization brings down my hackles enough for me to answer honestly. "Nothing. As far as we can tell, she's in perfectly normal health—and my healer has a lot of experience with all forms of bodily magic."

"Good," Madoc says, his shoulders sagging. "Thank you."

Whitt and I walk several paces into the shelter of the woods before my brother catches my arm. He murmurs a quick spell to the air around us to muffle our conversation from distant ears. "What do you make of him?"

"I was going to ask you the same thing." I rub my jaw. "He doesn't like talking to us, but I didn't get the impression he was holding back anything significant either."

"Neither did I." Whitt gazes back the way we came. "But what do we do with him now? We can't ask Celia to release him and let him run free simply because he's made friends with our mate."

"No." I pause. "But perhaps we could come to a more formal agreement with him after we've held him a little longer, had more chance to feel out his intentions. It might help to let Talia speak to him on our behalf. If we could count on him revealing more about the Murk's preparations, that would be worth a lot."

"It would." Whitt lets out a restrained snarl and meets my eyes. "But for all we know, this whole tale of a curse could be a lie. Just how far are we willing to trust him, no matter what he says?"

8

Talia

$\mathcal{A}$ tingle passes over my skin and into my flesh with each soft true name August murmurs. He seems to be casting his magic over every part of my body, starting from my head and working his way down. I hold still, fighting the urge to fidget.

What are we going to do if he *does* find something wrong? I might be the cure for the fae's curse, but Madoc indicated that there is no cure for the one Orion planted in me.

My stomach twists, but August finishes his examination with a smile and a squeeze of my shoulder. "I still can't see anything out of the ordinary. I'd say you're stronger than that rat king bargained for, Sweetness."

I smile back at him, only partly relieved. It's easier for him to say that when he never had to deal with Orion face to face or stand in the unnerving glow of the Murk's Heart.

All's well? Corwin asks through our bond in a hopeful tone. He's been checking in on me even more than usual during the times when his duties take him from my side.

As far as August can tell, and bodily magic is his specialty, I reply. *Maybe we'll be able to find out more about what I need to watch out for after I talk to Madoc again.*

My mention of the Murk man provokes a ripple of uneasiness from my soul-twined mate, but he doesn't argue against it. He already knew that was the plan. I'm supposed to go to Madoc and try to negotiate some kind of deal, his help in exchange for his freedom. I don't think it's exactly the kind of negotiation he wanted to be having, but I can't blame the fae of the Mists for being even warier of the Murk after the attack a few days ago and now this news of a fatal curse in me.

"Ready to go downstairs?" August asks. "If you need more time, they'll wait, arch-lords or no."

I square my shoulders and turn toward my bedroom mirror, taking in my reflection. August has touched up the pink and purple in my hair again since I returned from the Refuge. The turquoise dress I've picked, formally long but not particularly ornate, brings out both those vivid hues and the green in my eyes.

I'm Lady Talia. My opinion matters too. I will not let myself be bullied into saying anything I don't agree with.

At least I'm less worried about that from the Seelie arch-lords than I would be if it was someone like Laoni who'd captured Madoc. I'm not sure he'd even have stayed alive long enough to deliver his message if her warriors had come across him.

The thought of him slaughtered makes my stomach twist tighter. I shake off my discomfort and nod to August. "I'm fine. As good as I'm going to be." My broken sleep has left my mind a little bleary, even with catching up on some in Sylas's carriage this morning, but I've been equally tired in the past week just from being pregnant. If I've got eight more months of this ahead of me, I'd better get used to working around it.

It'll be worth it. As August walks with me into the hall, my hand drifts to my belly. It'll be worth it for him… or her… I wonder if some fae magic will tell me whether I'm expecting a son or a daughter before the birth.

Those warmer thoughts fall away as we step into the border castle's main meeting room. Sylas and Whitt are already there, Astrid having stayed behind with Madoc to keep an eye on how he's treated. Donovan and Celia are waiting for me as well, standing by one end of the long table, each with a cadre member of their own. Donovan's eyes glint, bright with what looks like excitement at the possibilities we're going to discuss, but Celia is much more solemn. The oldest of the Seelie arch-lords is always the most pessimistic of the trio.

"All right," I say. "I'm here. I think this is going to be pretty straightforward, though, isn't it? I'll explain to Madoc that if he'll agree to pass on more news to us about Orion's plans, we'll let him go. I think he'll agree to that." It isn't as if he wants to stay locked up here.

Celia looks at Sylas instead of me. "Does she have no sense of the necessary precautions?"

Sylas gazes steadily back at her. "That's why we're having this discussion, is it not? To come to an agreement on what precautions are necessary?"

I frown at Celia. "What are you talking about? Obviously I'm not going to put myself in harm's way or say anything that could hurt anyone here in the Mists. I'm not an idiot."

She finally turns to me. "Offering this vermin his freedom could hurt us greatly in itself. We'll have no guarantee of him giving us any aid at all. And who knows what he might have discovered before my guards caught him that he'd run off to report to his 'king'?"

I bristle automatically at her disdainful tone. "He's already proven that he isn't totally loyal to Orion by coming here in the first place, hasn't he? If you treat him like he's attacked us instead of helped us, which is all he's done so far, you'll just be encouraging him not to trust the fae of the Mists."

Her eyes narrow. "It isn't our fault if the rats want to blame us for a natural wariness founded on their own horrible actions for centuries upon centuries past."

Before I can point out the horrible actions the other fae have taken against the Murk as well, Sylas breaks in. "This Madoc *has* helped us, or at least attempted to, and he's helped Talia in the past at great risk to himself. I don't fully trust him either, not only because of his divided loyalties but also because we can't know what greater sway his king may force on him later on. But I agree with Talia that we have to appeal to his *better* nature at least as much as the aspects we fear."

"It's not a matter of fear," Celia mutters, and then sighs. "We do need to have some kind of failsafe in place. I won't order my people to free him otherwise."

"Of course," Donovan says, his eagerness brightening his voice as well. "But it is an excellent opportunity we're getting. We've never had a rat on our side, a way of finding out what's going on within the Murk community. No matter how much magic they have, we couldn't ask for a better advantage than that."

Celia gives him a cool glance. "Assuming we don't end up double-crossed. And an even better advantage would be if he'd point the way straight to his king so we can cut off this rebellion at the root."

Sylas clears his throat. "He's already made it quite clear he won't betray his people to that extent. Pushing him will only make him more resistant to offering us anything at all."

"Fine. But we still need some guarantee of his loyalty, however little of it he's going to offer."

I wasn't feeling queasy before, but all this tense back-and-forth has brought out a twinge of nausea. I sink into one of the chairs. "What do you even mean by a failsafe? We can't enforce a vow or anything like that, can we, when the Murk aren't tied to the Heart out there anymore?" I motion toward the Heart of the Mists, its resonant energy humming through the air even with the walls hiding it from view.

"I've been thinking on that," Celia says. "You've mentioned that the Murk king lashes out against any of his subjects if provoked, haven't you? Does that mean this one would face severe punishment for a misstep despite his high status in their false court?"

I can only imagine what Orion would do to Madoc if he found out how his knight had betrayed him, and I don't want to. "Yes. His position wouldn't guarantee any protection. He'd probably face worse punishment so Orion could make an example of him to discourage anyone else from turning traitor."

Sylas is nodding, apparently having picked up on the direction Celia is heading in. "Then we have some leverage over him in the fact that he's come to us at all."

Her eyes gleam. "Exactly. All we need is some basic proof of his complicity. Perhaps we could ask him to mark an object in a clearly identifiable way or cast magic into it —something he wouldn't have done as part of his regular missions and that we couldn't have obtained without his cooperation. If he makes any move to harm us after we release him, then we can reveal the proof to the rest of the Murk. It sounds as though that should give him plenty of motivation to keep his word."

I can see her logic, but the idea doesn't sit totally right with me anyway. Maybe because it's essentially threatening the man who's looked out for me more than once—and relying on that threat rather than trust to ensure his continuing help.

But how can I blame the fae around me for not being

willing to fully trust one of their long-time enemies, one who clearly still doesn't like them particularly? I'm not sure *I* even trust him to come back after they've held him captive once, no matter what he hears from Orion next.

"He wouldn't *have* to come back, right?" I say slowly. "If he hears nothing he feels we need to know, he'd have no reason to. I wouldn't want us to destroy his life just because we got antsy about a long period of silence."

"That's a fair point," Sylas says. "We'd strike against him only if he actively struck against us."

Celia looks as if she's going to argue, but Donovan jumps in first. "And we could test that pretty easily. Let him see one thing that he'd think was damaging before he goes, something that would suggest an obvious target or tactic to the Murk. Then we wait and see if they make use of that opportunity. If they don't, then we know he didn't pass the information on to his king."

I don't love the idea of setting Madoc up for a fall either, but... if he *would* use his time here to help Orion attack us, then he isn't any kind of ally or friend to me, not really.

"I'd agree with that," I say.

Celia purses her lips. I don't think she considers my opinion on the same level as her own and her colleagues', but at least she doesn't make that as obvious as some of the winter arch-lords have. "All right. We can work out the exact details while Talia speaks to the man. If we're going to make use of him, we should do it quickly. The longer he's here, the more suspicious his king might become of his absence."

Whitt rests his hand on my shoulder. "I'll take you to speak with him, mite. I'll hang back so I'm not obviously part of the conversation, but I'd like to listen in so I can judge his answers for myself."

I drag in a breath, suddenly not sure *I'm* ready for this conversation after all. "Okay."

Whitt leads me out to a small carriage. "No wolf-back riding today?" I tease.

The spymaster arches an eyebrow at me. "I wouldn't have thought that much jostling would be ideal in your current state."

My hand drifts to my belly again. It's true that I have been getting queasy in general much more easily than usual. "I never had a problem with it before, but maybe it's better to be careful."

As he guides the carriage toward the woods where Madoc is being held, Whitt lowers his voice. "Celia has agreed that the guards will draw back out of hearing while still monitoring the holding cell magically. We want Madoc to feel he's speaking just to you, since you're the only one he seems to trust at all. But I'd like you to use my true name to ask me to hear what you hear, so I can follow the conversation completely without being close myself. It won't be as smooth as your conversations with your soul-twined mate, but the outcome is similar."

"Of course." I reach for his hand and squeeze it, abruptly needing that contact. I haven't used Whitt's true name since the second time I tried to reach out to him from the Refuge. It still sends a flare of happiness through me that he shared something so intimate with me to begin with.

Now I have to see whether I can convince Madoc to trust me even a fraction that much.

As before, we get out of the carriage farther up the hill where the forest starts to thicken and walk the rest of the short distance to the clearing on foot. As we come into view of the holding cell, Whitt motions to the leader of the guards. They all fade back into the trees as if they were never there.

I pause, and bob up on my toes to whisper Whitt's true name right into his ear. "*Wye-con-ell.* Hear what I hear." A giddy shiver travels through my chest, and he smiles before pressing a kiss to the top of my head. Then he escorts me the rest of the way to the shimmering wall before turning and walking away to give us our space.

Madoc sits up on the mat he's been given to rest on. Someone's brought him a small pillow and a blanket too. The cut on his face has been healed, only a faint pink mark showing where the skin was broken before. His expression doesn't exactly brighten at the sight of me, but the shadows darkening it draw back a little.

I sit down on the other side of the shimmering barrier so I'm not looming over him, which would feel uncomfortable. "Sorry it's taken so long for me to come back. I'm glad to see they've made you more comfortable at least."

"It hasn't been that long as far as I can tell," Madoc says with a hint of wryness. "Am I right in assuming I can thank you for this incredible generosity?"

I did insist to Sylas that he needed to get Celia to show a little consideration to our prisoner. I shrug awkwardly, not wanting to make a big deal of it, and have to ask, "Have they brought you any food?"

"Oh, yes, I'm not going to starve." He chuckles darkly.

But no doubt being locked up in this holding cell is only confirming his beliefs about how the fae of the Mists see the Murk. I swallow thickly. I know I need to be cautious of him still, that my mates all feel he could still have some ulterior motive up his sleeve, but I can't help wishing this could be a proper conversation across a table in a regular room, like the one I just had with the Seelie arch-lords.

"I'm sorry about all of this," I say. "I don't like seeing you locked up like a criminal."

Madoc shrugs. "I know it wouldn't have been your doing. And I know it'd be asking a lot for the fae of the Mists to see me as anything *other* than a criminal."

"Still… I know what it's like being in a cage, and I wouldn't wish that on anyone."

We look at each other for a moment, and I can tell he's remembering the night he opened up Orion's cage for me too. His tone softens. "At least this one is more spacious than the ones you've had to suffer. And it is a little relief to see they haven't decided to kill me just yet."

There's more truth than teasing in that statement. I meet his cloud-gray gaze, my stomach knotting all over again. I *need* him to listen to me, for both our benefits.

"They don't want to kill you at all," I say. "They're

hoping we can come to a deal, which would mean not just keeping you alive but releasing you."

Madoc blinks at me, genuinely startled. "What could they possibly think was worth letting one of the dreaded vermin run free after they've caught him?"

I gather my words and my resolve. "You want to see the Murk get a better life without war if you can, don't you?"

"You know I do," he says, his voice roughening with the passionate determination I have to admire. "That's why I'm here."

"Well then… The Seelie—and the Unseelie too, I'd imagine—would find it easier to trust the Murk, and you as their representative, if they see that you're willing to work with us. They'd let you go back to Orion under the condition that if you heard about any plans he's making that would hurt us—something like the curse you say he's tried to spark in me, or an attack or an ambush—you'd warn us ahead of time."

Madoc doesn't look unwilling, only skeptical. "I won't tell them anything that would harm *my* people."

"Of course not. And if there wasn't any news to pass on at all, that would be fine too, although I guess then we'd be at a standstill." I pause. "I think this could be a solid step in the right direction. You'd have a chance to talk more with the other Murk who might be willing to negotiate and let us know about any progress there as well."

"And that's it? No catch?"

I grimace. "They do want a show of faith to give us

some security that you wouldn't turn against us." I explain about Celia's suggestion as quickly as I can. "But if you don't instigate anything, none of the Murk will ever know. I'll—I'll make the arch-lords all take a vow to that effect before you agree to anything if I have to."

Madoc is silent for a long moment. He studies me, his expression unreadable. "What do you think?" he asks abruptly. "Do you honestly believe that going through with this deal would be better for all of us—not just the fae of the Mists?"

"Yes," I say without hesitation. "I wouldn't be here talking to you about it if I didn't. I argued with *them* about what was reasonable to propose before I even got here."

The corner of his mouth twitches upward. His expression may be shadowed and his cheek bruised, but that hint of a smile shows how handsome that face can be in unexpected ways.

"I can imagine you doing that," he says. He leans back on his hands, the hint of a smile falling into a pensive frown. "I'll need to think about it. I won't take too long, but—it's a lot to decide on."

"I'll tell them that. Thank you for at least considering it."

His smile doesn't come back, but a glint that's almost playful comes into his eyes. "It's a good thing for them they've got you on their side."

I get up, and he lies down on his back to gaze up at the sky as he does his thinking. How often has he gotten such a clear view of that sunlit expanse while living in the Refuge?

Can he even enjoy it while he's trapped in that cell?

A deeper urge grips me, to offer him even a fraction of what he's offered me by coming here. I wet my lips. "I have to report to the arch-lords, but I'll come back. I could bring a book if the guards will let me give that to you, or we could just talk. If you'd want."

Madoc pauses, tipping his head to the side to consider me. For a second, he looks so uncertain I want to reach right through the magical barrier and squeeze his hand. He really isn't sure what to make of my kindness either, is he?

The sudden vulnerability fades away behind an impassive front, but I know he means it when he says, "I'd like that."

As he leans his head back again, I limp toward the trees, watching for Whitt to come to meet me. The guards draw forward first. They must have been tracking my movements well enough to realize the conversation is over.

I've nearly reached the edge of the clearing when an odd prickling sensation races through my chest. I keep walking, not paying it too much mind after all the other twinges I've experienced with the pregnancy, but as my foot hits the ground with my next step, the prickle explodes into a lance of pain.

I gasp, my lungs seizing as if they've been stabbed through with a spear. My legs wobble. I grope for something to catch my balance, but the rush of agony has stiffened my arms and blurred my vision.

"Talia?" Madoc calls in alarm from behind me with the thump of him leaping to his feet.

I can't form words to answer him, to cry out to Whitt, anything. Two of Celia's guards rush to my side, but I crumple before they can reach me.

9

Talia

I don't remember much of the hustle back to the castle, most of it in Whitt's arms. The pain washes through my nerves in waves, always sharpest in my chest. In the moments between waves, I feel utterly weak, my muscles refusing to move, my limbs gone slack. And through it all courses a deepening fear.

I haven't escaped Orion's curse after all. It just took its time kicking in. And this is only the beginning. Who knows how horrible it might get from here when it was dreamt up in the mind of that brutal tyrant?

After a while, I can hardly think at all. I'm vaguely aware of being settled onto soft sheets in the amber light of my bedroom's glow orb. Words are murmured over me, but all they do is numb the barest edges off the pain. Whatever spells are being cast on me, they can't quite reach into the center of me where the attack seems to be coming from.

For I don't know how long, I'm lost in a daze. Then gradually the agony eases back. When it's dulled to the point that it's only a constant but faint prickling behind my breastbone, I open my eyes and look around.

All four of my mates are in the bedroom with me now. Sylas, Whitt, and Corwin are standing in quiet, anxious conversation off in the corner. August paces by the foot of my bed. Corwin turns with a flicker of relief through our bond at the realization that I'm more aware now, but August speaks before my soul-twined mate can say anything.

"I don't know how—it couldn't have been more than an hour beforehand that I checked her. There wasn't even a hint that anything was wrong. I don't see how I could have missed it… but I must have."

"The Murk appear to specialize in magic that catches us off-guard," Whitt says. He and Sylas follow Corwin around the bed.

Corwin grasps my hand. "I'm glad to feel you in a more comfortable state now, my soul. We're going to do everything we can to stop any future fits." He glances at Whitt, his jaw tightening. "What exactly did the rat say to her before the pain came over her?"

Whitt opens his mouth, but I get there first, my voice croaking a bit as I push the words from my throat. "It wasn't Madoc. He didn't do anything to me."

Corwin frowns. "You can't be sure of it. You were near

him when this curse or whatever it is hit you. *He* could be the trigger."

I push myself into a sitting position, ignoring August's noise of consternation. "I was near him for just as long yesterday night, and nothing happened then. I was walking *away* from him when it happened. I don't think we have any reason to blame him."

Whitt clears his throat. "I'm not saying we should remove the rat from all suspicion, but to my eyes he appeared very honestly distressed by Talia's collapse."

"If he is some kind of trigger, he may not even know it himself," Sylas says. "His king may have used him without him knowing."

"But how would Orion even be sure that Madoc would be able to get close enough to me to trigger anything, if that's what was needed?" I ask. "Even when he kidnapped me after the mating ceremony, he didn't dare come too close to the celebration, and that was before we were quite as guarded against the Murk. He obviously couldn't count on going undetected. I don't think that makes any sense either."

Sylas exhales roughly. "That may well be true, my love. And it's true that you suffered no ill effects from being in his presence earlier. Still, I think we need to proceed even more cautiously than before. He didn't agree to the conditions you offered him. He clearly thinks we're more the enemy than his king is."

I don't think there's anything else I can say—and to be honest, I wouldn't put it past Orion to have come up with some cruel scheme that would punish both Madoc and me. I just can't imagine him leaving a task that important so much to chance: the chances of Madoc getting so close without being caught, the chances that if he was caught, the fae who had him wouldn't kill him outright or refuse to let me anywhere near him.

The Murk king never believed the other fae really respected my opinions on anything. *He* certainly didn't when push came to shove. Even if he realized I'd want to defend Madoc, he'd have trouble imagining my mates allowing me to.

I pull my knees up under the sheets and tuck my arms around them. "So what happens now? I do feel reasonably all right." I glance at August. "Did that 'fit' do any actual damage to me?"

August's mouth twists. "I can pick up on a few traces of very minor internal injuries to your lungs and heart. Not so much that they wouldn't heal on their own given time, but if you continue to suffer from spells like that—if they get worse..."

"There has to be a way to tackle it," Whitt says firmly, though his eyes are dark with worry. "No magic exists that doesn't have a counter spell. It's only a matter of finding it. We can call in the best healers in both realms—and there's always places like the Serene Springs too."

But we've gone this long without finding a real cure to the other curses plaguing the fae of the Mists. I bite my lip.

The unexpected knock on the door makes all of us startle. Sylas goes over to answer it.

One of his staff stands outside. "My lord, Arch-Lord

Celia has come to speak with you. She has news about the prisoner."

I tense on the bed. She hasn't decided Madoc was responsible for my curse activating and taken matters into her own hands, has she?

"Tell her to come up," Sylas says. "My mate will want to hear whatever she has to say and to have the chance to weigh in too."

The woman hesitates as if she's afraid of Celia's reaction to that order, but only for a second. Then she darts off down the hall.

I pull back the sheets and slide to the edge of the bed, though I'm not in any hurry to try standing up. My mates look ready to spring to stop me if I did. I'm still wearing the same dress from before, so I'll look reasonably put together in front of the other arch-lord, even if I am technically now an invalid.

A shiver runs through me. I push my worries about the future away. The one thing I do know for sure is that the men around me will stop at nothing to protect me from this and every other threat I might face.

Celia arrives at the doorway looking typically stern but a little puzzled as well. She takes in the five of us and offers me a small dip of her head in acknowledgment. "It's good to see you somewhat recovered, Lady Talia."

I'm not sure what prompted that gesture of respect—maybe her thoughts about what her people would face if I didn't recover—but I'll take it.

"What's the urgent news?" Sylas asks.

Celia turns to him, her jaw working for a second as if

she doesn't totally want to tell him. "The rat shifter. Madoc, or whatever his name is. He's agreed to the deal."

My heart skips a beat. Whitt raises his eyebrows. "Just like that?"

Celia smiles thinly at him and then me. "I believe we may owe the credit to your mate. Not only did she pitch the terms to him well enough, but he seems motivated to see what else he might be able to find out from his king about her ailment. If he's to be believed."

A swell of tender emotion momentarily numbs the lingering prickle of discomfort in my chest. Madoc is willing to put his future safety in the hands of the people he hates so that he can help me yet again.

"We still need his proof," August says, flexing his shoulders as if he thinks he'll need to march over and demand it right now. "We can't assume—"

"He's already given it," Celia interrupts. "I wouldn't have come to report his decision to you unless it was firm. I arranged a clay tablet for him to mark, and he's done so. I only wanted to speak with you before I tell my guards to actually release him."

There's a pause between my mates. I suspect now that they're faced with the reality of letting a rat shifter loose, they can't help being unsettled, no matter how much this one has proven himself. I'm preparing to speak up in Madoc's favor again when Corwin slips his arm around my shoulders.

"The deal was made with the Seelie, so I can't speak to that. I don't object to him going free if he's committed to terms you feel will ensure he sticks to that deal. But before he leaves for however long he may be back with his kin for, I think we should speak to him about Talia's curse now that it's started to act on her. Perhaps he'll be able to observe something about it that we wouldn't, since he's much more familiar with the new magic of the Murk, or to suggest treatments we wouldn't normally make use of."

Whitt nods, a faint grin crossing his face. "Lord Bird is no feather-brain."

Celia considers the suggestion with a tilt of her head. "You'd let him get close enough to Lady Talia to examine her?"

Sylas hums. "We could start at more of a distance. We are putting a lot of trust in him as it is. I say we should extend that trust at least somewhat to this urgent situation. Show him that we'll keep *our* end of the deal before we ask more of him." He looks at Celia. "Can you have your guards escort him to the field just outside the summer entrance to this castle?"

"Are you sure?" she asks.

"We won't throw caution utterly to the wind. If he can offer any insight, it'll be worth the attempt."

Corwin supports me as I rise onto my feet. I test my balance with a couple of typically uneven steps and find I can walk like normal, no additional pain waking up inside me and no weakness gripping me. I squeeze his arm. "I think I'm okay for now."

My mates all stay within easy reach as we head down to the summer-side entrance. Corwin is monitoring my internal state so closely I can practically feel his attention brushing through me.

We'll get through this, I tell him. *We've gotten through so much else. One little curse isn't going to stop me now.*

But for the first time since I started reassuring myself that way in the face of the various threats I've encountered among the fae, I don't know that I totally believe it myself.

Sylas leads us to a spot about halfway between the border castle and the pack village of Hearth-by-the-Heart, as if he doesn't want Madoc getting too close to either of those sites. He and Whitt quickly conjure a narrow wooden table and chairs, so it'll even feel like a proper meeting—although from the words they continue to murmur around the furniture afterward, I suspect they're also building in protections against whatever they're worried the Murk man might do.

They arrange it so that there are five seats along one side, with our backs to the castle, and one chair on the other. The setup gives the sense of an interrogation, but it's a big step for them to accept Madoc this near our homes to begin with, so I don't complain.

Sylas has me sit at the far right of the table. He sits in the middle where he'll be most directly facing the rat shifter, with August between him and me, Corwin at his other side, and Whitt at the far end.

We've only just sorted that out when a cluster of figures comes into view, emerging from the path that leads into the nearest stretch of forest. Five of Celia's guards stand in a ring several feet wide with Madoc in the center, swords in their hands, a shimmer in the air that suggests they've brought some of the holding cell's barrier with them.

Madoc looks uneasy, but when his gaze veers from us to the pulsing glow of the Heart just down the border, something in his face softens. I can see even at a distance that the source of magic he either rejected or lost so long ago still stirs awe in him.

When they reach us, Sylas motions to the guards. "You can leave him in our care. He's soon to be completely released regardless."

The guards stiffen a bit at that order, but they bow and remove the magical barrier around Madoc before shifting into wolf form to lope back to their own domain. Madoc stands tensed with his hands braced against the back of the chair, taking us all in.

His gaze stops on me. "You're all right," he says, relief and horror warring in his tone. "I was afraid—it came on you so quickly—"

"I get the impression that your king enjoys drawing out his torments rather than seeing them to the end immediately," Whitt remarks dryly from the other end of the table.

Madoc's mouth tightens. "He does indeed."

Sylas inclines his head toward the chair. "I hope you'll take a seat. I understand you've accepted our terms and confirmed our deal through Arch-Lord Celia. We were only hoping to have a short discussion before you're on your way—since you seem concerned about our mate's wellbeing."

Madoc's stance relaxes just a bit. I can't tell whether it's because Sylas has confirmed that he's being released or because of the realization that this meeting is about me.

He tugs back the chair and sinks into it, keeping a careful pose as if he might need to leap away quickly. I guess he can't help his instinctive guardedness.

"If there's any way I can help you ensure Talia's safety, I'd be happy to do it," he says. "That was the only reason I came here in the first place. I won't be able to question Orion too insistently or he'll get suspicious, but I'm sure I can find out *more* about what the curse entails, maybe even some hint about curing it."

"There's one obvious way," August says. "I know you dismissed this idea before, but it's more pressing now. If we could get at that false Heart of yours and destroy it, then all the magic that came from it would vanish too."

"Yes," Corwin agrees. "And that would end our curses as well. It seems a simple solution."

I didn't know they were going to make that argument, but the vibe along my side of the table tells me it was planned. They must have discussed it earlier while I was too out of it to pay attention.

Madoc grimaces. "That depends on what you mean by simple. It took Orion decades to develop the magic to create our Heart and over a century to build its power. I have no idea how you'd destroy it. You'd have a hard enough time getting to it, even if I was willing to show you the way to the Refuge. You'd better believe Orion has sentries all over watching for any sign of Seelie or Unseelie presence through any portal within reasonable traveling distance."

"*If* you were willing," Sylas repeats.

Madoc narrows his stormy eyes at the Seelie arch-lord.

"I thought I made it clear that I'm not willing to throw so many of my people to be slaughtered by yours over one ruler who's taken things a step too far. I swore to report back any information that might protect your people and Talia's, and if there's a chance to remove just Orion, I'll inform you of that. But if we can find a way to end the curses that doesn't touch the Heart, I'd rather we used that."

Whitt raises his eyebrows. "Awfully attached to it, are you?"

"You don't understand." Madoc's gaze drifts to the Heart of the Mists again. He jerks it back to my mates. "Most of us can't reach *your* Heart anymore. Orion's is the only source of magic we can draw on. We've used it to grow things and heal and all sorts of other purposes that have nothing to do with hurting anything. There's nothing harmful about the Heart itself."

"It sounds as if we need to table that possibility for the moment anyway, until we can be sure of getting the upper hand," Sylas says. "The magic acting on Talia comes from that Heart, from the powers you're much more familiar with than we are. I know you aren't aware of any definite cure right now, but we want to hear any ideas you have about healing or dispelling strategies that are common among your kind."

Madoc studies me. "I'm not sure. We don't typically curse each other or lift the curses we cast on others. The curser sets the conditions." He pauses. "We make a lot of use of shielding—to stop bleeding, to section off wounded or sickly parts of the body so they don't affect the rest...

It's possible something like that would at least slow down the progression."

I'm tired of sitting here being talked about as if I'm in a coma, unable to contribute. "Can you sense anything about the curse now that it's active—what it'll do, how it'll affect me?"

His gaze becomes more intent. Then he shakes his head. "Not from here."

I resist the urge to roll my eyes. "You can come closer."

Sylas coughs. "I'm not certain—"

He cuts himself off, taking in the Murk man's reaction. Madoc has gone even more tense in his chair, his shoulders rigid. Sylas's brow furrows. "*You* don't want to get closer to her."

Madoc seems to grapple with his words before he speaks. He doesn't look at me. "It's occurred to me that it might not be a coincidence that she got sick right after she spoke to me. I don't have any awareness of anything in or around me affecting her, but if there's any risk at all—"

"Oh my God, enough!" I burst out. "Between the bunch of you, you'll end up missing the cure because you're too afraid of doing anything." I push to my feet and limp around the table as forcefully as I can. The men all leap up too, Madoc included. Before he can back away, I snatch his wrist and pull his hand toward me so his palm rests against my dress over my breastbone.

He freezes, not jerking out of my grasp but looking utterly miserable. "Talia, if there's a chance that I—"

"If there's any chance that you being near me is going to set off another fit, then we might as well find that out in the early stages, don't you think?" I fix him with my firmest look and then glance at my mates, who don't look all that much happier about the situation than Madoc does, but have settled for coming up around us at a short distance in case they need to intervene.

Madoc gradually relaxes again, letting his hand rest against me. The warmth of his palm, a little more potent than the pleasant summer air around us, seeps through the fabric into my skin. He adjusts his fingers a tad and murmurs a few words, his gaze darting briefly to our audience as if worried my mates will pounce on him. A tingle carries through my chest that doesn't feel particularly different from when August has checked me over.

Madoc's mouth slants downward. "I can feel the spell. I can feel Orion's influence in it." He closes his eyes and intones a couple more syllables.

Nothing changes inside me except that brief tingling sensation. The prickling patch between my lungs remains, but it doesn't expand or intensify. That only makes me surer that Madoc wasn't the trigger.

If we let paranoia like that interfere with how much we trust each other—or ourselves—then Orion will have already won.

"I've never encountered anything quite like that," Madoc says after a moment. "I don't know—the barrier suggestion I made earlier would be difficult to attempt even at this stage, with the lingering energy of it being so close to her vital organs. But maybe, now that I have a clearer sense of the curse, I'll come across something that would point me in the right direction once I'm home."

He opens his eyes, moving to withdraw his hand. I release his wrist. As his fingers and their warmth leave my chest, his gaze catches mine from where he's standing over me, just a couple of feet away. His fleeting touch brings me back to the brief brush of his lips against mine just before I left the Refuge—and stirs up a sudden curiosity about how it would feel to have him claim my mouth more thoroughly.

My cheeks flush. I step back toward my chair, willing away those thoughts as fast as I can.

He didn't hurt you, my soul? Corwin asks through our bond, with no sign that he's noticed the odd direction my emotions momentarily veered in.

No, I feel perfectly fine. "Madoc didn't have anything to do with setting off the curse," I say out loud. "So let's stop worrying about that and focus on finding a real solution."

Whitt chuckles. "You are adept as always at putting us in our places, mighty one."

"I suppose I should go and see what I can learn, then?" Madoc says with a doubtful note in his voice. Is he still waiting for the other fae to reveal this was all a ploy and he can't leave after all?

Sylas nods. "Yes. Report back with anything you hear that it'd benefit us to know as soon as you can."

"It's likely that Orion will send me back here of his own accord once I make my report to *him*. But I can't promise I'll have come across anything all that useful in the meantime." Madoc turns from them to focus on me again. "I'll do as much as I can. If there's any way I can help you, I will."

"I know," I say quietly, still grappling with the unexpected feelings stirred up by his nearness. "Thank you."

"Thank *you*," he says. "For being willing to believe in us despite what the man ruling us has done to you."

Without hesitation now, he nods to my mates and walks away toward the forest. One moment he's a man, striding along, and the next he's vanished—or almost. All that's left is a small, pale-furred shape darting through the grass.

Back to his home and to the king who'll destroy us all if he has his way.

10

Corwin

I've always been an early riser, and that tendency has only deepened while my worries for Talia dog me. The sun is barely painting the horizon gold when I cross from the palace of Heart's Cadence to the border castle to check on her. When I stop outside her bedroom, I can tell from the muted impressions through our bond and the rasp of subdued breaths filtering through the door that both she and Whitt, who stayed by her side tonight, are still sleeping.

I have no interest in waking her from her much-needed respite, but I don't find I can sit calmly in the common rooms or my own bedroom waiting for her to awake. My restless feet carry me back through the halls and out the door to wander in the briskly cool breeze that dances across the icy plain. Not even the melody that breeze summons in the diamond walls of my own palace soothe my nerves.

A couple of healers arrived last night and tried a few spells on Talia, and she hasn't lapsed into the same pained state that took her yesterday morning so far. But it might have been days from the curse being triggered until she first showed symptoms. Who knows how it'll pace itself? The healers couldn't discern those kinds of details in their examination of my mate.

A few more, the most skilled fae in the healing arts from across all the domains of the Mists, will be arriving throughout the day as the messengers we sent reach them. Heart willing, we won't even need them. But after everything I've seen from the Murk and their wretched king at this point, I'm not feeling particularly optimistic.

Our best chance may lie in the rat who came bearing the warning. A rat Talia has softened to more than I'm sure I like. She cares so deeply and is willing to forgive so much, my kind-hearted love. It worked to my benefit when she and I barely knew each other, but now...

There was a flicker of something deeper than gratitude in her after he checked her curse. And I may not be the most experienced in romantic relationships out of all fae kind, but his response to her strikes me as more devoted than simple compassion.

If *he* ends up hurting her...

As I shake that thought away, one of my colleagues who's perhaps even less successful in her personal relationships than I've been soars into view. I recognize Laoni from the turquoise tint to her feathers and the quality of her movement before she lands, transforming into her usual form an instant later.

She swipes her hand over her thick hair that's a lighter shade of the same hue as her feathers and tips her head in acknowledgment. "I thought… I'd see how you're faring, with the new developments."

I'd informed my fellow arch-lords of Madoc's claim about the curse shortly after I heard it, of course, and of the fact that it appeared to be taking hold the first time I forced myself to leave my mate's side after her fit. Talia's fate affects the entire fae world. I can't help wishing just this once that I could set aside my duties as ruler and focus only on her, though.

"It's distressing, of course," I say to Laoni, who's probably inspecting me for signs of my mother's sort of grief-stricken deterioration as we speak. "But we're tackling the problem every way we know how, quickly and decisively. If there's a solution within our grasp, we'll find it."

If there's not… I'm not thinking about that yet.

Laoni rubs her mouth. For a moment, she just gazes off across the glittering landscape alongside me as if we're contemplating the same topic together. I haven't typically seen her this pensive. I'm not sure whether to be relieved or concerned by her new demeanor.

"I'm sorry you're having to face yet another threat to your mate," she says finally, without looking at me. "I can only imagine how difficult it must be to have her right there and yet not be sure of how to save her."

I blink at her, taken aback by the unexpected

condolences. Of all the fae I might encounter, Laoni is the *last* I'd have expected to express any sympathy. She's spent most of the few months since Talia joined us doing everything she can to undermine my mate and our union.

But things have changed. Talia became Laoni's savior as well as that of so many of our people. Just a few days ago, she delivered her cure to my fellow arch-lord a second time—at Laoni's palace, keeping it secret as Laoni prefers.

And perhaps my colleague *can* imagine how I feel better than she might have before. She lost someone in a much more final way—someone she wasn't there to save.

"The rats have a lot to answer for," I say tentatively, knowing how she reacted to Talia's gentle overtures on this subject. "Including one of your long-time guards, I know."

Laoni keeps her gaze fixed on the distant mountains, but I've worked alongside her long enough to know from the flex of the muscles in her broad neck that the remark affects her. She lets out a huff, and her voice turns just a little ragged. "We should have exterminated all those vermin ages ago before it could get to this point."

She still won't acknowledge the feelings she held for Kesral or even the childhood friendship they once shared. What did her father say to her, how did he push her over the years, for her to get to the point where she'd distance herself so much from a man she cared about deeply, simply because one of his birth parents was human?

I hardly think she'd answer that question, so I speak to the actual words she said. "I believe we were slaughtering as many of them as we encountered. It does get difficult to interfere much with those living in the human world without exposing ourselves to mortals more than is wise."

"We should have cut them all down before they fled there from the Mists." Her expression hardens. "We may need to make some compromises on our typical rules about exposure. I want to see that king of theirs, his Heart, and everyone who stands with him torn to shreds."

The furious vehemence in her voice resonates with my own inner turmoil. A picture flashes through my head of a horde of ravens descending on the swarming rats, slicing through them with our talons, tossing them into their false Heart until it suffocates with their bodies.

The thought brings a twinge of satisfaction into my chest, but it's a sickly sensation that turns my stomach as well. If Talia were awake and aware of me, she'd recoil from the images. I know she hates what Orion stands for and she wouldn't regret seeing him fall, but she doesn't want this to turn into a full-out war on either side if she can help it.

After the blood she's already seen spilled, her parents' and her brother's, and how much she's had to give of herself, I can't say I blame her.

"I want to see those who'd harm us dead too," I tell Laoni. "But I think we need to proceed with moderation. We once thought the Seelie were all villains, and clearly that isn't the case. None of us has really had a conversation with one of the Murk in centuries. Madoc seems reasonable enough."

Laoni scoffs. "Because it benefitted him to appear that way."

"It's because of him we have Talia back with us at all," I remind her and myself at the same time.

"Well, some people *can't* be brought back," she mutters. Then her gaze flicks to me finally, with a hint of anxiety. "Your mate had some specific ideas about my associations with my staff that—"

Is she going to outright deny it even after she's been calling for the blood of the ones who killed her old friend?

I shake my head before she can go on. "I know about the conversations you had. I make no judgments of you based on them. I'm still sorry that you've had to experience the loss. We need say no more about it."

Laoni's mouth tightens. I get the impression she feels she should thank me for how I've handled the situation but also doesn't want to acknowledge there was anything to handle. She settles for sighing. "I will stick to the agreement we came to that we will question any Murk caught venturing into our territory or by the patrols in the human world. But only because I want to squeeze every clue I can out of them that might allow us to wipe them from existence."

She takes off as a raven before I have a chance to answer her last proclamation. There wasn't much I could have said in response anyway.

A sense of groggy movement passes through my awareness—Talia is emerging from sleep. I'm about to turn to go in and greet her for the morning, to take some small pleasure in the fact that she's still well, when a carriage comes into view against the backdrop of the mountains. My heart sinks.

Of course, the other curses we face haven't disappeared just because a new one has emerged.

I head over to meet the vehicle as soon as it reaches the plateau. Since Talia's kidnapping, our brethren have been more frugal in how many flock-folk they send to accompany a curse victim. As the carriage slows, I make out just four figures—the man who's the afflicted one from the bluish pallor of his face, a woman sitting close to him who appears to be his mate, a younger man with similar features who's probably a son, and an older woman who's directing the craft while the others are distracted by their loved one's illness.

"I'm sorry to see you but glad you've made it here before the worst," I tell them. "Make your way over to the area in front of the Heart, and Lady Talia will be out to perform the healing as soon as she's able."

My mate has already picked up on the activity, though her thoughts still feel a little muddled from the earliness of the hour. *I'll get dressed and come right down.*

You'll eat something first, I insist as I head to the border castle to make sure that happens. *He isn't going to freeze in the next hour. You need to look after yourself now more than ever.*

I'll eat a quick *breakfast,* Talia retorts. *I definitely don't need an hour. I'm not going to leave that man and his family in misery any longer than I have to.*

By the time I reach the castle, I can hear her and Whitt chattering in the kitchen already. I find them digging into stuffed rolls that August prepared in advance alongside dinner last night. He wanted to be sure of Talia having a breakfast that met his stringent approval while he was overseeing some of the current patrols this morning.

I pick up one myself and can't help savoring the crisp pastry as it melts in my mouth around the center of softened vegetables and fried meat in their tangy sauce. One reason not to mind my mate having three others: it's somehow brought even better meals into my life. Not that I'd mention that to Charles and Beth, whose offerings are still quite impressive as well.

"Is everything all right?" Talia asks me, maybe picking up on the lingering uneasiness from my conversation with Laoni.

"Laoni came to speak to me briefly," I say, deciding no more detail is needed. "She does tend to have a rather… chilling effect on my mood."

Whitt guffaws and then coughs when he nearly chokes on his bite of roll. "I like your sense of humor when you choose to bring it out, my feathered friend."

I half-heartedly glower at him, and Talia swats him. "You need to come up with some better nicknames for him. If 'mite' could become 'mighty one,' you're obviously capable of it."

Whitt smirks and tugs Talia close to press a kiss to the side of her neck. "You're still my mite, no matter how mighty you become."

"Well, your mite needs to go cure one of the curses I *can* tackle." She leans over to kiss him quickly on the mouth and hops off her stool. "I'm ready. Let's see to them."

Whitt follows us across the icy landscape to the Heart

where the four petitioners and their carriage are waiting. His keen eyes skim over the snowy plains, and I know he's searching for any hint of rats or their illusions.

Talia smiles at the hunched man, bending a little to bring herself level with his face. "You'll feel better soon. It barely takes any time at all."

She drags in a breath and closes her eyes, raising her inner wall at the same time. She doesn't like having me see the horrible memories she has to bring up to provoke her tears, ones I've witnessed through her before but that it pains me to be reminded of. I'd share them with her if she wanted, but I won't demand it.

It takes a minute or so before the first tears streak down her cheeks. She swivels away from the cursed man to pretend to hide them, covers her eyes, and then turns back to him with damp fingers. As she strokes those fingers down the side of his face, the curse retreats like a light going on inside of him. His body starts to relax—

And Talia's seizes up.

The pain lances through her so abruptly that I double over with it too. I stagger, throwing myself the few steps between us as Whitt also rushes to her side.

Her whole body is shaking, and I can feel why in the agony that radiates from her into me.

"What's wrong?" the now-cured man asks, his voice rasping but steady, his eyes wide.

I wrap my arms around my mate, not knowing what to tell him. She's sick too, no matter what those first healers did for her.

And we don't know if there's a single person in the

world who can cure her the way she just cured him.

11

Talia

The newest healer frowns and tweaks her bulbous nose the way she has a dozen times already, as if it's a switch that'll activate more of her skills. She murmurs a few more magic-laced words with her hands hovering above my chest.

I don't feel anything except a faint tingle of energy passing through me, the same as during all her other attempts. I can tell she hasn't noticed any difference either from the way she knits her brow afterward.

"I'll do some more searching of the records and meditation with the Heart, and return when I have more ideas," she tells me.

I nod my thanks and hold myself still and somewhat regal on the bed until she's stepped outside. Then I flop back into the pillows with a groan.

Corwin's voice flits into my head in an instant. *All right?*

Yes, I reply quickly. *Just no progress either. I know they're all trying to help, but I'm starting to feel like a test subject in a lab.*

Corwin sends a tendril of apologetic sympathy my way. *That's the last healer we've called on. I believe Sylas and Whitt should be returning soon with the results of their investigations. In the meantime, I'm sending someone up who will hopefully make you feel more like a person again.*

I sit back up, my curiosity piqued. *Who?*

All I get from my soul-twined mate is mischievous silence. I don't totally mind, seeing that he's been able to find a little good humor in spite of the situation.

It's only a minute before a soft knock sounds on the door and a cautious voice travels through. "Talia?"

A smile springs to my face. It's Harper. I haven't seen my best friend from the pack in days with all the upheaval.

"Come in," I say, scooting to the edge of the bed.

Harper slips inside, her slim form as graceful as ever. She takes me in with her over-large eyes, looking as if she's a little worried that I might collapse right in front of her at any moment.

"I'm fine," I say, my smile softening. "For now, anyway. It's good to see you." My gaze drops to the bundle of fabric she's hugging against her. I don't even need to ask the avid dressmaker what that is. My cheeks flush in sheepish embarrassment. "You didn't have to bring me any presents."

"It's not because you've been sick," Harper insists,

relaxing enough to hop onto the bed next to me. She pinches the shoulders of the new gown and gives it a shake to unfurl it. "I started working on it as soon as Sylas announced that you're with child. An expecting mother deserves the clothes to honor that fact." She grins at me.

As my gaze slides over the dress, I have to catch my breath. "It'll be an honor to wear something that gorgeous."

Harper's work is always impressive, but this... She's combined sections of deep green and rosy pink so that the wearer will look as if they're embraced by vibrant brambles bearing roses. A line of the delicate blooms arcs along the belly area as if to cradle the growing child. I can see in it how much any new life matters to the fae, how much the entire pack will be celebrating the baby growing inside me.

I rest my hand over the spot where it's growing, even if there's no outward sign of it yet just a few weeks in, and add, "Thank you. I love it." Now I just need to get my men to come up with an occasion for me to wear it. It's way too fine to act as a nightgown.

Harper grins even wider. She folds the dress with a few swift gestures, sets it farther back on the bed, and leans over to give me a quick hug. "I want to see you in it so many times on your way to becoming a mother and afterward."

There's an unspoken wish underlying those words. She wants me to survive long enough to wear it all those times.

I swallow hard. "I intend to," I say with all the confidence I can summon. I bring my legs up and turn to sit cross-legged against the headboard. "I haven't had much chance to see the rest of the pack lately. How's everyone doing? Anything interesting to report?"

I don't need to tell Harper that I'm looking for light-hearted news because there've been so many serious developments I'm already very aware of. She tucks the smooth strands of her flaxen hair behind her ear and tips her head to the side with a thoughtful smile.

"Well, the sheep made a break from their pen, and Elliot had to chase a few of them all the way onto Arch-Lord Donovan's domain. The way they were bleating when he brought them back, you'd think he was going to carve them up for dinner instead of just milk them to make cheese." She lets out a giggle. "And a couple of women from Arch-Lord Celia's pack asked me to make them matching dresses. You won't believe the theme they wanted…"

She chatters on about the day-to-day activity in the domains around the Heart, and I mostly sit back and listen. A bittersweet ache forms around my own heart that despite the possibility of impending war, normal life is still carrying on as well as it can—but I can't really take part in it.

Is Whitt still holding revels? I can't imagine him being in much of a partying mood these days, but I should encourage him to host one. The pack needs a chance to unwind and be happy even while we're guarding our home so carefully.

Harper is just finishing an animated recreation of a silly argument between Brigit and Pomya when footsteps sound in the hall outside. When the door swings open,

Harper's mouth snaps shut. She pulls her posture straighter as Sylas and Whitt come in. She's always a little awkward around the ruler of the pack, maybe remembering how close he came to banishing her after a few of Ambrose's pack-kin caught her up in a scheme against me.

Sylas shows no lingering animosity, though. He nods to her. "It was good of you to come. I can see my mate has been enjoying your visit." He gives me one of his quiet but warm little smiles.

"I'll come back again soon," Harper says to him and to me, giving me another quick hug, and hops off the bed. "I don't want to get in the way, though." She dips into a low bow, waves good-bye to me, and leaves me with my mates.

For a little while as she and I talked, I'd been able to avoid thinking about the reason Sylas and Whitt were out "investigating." Now, taking in their relatively somber expressions, my spirits sink. Everything isn't normal, especially with me.

"Was there nothing?" I ask. They'd been following up on a few mentions of rare curative plants from Whitt's records, but they hadn't been sure how accurate the brief details were or, in at least one case, whether the plant even existed to begin with.

Sylas sits down on the edge of the bed by my tucked feet and nods to Whitt, who detaches a leather pouch from his belt. "We were able to track down a couple of the herbs we were seeking. Neither of them gives off an aura that's particularly potent, but they show no sign of being harmful either, so we may as well see what they do."

The first sprig Whitt pulls out has shiny round leaves and puffy blue flowers. He pulls off one of the flowers and starts to crush it between his thumb and his opposite palm. "One story suggested that skybloom might dispel hostile magic if the mashed petals of the flower are rubbed over the afflicted area. It's only noted in one place, so it obviously hasn't been tested much."

I loosen the bodice of my dress so I can tug it down over my shoulders, letting the neckline settle against the slope of my breasts. Whitt swipes the blue paste across my sternum with some murmured words. The stuff absorbs into my skin over the next few minutes, leaving behind only a pale blue tint.

"Do you feel any different?" the spymaster asks.

I concentrate deeply, but I can't pretend the prickling sensation that's been with me since the curse first struck me has disappeared. It remains as always between my lungs. "No," I admit reluctantly. "As far as I can tell, the curse is still there the same as before."

"Well, the effect may take some time to kick in. In the meantime, we also managed to dig up a clayvin root." He brandishes something that looks like a knobby yellow carrot.

"*I* managed to dig it up, you mean," Sylas says with a hint of a teasing tone.

Whitt holds up his hands in mock self defense. "It's not my fault clayvin only grows in the deepest of crevices and you're a significantly better climber than I am. If I'd gone down, I'd never have come back up. It was my spell that found it, though."

Sylas chuckles. "I'll give you that."

Seeing their easy banter, hearing the way they worked together on their mission, brings a welcome warmth into my chest. I tip my head toward the root. "So what do we do with that one?"

Whitt waggles it. "This is meant to be made into a tea that you'll drink. But it's supposed to be brewed at sunset and drunk at midnight for the best effect. We've got a bit of a wait to try that one out."

"So much to look forward to," I joke, but my own laugh falls flat.

A cloud of gloom passes over both my mates again, and the warmth that formed before tightens into an ache. We *should* have so many things to look forward to: the newfound peace between the realms, our lives together as mates, the child I'll be bringing into that union. But the threat of the Murk has cast a shadow over all the joy we should be sharing.

We should celebrate anyway—because who knows if we'll have the opportunity to later.

I slip across the bed to tuck my arm around Sylas, leaning my head against his shoulder. He hums happily and hugs me to him. Whitt takes the opening to sit down at my other side, giving my shoulder a quick peck.

It's all very gentle and comforting, but being enveloped between their bodies and their contrasting scents, a spark of deeper heat flares low in my belly. I don't question the urge, just push myself up to plant a kiss on Sylas's mouth.

He kisses me back tenderly, his hand stroking over my

hair, but when I move to swing my leg over his lap, he catches me around the waist. "I don't think we should push the limits of your body right now."

I tug at his shirt. "I think we've discovered plenty of things my body is definitely capable of that wouldn't require pushing it to any limits."

"That was when you were well."

I balk at accepting the concern that's turned his brown eye even darker. I'm still their mate, and I want the full benefits of that relationship, thank you very much.

Keeping my fingers curled in the front of Sylas's shirt, I glance at Whitt and then back to the arch-lord. "I feel fine right now, other than missing getting properly close with my mates. It sounds like you two worked very well together finding me possible cures. There are lots of *other* ways I enjoy having you work together."

I do my best coy gaze through my eyelashes, but I'm not sure it works. I'm not exactly an expert at flirting. Sylas hesitates. Whitt teases his fingers over my outer thigh, but he doesn't move his hand any farther. I don't think he'll take me up on my invitation if his lord won't.

With a determined huff, I grip Sylas's shirt harder and straddle him before he can stop me again. I stare firmly into his mismatched eyes. "I want the men I'm mated with. The Murk are trying to take everything from me, and I'm not letting them take this away too. Don't you dare help them do it."

Then I press my mouth to his.

Whether it was my speech or the fierceness of my kiss or both, Sylas's reluctance flies out the window. He kisses me back with a growl, hard and hot, the hand on my waist sliding down to my bottom to pull me closer against him. I rock into him, gasping against his lips as I feel his shaft hardening beneath his trousers.

Yes. I want this. I want him, and Whitt, and all my mates when I have the chance.

I'm still alive. Orion hasn't broken me. We're together, and we'll celebrate that, no matter what other troubles come our way.

Another hand travels across my shoulders, brushing aside my hair. Then Whitt's skillful mouth is branding the side of my neck. As I continue kissing Sylas, the spymaster nibbles a path up to the crook of my jaw and then nips my earlobe with a jolt of pleasure that propels another gasp from my throat.

"I think our mighty mate should have what she wants when she's asking for it so very clearly," he murmurs, nuzzling my hair before marking another trail of heat down to my bared shoulder blade.

Sylas lets out a sound somewhere between a grumble and a groan. He tugs the bodice of my dress farther down, the neckline flicking over my nipples, and cups one of my breasts. The swipe of his thumb over the peak mimics the sweep of his tongue into my mouth to tangle with mine.

Whitt strokes his deft fingers over my other breast until my chest is awash with quivers of bliss. They drown out the faint prickling sensation completely. I arch into my mates' combined touch, kissing Sylas even harder and then turning my head to seek out Whitt's mouth as well.

How lucky I am to have this at all, to have found not

one but four mates who can take me to such heights and who're happy to do so alongside each other.

I grasp Whitt's shirt and pull back just enough to meet his eyes and then Sylas's. The declaration sears up from deep inside me. "Whatever happens, whatever Orion puts me through, I'm glad I'm here. I'd rather be here with you even with his magic in me than living a normal life in the human world. Even if giving you up would cure me, I wouldn't do it."

"Talia," Sylas says in a strained voice. He kisses me again, roughly, as if he doesn't know how else to express his response.

Whitt wraps his arm tight around me in the joint embrace. "The only way I'd ever give you up is if it was the only way to save you. But we won't let it come to that. And right now, all I want to do is see you writhing with all the ecstasy we're going to bring you."

The promise in his heated words sets off a giddy tingling over my skin. I yank at his shirt in an effort to hurry us on toward the writhing in ecstasy part. Chuckling, Whitt pulls it over his head.

I turn to him, sliding off Sylas's lap to mount my other lover in turn. As I trail my hands and my mouth over the toned planes of muscle defining Whitt's chest, he tips his head back with a strangled but pleased sound. I lap my tongue over one of his nipples, and then he's cupping the back of my head, drawing me up to claim my mouth as thoroughly as he can.

Sylas tosses aside his shirt and leans in, his bare skin scorching against my back. He kisses the back of my neck and down my spine, his hands teasing around my hips and between my legs, just shy of the spot now throbbing for contact.

I push Whitt down on the bed, unable to stop myself from grinding against him. He hisses through his teeth. Through some silent communication, he and Sylas lift me up to peel my dress and my panties off me. I tug at their trousers.

"So impatient, mite," Whitt teases, stealing another kiss as he unfastens his pants. While he kicks them off, Sylas tucks his hand right over my core.

I moan at the rush of delight. For a few seconds, all I can do is lean back into Sylas and ride his hand. When he pulls his fingers away, I whimper in protest, but it's only an instant before Whitt's hardness settles against me.

My mouth waters with the deepest kind of hunger I know. I shift forward over Whitt, knowing his body so well now that I can line myself up without even thinking. He caresses my cheek, his eyes alight with both desire and adoration, and thrusts up into me.

Pleasure sweeps through my sex and up into my torso. I sway over Whitt, meeting the rolls of his hips as my hands brace against his chest, adrift in the haze of sensation.

As Whitt pushes himself up to bring my breast to his mouth, Sylas traces my other opening with magically slickened fingers. My body trembles with eagerness. I reach back with one hand to squeeze his arm encouragingly, and he lets out a rumble that sounds almost desperate with his own hunger.

"My love," he murmurs as he stretches me with one finger and then two. An embarrassingly needy cry tumbles out of me. "You deserve every pleasure we can give you. Never be afraid to ask for what you want."

I ask now with the motions of my body, pressing back into his touch over and over as I rock with Whitt. An intoxicating heat spreads all through my abdomen. Then the head of Sylas's thick shaft tests me. He pushes inside slowly, a little farther with each bob of my hips over Whitt. The blissful burn of my stretching muscles nearly shatters me apart right there.

"Mmm," Whitt says. "This is indeed an excellent cooperative effort. We'll have to come up with them more frequently, I think."

He winks at me, and my breathless giggle is lost in a moan as both men plunge into me together. I clutch Sylas's arm braced next to me and Whitt's shoulder beneath me, riding the wave of ecstasy they've conjured inside me higher and higher.

With each gasp and whimper that slips out of me, they speed up their pace, their muscles flexing with the effort. Our skin dampens with sweat where our bodies brush against each other.

Whitt pinches my nipple and swivels his thumb over my nub at the same time, and I feel the wave start to break. The tremor shakes me, pleasure whirling through every nerve before it bursts like the flare of a bonfire.

Sparks fill my vision. As I cry out, my inner muscles clenching, both of my men groan. Sylas comes with me, Whitt following at his heels.

We collapse together in a jumble of sweaty limbs and sated breaths. I tug my mates closer on either side of me, seeking as much of their heat as I can get as my body coasts in the afterglow.

But even that contentment can't completely mute the faint, inescapable prickle that rises up through my chest once more.

12

Whitt

hen word comes at night that our rat of divided loyalties has returned to us, Sylas has him escorted to one of the meeting rooms in the castle of Hearth-by-the-Heart. We want our privacy for the discussion to come, but none of us wants the Murk man in the same building as Talia if we can help it.

The fact that he's returned so quickly, and not leading an army—at least not any we've spotted so far—bodes well. No Murk has acted on the bait Donovan arranged, a stray comment one of his pack-kin ensured Madoc overheard about a vulnerable town we're supposedly relying on for weapons, so it appears the rat shifter didn't pass that information on to his king. But I'm hardly going to throw caution to the wind.

Corwin and one of his older coterie men, Verik, join the three of us in the broad room with its gleaming wooden table, the two Unseelie looking a little out of place in the summery space. August, Astrid, and a couple others of Corwin's people have remained back in the border castle along with the usual assortment of guards. I kissed Talia good night there just an hour ago.

Madoc comes in escorted by four of our pack warriors. He looks a bit peeved about the level of security we're still enforcing, but he should just be glad that we arranged a signal for him to use to alert us that he was arriving, so it'd be our warriors going to bring him in and not Celia's or some other more hostile lord who might not care for the deal we made.

The rat shifter sits down at the end of the table we've left open for him. The guards hesitate behind his chair, glancing at Sylas for instruction. Even when he waves them off with a thank you for their service, they appear to balk momentarily before leaving us alone.

But I think two arch-lords and one near true-blooded fae are up to dealing with one Murk, no matter how good he is with illusions. I've already cast a spell that's now subtly humming through this space that will warn us if any magic is enacted by anyone other than the three of us.

"You returned quickly," Sylas says, leaning his elbows on the tabletop where he's sitting a few feet from the rat shifter. He keeps his tone as even as always, his expression a mask of authoritative confidence, but I recognize the keenness in his eyes. He's as eager as I am to hear what news our theoretical ally has brought from his fellow vermin.

"Yes," Madoc says, his gaze sliding from one to

another of us before settling back on Sylas. He flexes his hands as if confirming that they're not bound. "During my assignments, I typically spend long periods of time in this realm with only brief trips back to report to Orion. I couldn't linger in the Refuge for long without him questioning it. I told him that the curse had started to act on Talia and that all of the fae were concerned, because that's what he'd want to hear, and he sent me back here to monitor how the situation progresses."

He pauses, and his gaze darts around the table again. The wary edge leaves his voice. "Is she still all right? I'd hoped—is she not well enough to leave her room?"

He expected Talia to be here when we spoke with him. I suppose that's not surprising, seeing as she played by far the largest role in making this deal happen. I can't stop a little dryness from creeping into my tone when I respond. "She's perfectly well at the moment, other than future concerns, but seeing as it's the middle of the night, she's asleep. You aren't so important that we were going to disturb her rest just because you showed up."

I anticipate a sharp reply, but instead Madoc looks a bit chagrinned. He does care about my mate in his own odd way, doesn't he? I'm not totally sure what to make of that or how to feel about it.

"Of course," he says. "I wasn't thinking—we're typically awake all night and sleeping most of the day unless there's something specific to take care of." His jaw works. "What exactly does 'perfectly well' mean? Has she had any more bad spells from the curse?"

The three of us exchange a glance over the table,

debating how much to tell him. Corwin clears his throat, and I figure he's the most cautious of us, so I'll accept whatever he feels is an acceptable level of detail.

"She's had two more fits since you left," he says. "They seem to come over her relatively briefly about once a day, though the timing hasn't been at all predictable." He stops there, and from the shadow that crosses his face, I suspect he's remembering how she crumpled during our dinner together in the joint castle just hours ago.

"Were you able to learn anything more about the curse in the short time you spent back in the Refuge?" Sylas asks, bringing us back to the most important subject. "I assume you have something to share with us, or you wouldn't have announced your arrival."

Before he even speaks, the twist of Madoc's mouth reveals that he hasn't got much. "I thought it'd be best if I came straight to you in case there's any way I can contribute. Orion will think it's strange if I return home again too quickly with no major news, so I might as well be here offering what I can." He exhales roughly. "I did press him as much as I felt I could get away with about the nature of the curse. He indicated that the pattern you've seen of short attacks and then seeming recovery was normal. It's his way of jerking around your hopes."

"Wonderful," Sylas mutters. "Anything else?"

"He seems very sure that nothing you could attempt to cure her with will work," Madoc says grimly. "Which is another reason it seems better for me to be here than wandering around accomplishing nothing. He thinks the Seelie and the Unseelie don't have the powers or knowledge, but he doesn't know there are any Murk willing to help."

How much is he here because he doesn't want to see Talia suffer and how much because he's worried that if he can't come up with some other cure, we'll find a way to destroy his false Heart, the source of his people's magic? I could tell how much *that* means to him from his protest about destroying it.

I suppose his motivations don't really matter as long as we can make her well again in the end.

Corwin's head droops for a moment, and I can't help feeling a pang of sympathy for the man who's experiencing Talia's curse nearly as vividly as she herself is. He knows exactly how much agony it's already put her through.

"It's true that none of our attempts so far have appeared to make any difference to her condition," he says. "Nor have we been able to work with the barrier magic you mentioned to prevent the fits—as you suggested, the curse appears to be in too close contact with her essential organs to be sectioned off."

Madoc frowns. "I wish I was better at the healing arts myself. This far from my own Heart... And we can't exactly call on the Murk medics I know."

He halts there, and his gaze goes momentarily distant. My senses spring to the alert. He shakes himself and doesn't add anything to that thought, but he was obviously remembering *something* relevant. I file that knowledge away for later.

"What about your king's preparations for war?" I ask.

"Did you get a sense of how soon he intends to move on us?"

Madoc inclines his head. "He's continuing to stockpile equipment and gather as many Murk as are willing to fight. He hasn't mentioned any specific plans to launch an attack soon. From what he's said, I believe he's waiting until Talia's curse has gotten significantly worse—or perhaps even reached its… end. So that you'll be distracted by your worries or your grief."

My lips curl back at the vileness of the strategy. We're working on a timeline directly connected to Talia's wellbeing, then. Keep her well, stave off the war.

If only it were so easy.

"Well, at least we don't have to be concerned about an immediate offensive," I mutter.

Madoc turns to the arch-lords. "I also know that Orion is trying to make it as painful as possible for you to intrude on the human world. He's had sentries observing the portals your patrols are most frequently coming through and has put out the word that any Murk who can bring back the heads of fae of the Mists will be well-rewarded. If you want to protect your people, you may want to stick to defending your borders on this side of the divide."

Corwin gives him a pointed look. "Which would also mean it'd be much harder for us to keep track of most of the Murk activity ourselves."

Madoc spreads his hands. "I can only tell you what I know. It's up to you what you do with the information. If you think it's worth getting into who knows how many skirmishes and potentially losing a bunch of your soldiers before the war's even really begun, have at it."

I think of August returning from his foray in Munich with the corpses of several loyal warriors and wince inwardly.

"We'll discuss the best strategy in more detail among ourselves," Sylas says. "Do you have anything more to add?"

"Those are the only things I picked up that I thought might be useful to you," Madoc says. "If I notice anything while I'm here that makes me think I have other information that's relevant, I'll tell you then."

My brother looks as if he's restraining a frown, but he simply nods and pushes back his chair. "Then I'd suggest we all get some sleep of our own and discuss the situation further in the morning—at which point you can also speak to Talia, as I'm sure she'll want to see you. I've set up a small cabin for your use in my domain. I hope you'll understand that for the time being we'll continue to have it guarded and magically secured when none of us is around to accompany you elsewhere."

Madoc's mouth flattens, but he seems to be putting forth his best behavior too. "I hope that in time you'll determine that those precautions aren't necessary, but considering it's a step up from the hospitality offered before, I'll take it."

As he stands, I follow suit, raising my hand. "Actually, I'd like to speak with our Murk companion a little more. You two don't have to wait up."

Sylas hesitates, and I can practically feel Corwin's

apprehension radiating off him, but they both trust *me* enough now to sense that I have a private conversation in mind. The rat may reveal more when he doesn't have two menacing arch-lords breathing down his neck. They bob their heads in acknowledgment and leave the two of us.

Madoc sits back down as I do, eyeing me with twice as much suspicion than before. "What else do you want to talk about? I've answered all of your questions as well as I can."

I hum to myself. "Perhaps, but I'm not sure you've shared all the answers to questions you came up with yourself. You had an idea when you talked about the Murk healers you know, didn't you?"

Madoc tenses in his seat. "If I thought it was worth bringing up, I would have."

"Why don't you let me decide what's worthwhile and what's not? I'm the strategist here—don't put me out of a job."

Obviously despite himself, Madoc's lips twitch with a hint of a smile. It disappears as quickly as it showed itself. "Even if you'd want to do something with this information, I'm not sure *I'd* want to pursue it. And you'd need my cooperation."

"I accept those terms," I say. "Let's see what we can hash out. You're used to working around obstacles and tackling challenges in unexpected ways, aren't you? That's what Murk are known for. Add in a little wolfish wisdom, and we'll see where that gets us."

My nonchalant demeanor appears to put the rat shifter a little more at ease. He sighs and rolls his shoulders. "I only— There is a Murk woman I've heard of who's very powerful with magic. I don't know if she has any specific affinity for healing, but there've been rumors that she's second only to Orion in power. Which is a good thing for Orion—that he's still on top—because she doesn't like him much. She has her own small colony that she's refused to unite with his empire."

I tap my mouth. "Interesting. And you think we might appeal to her to see if she can break his curse on Talia, on the grounds that she'd get to really piss him off by doing so."

Madoc's mouth twitches again, how much because he's surprised that I followed his train of thought and how much because my phrasing amuses him, I'm not certain. "That's the gist of it, yeah. But I only know *of* her—I've never met her myself. I have a basic idea of where and how I could reach out to her, but I'd also need to ensure that no one associated with Orion ever finds out I did, or I won't be around to help anymore. It's also possible that she hates the fae of the Mists even more than she dislikes Orion."

"Reasonable concerns." I set my hands on the table, clasping them together. "Let's see if we can address them. I wouldn't think hiding yourself would be so hard. Are you a master of illusions or aren't you?"

Madoc grimaces at me. "My magic will definitely help me avoid notice. It won't help me convince her to speak to me."

I shrug. "From the sounds of things, she'll be more

inclined to talk to you if she *doesn't* know who you are than if she's aware you're one of Orion's 'knights.'"

"All right, you have a point there." Madoc lets out a short chuckle. His eyes narrow, not at me but at the problem he's picturing, and all at once I can see the schemer in him, a mind that could align with my own.

"What would probably be *even* better is if I put an illusion on one of your people to help you reach her unnoticed by any spies. Then you could present your case directly along with a reward to encourage her to listen…" He pauses, and one of his eyebrows lifts. "I hear she's particularly fond of barbtooths and duskapple wine. We don't get much of either in the human world."

"I'd suppose not." I laugh and let a smile cross my face. I may not trust the man in front of me farther than I could spit him, but weaving a plan with him might actually be enjoyable. "Now how would we get her attention in the first place…"

13

Talia

I stop outside the cabin hidden away in the woods just beyond Hearth-by-the-Heart's castle, not sure whether to be more grateful to see that Madoc's living quarters here are significantly more private and comfortable than the holding cell he was stuck in last time, or unsettled by the guards and the hum of magic that still hold him captive. I understand Sylas's need for caution, but how long will my mates continue treating Madoc like an intruder rather than an ally?

August speaks to one of the guards, who at least does Madoc the courtesy of knocking on the door before opening it. "You've got visitors," she says gruffly. "You can come out."

The Murk man appears in the doorway with the wary expression that's his primary mode around the fae of the Mists, but when he finds me there, it relaxes a little with the start of a smile. "I wasn't sure they were actually going to let you come see me."

"My lord keeps his word," August says with a hint of a growl.

Madoc holds up his hands. "No criticism intended. You're protecting your mate from the disreputable rats. It's very admirable." His tone walks the line between sympathy and sarcasm.

August frowns as if he's not sure which way to take the remark and seems to decide he'll just ignore it altogether. He sets his hand on the small of my back as if *I* need reassurance. "She's here. If there's anything you want to say to her, you can now."

Madoc's stormy gaze takes me in, and his voice gentles. "They said you've been mostly all right other than a couple more short spells of the curse."

It isn't exactly a question, but I hear the need for confirmation in it. "That's right," I said. "I feel pretty much fine most of the time. Just every now and then…" I shrug as if it's no big deal, as if my stomach doesn't clench up with the worry about when another attack might hit me, how it'll be if they intensify or start coming closer together—or both.

Madoc's mouth twists. "I suppose they've told you that I haven't been able to bring much news. Orion likes to keep his cards close to his chest."

"I know. I'd rather you stayed cautious than made him suspicious of you. Whitt did say that the two of you have come up with a possible plan."

He lets out a rough chuckle. "We'll see how that goes.

He's supposed to come around later to work out the rest of the details. After he's consulted with his colleagues who aren't rats, I guess, to make sure I'm not leading you all astray."

I fix him with a firm look that I hope conveys as much confidence as I want it to. "It'll take some time, but they'll see that you really do want to help. It isn't as if you're all that happy to be working with them either."

"Fair point." He exhales in a rush, and I notice the shift of his weight on his feet, from one side to the other and back again. He's been stuck in the little cabin for hours.

"Do you want to take a walk while we talk more?" I ask with a twinge of concern. "Stretch your legs, enjoy the fresh air…?"

Something flickers in Madoc's eyes before his small smile returns. "I'd like that very much if my keepers will agree."

I glance at August, who knits his brow and then motions to the guards. "We'll give you some space," he says, "but I'm not letting you out of my sight."

"I wouldn't expect you to," Madoc says before I need to reply. He studies the guards as if making sure this isn't some kind of trick and then steps over the threshold.

It's still odd seeing him walk around without his tail, as if he's missing an essential limb. But having it out would *definitely* draw the wrong kind of attention around here. I wonder if it bothers him to hide it away after spending so much time with it out in the open in the

Refuge. But then, he must be used to sticking to his purely man form when he's on his missions to the Mists.

The thought of all the times he spied on us in the past with nothing but hostility in his heart makes my gut knot. But he didn't know me then, just as we didn't know him. A lot can change in not much time at all.

I let him direct our path, and he ambles through the trees in the general direction of Hearth-by-the-Heart's castle. August and the guards follow several paces behind us. I can't see her, but I know Astrid is standing guard somewhere nearby too. Corwin is a constant presence inside me, watching through my eyes.

"No one's been too hard on you since you came back, have they?" I ask, not knowing if Madoc would even admit it to me if they had been. Whatever the fae of the Mists might say about the Murk, they do have their pride.

"No," Madoc says, in a tone that's bemused enough that I believe him. "Your pack has been downright gracious compared to my reception last time." He sucks in a deep breath, and his eyelids dip for a moment as if he's savoring the warm forest air with its tang of pine and spruce. Then his gaze veers to me again. "If you don't mind talking about it, what exactly are you feeling from the curse? I got my own sense of it, but knowing the 'symptoms' might help."

My hand rises to my chest automatically, settling on the spot right over my breastbone where I guided his hand a few days ago. "Most of the time it's just a faint sort of prickling sensation that feels like it's right between my lungs. When it's bad, it's like that spot… bursts, with no warning at all, into a bunch of knives jabbing into me from the inside." I wince at the memories. "Sharp pain, and a lot of it. It's hard for me to think or really pay attention to anything more specific than that while it's happening."

Madoc's jaw has tightened. "But it doesn't last very long?"

I shake my head. "About a half hour, I think, all three times so far." Will it affect me *longer* the next time? I'm probably going to have another fit sometime today… I swallow hard and push that thought away. "I'm managing. It could definitely be worse."

"There's nothing very surprising about your description," Madoc says grimly. "Orion does like to be unpredictable and keep his enemies on their toes. I wish he hadn't decided you counted among those enemies."

"Well, the alternative was becoming his ally, and I definitely wasn't going to do *that*."

"I know." Madoc falls silent. As we emerge from the trees into the sunlight, he tips his face to the brighter warmth. An odd hunger crosses his expression, and it occurs to me that while he might have gotten plenty of fresh air during his missions into the Mists, he probably spent most of that time staying concealed in the darkness.

He glances toward my feet as if checking whether my limp has worsened and slows just slightly, heading across the fields at an angle that'll give both the castle and the pack village a wide berth, which is probably wise. Those little gestures—the recognition of where both I and my pack are vulnerable and the consideration to those factors —bring an ache into my chest that has nothing to do with the curse.

My mates *have* to see that this man has no interest in harming us. All he wants is to be treated as an equal, his ideas and goals worthy of consideration.

I can relate to that struggle on a bone-deep level. I'm *still* fighting to get all of the arch-lords to give my opinions their due. In some ways, as a human, I have more in common with the Murk than the rest of the fae. And I know how set in their ways they can be.

But I've made progress. I have to make sure Madoc can too. He's definitely determined enough, as long as he doesn't give up on the fae of the Mists completely.

He might have no intention of hurting us, but he's under threat himself because of his deal with the Seelie. I swallow hard and then ask, "You don't think Orion suspects anything at all, do you? He hasn't shown any sign that he's skeptical of your reports or whatever?"

Madoc shakes his head. "No, not that I've noticed. I don't think he trusts *anyone* completely, but he's mentioned things in my presence that I can't imagine him saying if he thought I might pass them on. It just may become increasingly difficult keeping his suspicions off me as I get more involved."

I have the urge to take his hand and squeeze it, but I'm not sure if he'd appreciate the gesture. "If you feel like you're no longer safe with him—or he shows that you're not—you can come here. You don't have to face it alone."

Madoc gives a raw laugh, maybe thinking about the

irony of turning for protection to the fae he was recently planning war against—and still might wage war against if the fledgling alliance between him and the Seelie arch-lords falls apart. Then he looks ahead of us, to the glowing mass of the Heart of the Mists that's just come into view.

That's where he's been headed this whole time, I realize. He's taken us on a course almost straight toward it. The soft pulse of its energy over my skin is so familiar to me now that I only notice it when I focus on it, but he won't have been quite this close to it… maybe in all his time before he was captured the other day.

"Do you feel any connection to it at all?" I ask quietly.

Madoc's gaze jerks to me, startled and then sheepish. He turns back toward the Heart, which looms a little higher with every step we take toward it and the haze of the border. "No," he says, the admission sounding as if it wrenches at something deep inside him. "I—no."

And yet he wants it so badly. He wants to bring all of his people back here where they can be embraced by that light again, whether they can make use of its energies or not. Whatever you could say about the means he was willing to resort to, there aren't many dreams more noble than that.

I hesitate before saying anything else, afraid I might offend him by bringing up the tragedy he went through in the Mists so long ago. "You said when you lived with your parents on the fringes of the summer realm that they could use the Heart's magic a little."

Madoc comes to a stop about fifty feet away from the

Heart, still facing it. We're close enough now that the glow touches him, bringing a warmer tone to his pale skin and turning his straw-blond hair into gold. He looks like he's wavering between crossing the short distance to walk right up to it and staying here where it can't wash over him quite so intensely.

"They could," he says. "Not very well, but they had a small connection. I could feel it a little myself then, but I hadn't learned any magic I could actually cast. But—when any of us start drawing on the Heart Orion made, it fills in all the places where that old connection would have been if we'd kept closer to the Heart of the Mists all along. Whatever shreds of a connection I had left, it overwhelmed them."

He shakes himself and swivels toward me with a crooked smile. "But it's worth it. I can do much more with our Heart than I'd ever have been able to with the feeble scraps that one would still allow us. *It* dismissed us ages ago."

I'm not sure the dismissal was so one-sided. From what my mates have said, certain actions—lying, unjustified killing—weaken the connection to the Heart for any kind of fae. At least some of the Murk in the past choose to separate themselves from its power so that they had more freedom to carry out their schemes.

It doesn't seem fair that their decisions carried on to their offspring, though. How many generations made their own decisions that dwindled the magic of the Mists in their family line before Madoc was born with the choice between barely any magic and magic from a different source?

"I know you have a lot of reasons to hate the fae of the Mists," I say, "but I don't think the Heart is that vindictive. Maybe you could find your way back to it if you opened yourself up to it. The Murk haven't really had the chance to try to get closer to it in a long time, and that's something we should change."

Madoc's next smile is bittersweet. "Of course you would say that. It isn't that easy, Talia. Believe me, the Heart doesn't want anything to do with me or anyone else among the Murk."

"It hasn't turned *me* away," I argue. "Even though I'm only here because of Orion. Even though I've got Murk magic all twisted up inside me, and I'm tied to the curse that's been draining its strength."

"Well, it isn't going to shove you through a portal. But what has it *done* for you?"

A sudden resolve swells inside me. He needs to see— he needs to know. He *deserves* it, to know that he could bring an even better future to his people than he's been able to imagine.

Corwin, sensing my decision even from out of view, extends a waft of concern. *Talia, we still don't know if he might tell his king—*

It's okay, I insist before he can finish his protest. *I know Madoc. I think he needs to hear this. And even if he did tell Orion, it wouldn't change much now.*

Holding Madoc's gaze, I lift my hands with a little space cupped between them. "The powers Orion gave me

—it's just the ability to heal the curse on the fae of the Mists and the soul-twined bond with Corwin, right?"

Madoc peers at me, obviously puzzled. "Yes, which is plenty. Why?"

"Then it's the Heart of the Mists that gave me this." I draw in a breath, think back to the joy of being snuggled between Sylas and Whitt yesterday after the passion we shared, and say the true name for light. "*Sole-un-straw.*"

A glowing ball flares into being between my palms. Madoc blinks, staring and then staring harder. "You—how did you—?"

I dismiss the glow with a flick of my fingers and reach for my new bracelet. "How do you think I was working on the bolts on the air vent? No one gave me a tool. I *made* it. Orion just didn't believe me." I grasp the warm bronze, remembering the panic of the moment when the Murk sentry caught me in the act, and murmur the first true name I ever learned. "*Fee-doom-ace-own.*"

The bracelet splits and straightens into a wrench in my hand. Madoc's eyes widen even more.

"That power didn't come from Orion or his Heart, did it?" I say, clutching the wrench. "He had no idea."

"He didn't," Madoc says faintly. "But—"

I point to the Heart of the Mists with a rush of affection for the presence that has been on my side for so long without me even knowing it. "*That* Heart decided I deserved a little magic of my own. Even though I was a tool for someone who wants to destroy everything in the Mists. If it could see something worthy in me, then there's no reason you or any of the other Murk should give up on it. It hasn't given up on you."

Madoc's throat bobs. He looks from me to the Heart and back again. So many emotions are warring on his face that I can't pick them apart, but I don't think I'm mistaking the flare of hope that shows briefly. It's followed by something warmer that seems to send a wash of heat straight from his gaze over my skin.

Before he can say anything else, a guard comes loping over from the castle, breaking the moment we were sharing.

"Whitt is ready to speak with you," he tells Madoc. "He'd like you to come right away."

"Of course he would," Madoc mutters, but there's a lot less edge in his voice than there might have been earlier. He shoots me one last bewildered glance and follows the man toward the castle. Whitt has appeared in the doorway, waiting.

The guards from the cabin fall into step behind Madoc. I limp over to August, feeling abruptly drained, even though I didn't cast all that much magic. With a quick murmur, I fix the bronze back in its bracelet form around my wrist.

August slips his arm around my shoulders, ruffling my hair. He looks down at the bracelet. "Are you sure that was a good idea, Sweetness?"

I watch Madoc disappear into the castle. Another ache twines through my chest, thinking of how hard it was for him to accept what I was telling him, to believe he could ever draw on the Heart of the Mists again, even when he's shown more honor than a whole lot of the summer and winter fae I've encountered in my time here.

Am I sure? Maybe not one hundred percent. But—

"At some point," I say, "we have to open our arms like the Heart did for me. I'd rather take the risk than not."

14

Madoc

 don't remember ever noticing grass being quite so soft. Or maybe it only is this close to the massive form that powers all life in the Mists. Either way, the blades cushion my body like a welcome bed at the end of a long day, tickling the back of my neck and my bare forearms. I'm not used to this comfortable warmth either.

But it isn't the end of a long day, only the very beginning of one—and I'm not sure just how long it's going to get. I'm lucky that Whitt allowed me this brief reprieve to "collect myself" as he put it, before we set off for the fringes to see if Delta will meet us for the parlay one of Whitt's scouts was able to arrange after plying her with the gifts I suggested.

The sunlight beams through my closed eyelids with a muted glow. It wavers faintly with the rhythm of the other nearby light source. I'm lying within several paces of the Heart of the Mists, and its energy washes over me, tingling across my skin. I can't decide whether the sensation is a pleasurable reminder of what could have been or a wrenching reminder of what isn't. None of that energy seeps right to the center of me where it could help me spark any magic.

It's just a few feet from here that Talia stood with her Seelie men when they officially claimed her as their mate. I saw only a snippet of the ceremony before I made my preparations to draw her away, and even that snippet was from a distance, perched in my rat form on a partly obscured branch halfway up a tree. The memory rises up all the same of the joy that lit her face.

At the time, that joy only angered me—that she'd throw herself in so completely with the fae who've savaged my people so brutally. Having spent a little time in their presence, I can admit that her choice wasn't totally horrible.

The men she's taken as mates clearly adore her and are willing to stop at nothing to protect her. It's only too bad they all seem so convinced they still need to protect her from me. Whitt, with his sharp mind that many of the Murk would admire if it wasn't in a wolf, has at least offered me enough respect to listen to my input. I guess I should give him a little grudging credit for that, and for not prowling around quite as imposingly as the others while I shared my thoughts.

Of course, a few days ago even *I* wasn't completely sure they didn't need to defend Talia from my mere presence. Who's to say her association with me won't still hurt her in ways I can't predict or control?

Footsteps whisper across the grass from the direction of Hearth-by-the-Heart. I open my eyes and raise my head, expecting to see Whitt or one of his pack-kin coming over to call me to the carriages.

Instead, it's Talia. The sunlight beams around her vibrant hair like a shimmering halo, and my heart flips over. The images flash through my mind of a dream I had weeks ago, lying in the grass and her sinking over me, baring her body to me.

My cock twitches, and I push myself upright, both confirming that I'm not dreaming now and willing away the imaginary encounter.

"Hey," she says, stopping a few feet away from me. She looks hesitant, as if even *she's* wary of me right now. My throat constricts.

"Felt like another walk?" I ask her.

"I just—I saw you out here. Are you all right? I know going to this woman and seeing through the meeting could put you in a lot of danger."

Oh. Her hesitation wasn't concern for herself but for me. I should have known her well enough to realize that.

A pang echoes through my chest. I'm not all right. I'm walking a thin line between saving and betraying my people, I'm still not sure whether I've kept to the right side of it so far, and...

And I'm falling for a woman I can never have. My heart aches with the urge to reach up and draw her to me like I did in that dream, to discover the sweetness of her mouth with more than just a fleeting kiss, to press into her until she's moaning with so much pleasure she can't contain it.

But I don't for a second think even the slightest overture I could make would be welcome. She hasn't mentioned the quick kiss I couldn't resist giving her on her way out of the Refuge, and definitely hasn't encouraged another. With her habit of assuming the best of people, she's probably decided it was a random impulse in a desperate situation that no real meaning should be attributed to.

She'd never betray the men she's already devoted to. And what exactly could I offer that would tempt her to anyway?

Besides, I wouldn't want her if she was the kind of woman who'd so easily turn her back on those she loved.

I'm hardly going to tell her any of that, so I manage a smile. "I'll be taking all kinds of precautions and sticking to the sidelines. None of the Murk involved will have any idea what my part was." I glance back toward the Heart and get to my feet. "I just wanted to enjoy the atmosphere while I can."

A smile of her own tugs at the corners of Talia's lips. "Even you have to admit the scenery here is a *little* nicer than an abandoned subway tunnel."

I hum. "Subway tunnels have a lot to recommend about them." I inhale the scent of the grass in the air and find myself acknowledging, because she's the only person I can admit it to, "I might be a bit nervous about this parlay. I've never done any kind of business with Delta before—and to encourage a collision between the Murk and the Seelie…"

"It won't be a collision," Talia says with typical optimistic determination. "It's the beginning of a larger alliance. The more the Murk see that we're willing to work with them, and the more the fae of the Mists see that the Murk can keep their word, the easier it'll be to find some kind of compromise that doesn't mean attacking each other."

I think she's being *overly* optimistic there. Orion isn't going down without a fight, and there are plenty of my people who'll stick with him to the end no matter what. But I suspect Talia's aware of that too. It's just her nature to put a positive spin on dire situations.

"I'd very much like to see that," I say, which is true, and spot several figures beginning to assemble over by Sylas's castle. "It looks like my reprieve is over. Time to get going."

I'm trying to ignore the uneasy sinking of my stomach, but maybe it shows through anyway. Talia offers me another smile. "Thank you for doing this— for everything you've been doing. I know how hard it must be when you have so many reasons to distrust us. I promise you the fae appreciate your contributions too, even if they're still being cautious around you."

She moves forward suddenly, slipping her arms around me in what must have been meant as a hug. But the second her body brushes mine, my stance goes completely rigid, my pulse stuttering. The heat of her, the soft swell of her chest—the fae watching, will they think I compelled her, that I'll hurt her—?

Talia jerks back as if burned. Her face flushes, and I'm immediately kicking myself for my instinctive defensive reaction.

"Sorry," she says hastily. "I didn't mean to make you uncomfortable. I just—I want you to know it's important to me that you make it back safe too."

Her apology makes me feel even worse than I already did. I could have gotten to hold her close for just a few seconds, breathing in her scent and knowing *she* trusts me enough not to be afraid of me. But how awkward would it be to try to re-enact the moment now?

"It's all right," I assure her as emphatically as I can. "I wasn't uncomfortable, just surprised. We Murk aren't generally much for friendly gestures of affection, so I'm out of practice with the whole hugs thing."

My dry tone at the end seems to put her at ease, so at least I can keep the possibility of future hugs if she dares to try me again. I'm going to try not to dwell on that potential future too much after we part ways.

Whitt has appeared among the other gathering fae now. He waves to me, and I dip my head to Talia. "I hope you stay well while I'm gone, and that we can come back with good news."

"So do I," she says softly. I walk away with more reluctance than is probably healthy, the image of her bright figure lingering behind my eyes.

Whitt beckons me with a grin that's just shy of friendly. I don't think he's totally warmed up to me, but I won some kind of points by being willing to mention this strategy at all.

The fae around him watch me with much more hostile gazes. And there are quite a lot of them too. They've conjured five carriages, each big enough to hold at least ten fae.

I go straight to Whitt, ignoring the eyes that follow me with suspicion. "I'm not sure we need such a large delegation for the initial meeting. We look like we're prepared for battle."

"We are," Sylas says, just coming out of the castle. His gaze is still plenty wary when it comes to rest on me, his posture all arch-lordly dominance. "From what I understand, you said yourself that this Murk sorceress may see us as enemies rather than potential allies. We don't know what kind of force she'll have at her disposal if she comes. I think it's best to be prepared for the worst."

"If you bring them all through, she isn't likely to stick around at all," I have to point out.

"We're going to leave most of them on the other side of the portal with a spell to alert them if they're needed," Whitt says with no sign of concern. "It's only a precaution."

Like the guards and the magic around the cabin where I've spent the last two nights. Like the gazes trained on me no matter where I go in the Seelie's domains.

Maybe it's ridiculous of me to think there's any point in attempting negotiations. If the fae of the Mists can't see me as a true ally even after the lengths I've already gone to for them, what are the chances they'll fully accept any of the other Murk?

But that's another matter. What we're doing today is for Talia most of all. If Delta can dispel Orion's curse, that's enough of a victory for me. The rest I can decide later.

Sylas has me join him in his carriage, which includes a few warriors I'm familiar with from my rotating guard detail, and Whitt takes another. I guess they've already done all the strategizing they need to. I sink onto my end of the bench and spend most of the journey watching the landscape whip by, the wind ruffling my hair.

What would they think of the vehicles some of my people have been able to conjure? We've traveled through this realm many times in them without being spotted, but somehow I think the fae around me would turn up their noses at anything less elegant than their own crafts, no matter how well-constructed.

Sylas doesn't attempt any conversation, but I can sense him monitoring me and the fae around me. At one point a couple of his warriors mutter something between themselves, and he clears his throat with a sharp look.

Maybe he's watching us all for my defense as well as theirs. It's a strange thought, and not enough to let me relax in their presence. I doubt he sees any value in me as more than a tool to help build this potential alliance.

The fog and hunched trees of the fringelands come into view in what feels like no time at all. I tug at the collar of my shirt, the fabric starting to stick to my back with sweat. I definitely prefer the sharp chill of the winter-side fringe area to the sweltering humidity here, especially when this atmosphere brings back distant memories of my childhood and the violence that destroyed my family.

As we disembark, the horde of warriors gathering together, anxiety pinches my gut again. Have I been instrumental in setting up a parlay that could benefit both the Murk and these fae—or have I set the stage for yet another slaughter of my people? I might be insane to trust any of the fae of the seasons.

The man who came out here yesterday with my illusion spell cloaking him wasn't able to speak to Delta directly. He left the gifts and the request of the parlay, and one of her kin dropped off a reply. For all we know, we'll step through the portal where we asked her to meet us and find no one there at all. She might have changed her mind about trusting the message or about wanting to associate with the fae of the Mists even if she believes they're genuine.

Sylas assembles a significant portion of the warriors in a squad stationed around the portal in question, but it looks like we're still bringing through about twenty with us. My teeth grit against another complaint.

I said my piece. If I keep badgering them about it, for all I know they'll take that to mean I've set them up and decide to bring even more.

"Ready to go through?" Whitt asks me. "Your illusion looks solid to me."

I spent the last several minutes in the carriage constructing the magic to give a different impression of my appearance. Delta will expect to see a Murk man among the fae of the Mists for this parlay, but I don't want her or anyone looking on to recognize me. I nod and let my tail lash free from the base of my spine like a signal of my heritage. If any of the wolves around me have a problem with it, let them sneer.

As we pass through the portal one after another, my nerves stay on edge. In the sheltered cove on the other side, which contains a narrow strip of little-touched beach framed by a semi-circle of craggy rock, I step off to the side of the main Seelie force where I'll be visible but not the main focus of the discussion.

Waves lap at the sand. Salt laces the air from the ocean, stinging my eyes and burning in my throat. It's no wonder this pathway to the Mists is rarely used, but that also makes it an ideal spot for particularly secretive meetings.

The fae around me grimace and grunt in their discomfort. But they're disciplined enough to jerk stiffly still, erasing all signs of complaint, at the sight of a woman clambering over the jagged rocks to meet us.

Delta's face is a deep gold like the sand, burgundy curls falling around it to her narrow shoulders. She picks her way partway down the rocky outcropping with nimble hands and feet. There's nothing particularly impressive about her clothes, what looks like three tattered dresses of different faded colors layered on top of each other. But I know it's her from the moment she stops and draws herself up straight, still several paces above the beach. Her presence emanates confidence and power.

More figures pop their heads over the top of the rocks,

watching over the ruler of their colony. The Seelie warriors study them, a few hands moving to rest on the hilts of their swords. My body tenses, but they make no further move.

"You wished to speak with me, wolf," Delta says, crossing her arms. "What could you possibly have to say that might be of interest to me?"

Sylas steps toward her, his head held high. "I think we have a common enemy. I wondered if you'd like the chance to undermine King Orion's plans."

"*King*," Delta sneers. The stories I've heard of her disdain for Orion obviously didn't lie.

But my attention snags on some of the Seelie near the back of our formation who are easing away from the others, closer to the rocks. They aren't getting into position to strike at the Murk, are they?

"I understand that's what he calls himself, at least," Sylas says with a chuckle, and at the same moment, a few of the warriors I'm watching start moving their mouths with a quiet incantation.

My heart lurches with the sudden certainty that I've been wrong—I've led this woman and her followers into a trap. With no thought in my head other than interrupting the guards however I need to, I dart around the delegation toward them.

My sudden movement must put the Murk on the alert. As I scramble along the edge of the rocks, dozens more figures leap up on top of the rocks, braced for an attack.

The Seelie warriors whip around, taking in the Murk

force that's abruptly tripled in size, and must conclude that the colony is already launching an attack. With snarls, several snap out spells and draw their swords, others pulling in close around Sylas.

The rest happens so fast I can barely follow it. I'm not sure any of the spells are more than shields, but the Murk shout and start hurling needle-like knives and spells of their own down on the Seelie. Most bounce off the defensive barriers, but a few slice across the warriors' limbs.

A roar goes up, the Seelie warriors charging toward the rocks, Sylas hollering for order—and Delta springs up the ledges to vanish behind her people in the blink of an eye.

"Wait!" I holler. I clamber up the rocks to try to speak to the Murk from closer by. The next second, they're flooding down over the rocks to meet the Seelie's charge. I manage to dodge the ones that rush right by me, one of their blades cutting my cheek open.

In a matter of moments, blades are hissing and voices crying out in pain all around the cove. Sylas calls for the Seelie to retreat through the portal. A few Murk lie bloody on the sand, but the others jeer at the retreating wolf shifters.

I duck low into a crevice. The only way to reach the fae I arrived with is to push through the crowd of Murk who may see me as just as much a threat as they decided the Seelie were. It seems better to stay out of the way entirely. They're obviously not in any mood to listen to an explanation.

And why should I try to make one? I'm not totally

sure what did happen there, whether the Seelie were on the verge of launching an attack and the Murk caught them at it or whether all of us misread the situation.

Do I even *want* to follow Sylas's people? What exactly were they up to before everything went to hell? Maybe if I hadn't made a move at all, there'd be ten times as many Murk corpses sprawled around the cove.

I weave another illusion around me, hiding me from the eyes and noses of Delta's colony. They linger in the cove for several minutes after the last Seelie has vanished, but they don't follow the wolf shifters into the Mists.

Finally, Delta's voice rises in a brisk summons from somewhere beyond my view, followed by a snarky remark about the treachery of wolves. Her people quickly scale the rocks and follow her back to their colony.

I stay where I am, wedged between two rough walls of stone, my stomach knotting. That meeting couldn't have gone much worse, and I don't even know who to blame for its failure. The one thing for sure is that the Seelie started throwing around magic and waving their weapons before the Murk had done more than *look* at them.

Why had I trusted them even enough to attempt to arrange this parlay? I should have known they'd never trust *us* enough to deal with us fairly.

The only one back there who deserves any consideration from me is Talia.

That thought weighs heavily on me. I want to spit in the Seelie's faces and turn my back on them, but am I really going to abandon her too, after all the faith she's shown in me?

I remain crouched among the rocks for over an hour, grappling with myself. Then I squeeze out of the crevice and push on into the jungle terrain beyond, leaving the noxious salt of the ocean behind.

There's another portal in this area that's closer to civilization, one that'll let me travel back to the fringes to the doorway I need without me risking ending up in Sylas's company again.

If there's anything I can do for Talia, I can't manage it back there in the Mists, surrounded by jackasses who hate me for what I am. I have to go back to Orion.

15

Talia

The tension in the border castle's meeting room thickens with each new arrival. The arch-lords barely speak other than to mutter to their cadres and coteries, but everyone looks grim.

I brace myself on my chair near the head of the table, willing myself to stay focused. Another fit of pain came over me just a couple of hours ago, and I feel exhausted now. I can't tell how much it's left over from the curse's effects and how much it's the fatigue of early pregnancy.

Sitting next to me, Corwin wraps his fingers around mine with a waft of reassurance through our bond. Every other emotion I can sense from him is unsettled, though. Sylas has taken the head of the table, and frustration seeps through his normally composed expression. Behind him, Whitt's expression is similarly gloomy.

When the last of the arch-lords, Neve, arrives and

takes her seat, gazing around at us as if she isn't totally sure why she's there, Laoni clears her throat and leans forward. "So, from what I understand the rat you took into your confidence stayed true to his nature. He led you into a trap, did he?"

My heart skips a beat. "That's not what happened!" My gaze darts to Sylas. "That *isn't* what happened, is it?" He called this meeting so quickly after his return that I've barely had a chance to find out what went on after he, Whitt, and Madoc headed to their parlay, but no one said that Madoc betrayed them.

Sylas's mouth flattens into a taut line before he speaks. "We aren't entirely sure where things went wrong, but they did go very wrong. Our Murk collaborator may have played a role in that."

"He appeared to incite the other Murk," Whitt puts in, his tone even but hard. The flex of his jaw tells me he's angry with himself as much as anyone else. "And he didn't return with us. He appeared genuine when we worked out the plan, but I could have made an error in judgment."

Celia sighs. "It was always going to be a risky move. We have to dismiss everything else he's told us then too."

"And send out orders to kill him on sight if he tries to return," Uzziah adds with a menacing edge to his normally dour voice.

"If his own people don't take care of that for us," Celia says. "We can send proof of his duplicity to his king as planned and—"

"Hold on," I burst out, smacking my free hand on the table for emphasis. "We haven't even talked about exactly what happened. How did Madoc 'appear' to incite anyone? What did the Murk do? What did our warriors do? You all made it back safely." I fix my gaze on Sylas in an appeal. "We can't make life and death decisions without knowing the whole story."

He exhales roughly. "You're right, we shouldn't. The account we can give may not clarify the situation all that much, though."

"Let's hear it all the same," Terisse says in a tone I can't read. She's sided with my men and their more moderate views recently, but she was loyal to Laoni not long before that. I'm not sure how strongly she resents the Murk.

Sylas folds his hands on the tabletop. "We went out to the fringelands and through a portal to the agreed-upon meeting spot. The Murk woman that Madoc had arranged for us to parlay with did arrive, with what seemed to be a small contingent of her followers. We'd only just started speaking when Madoc, who was with us, made a sudden move, hurrying toward some of our warriors at the back of the formation. The sight seemed to provoke the other Murk, and many more converged on us. They attacked, and we fended them off while making for safety through the portal. None of them followed us—including Madoc. I don't know whether he stayed with them or went off on his own elsewhere in the human world."

"Probably running back to his 'king,'" Donovan growls. Even the normally mild-mannered Seelie arch-lord has his hackles up about this disaster.

I swallow hard, thinking through Sylas's story, noticing the gaps. I can't believe Madoc would have set up him and so many others of our people to be attacked. He gave every impression of thinking they might come back with a potential cure for me. I didn't see the slightest hint of guilt in him when we spoke right before he left.

I might not be as adept at reading people as Whitt, but the spymaster trusted him enough to go through with the plan too. There must be something more to the situation.

"What were the warriors Madoc ran toward doing?" I ask. "Do you have any idea why he reacted like that?"

"They'd stepped a little apart from the rest of us to cast additional spells we'd want to have at the ready in case we *were* attacked," Sylas says. "It was only a precaution. They didn't make a spectacle of it or aim the magic at anyone."

"Madoc obviously noticed it, though. Didn't he know they were going to be casting spells?"

Sylas pauses, and Whitt speaks up into his silence. "It didn't seem wise to inform him of every aspect of our plans ahead of time. If he was conspiring with the other Murk, we'd have lost any potential advantage. But if he was acting in good faith, he should have realized we weren't about to do harm to anyone who didn't provoke it."

"Why?" I have to ask. I don't like arguing with my mates, but I don't seem to have much choice. They hate the Murk so much they can't even see how unfair they're being. "If you didn't trust *him* not to be setting up an ambush, why would you expect him to have more trust in you? It sounds like you're the ones who made the first unexpected move."

Whitt opens his mouth and closes it again. He looks briefly chagrinned.

Sylas steps in. "That shouldn't have been enough reason for the other Murk to attack us. It was as if they were taking their cues from him."

I shift my gaze back to him. "Why wouldn't they? He was the only Murk with you—of course they'd be watching him to make sure everything was okay. Did they really attack the second he reacted to the spell-casting?"

Sylas frowns and rubs his temple. "My attention was mainly focused on the supposed sorceress. I saw a sudden surge of rat shifters appear along the ridge behind us—"

"They were all around us," Whitt puts in. "A huge force they'd been keeping in hiding."

"—but we'd done something similar," Sylas acknowledges, glancing back at his strategist. "So I suppose we can't fault them for that. Our warriors who were present responded to the sudden onslaught by casting shielding spells around us, and it's a good thing they did, because they got them up just in time to fend off the worst of the initial attack."

"Had any of the Murk actually tried to hurt our people *before* ours started conjuring those shields?"

Both Sylas and Whitt appear to consider, the rest of the table watching us in silence as our conversation plays out.

"I don't believe they had," Whitt says finally, slowly, "but it was almost simultaneous."

"Then it's possible that they were already worried because of Madoc's obvious concern, and then they saw a whole bunch of you casting more magic and assumed *you* were about to attack them?"

He grimaces. "I'll acknowledge that could be true. We can't know whether that's the case or they meant to turn to violence all along, though."

"And since we can't know, we have to assume the worst for the security of our people," Celia says, drawing her slim form up even straighter. "We gave them a chance, and they betrayed us."

"Or they gave *us* a chance, and as far as they're concerned, we betrayed *them*," I protest.

Laoni scowls. "If that's the case, then why hasn't the rat who's supposedly allied himself with you given any explanation?"

I glare at her. "Maybe because he's afraid you'll kill him the second you see him just like it looks like you tried to kill all the other Murk he brought to talk to you—like you were just talking about doing to him a few minutes ago." A sound of frustration escapes me, and another wave of exhaustion rolls through my body.

Corwin's hand comes up to grip my shoulder, keeping me steady. "We're all upset about what happened, and we clearly can't determine the motivations of anyone other than ourselves," he says to the table at large. "Talia is speaking from a good place, making sure we consider every factor. But..." He squeezes my shoulder. "I'm not sure how much more risk it'd be reasonable for us to take in the hopes that any of the Murk will really work with us."

"Exactly," Uzziah says. "We have the ability to track

them down with her blood now. Maybe the first attempt didn't go perfectly, but we learn from our mistakes. I say we track down every one of those vermin we can and end them, and their Heart too. Then we'll have peace and all the curses hanging over us will be cured."

The murmur that goes around the table sounds far too appreciative of that suggestion. Even inside me, there's a tiny twinge of relief at the thought of taking a simple route, what could be the fastest and surest way to ensure all of us are safe so that I can live on and my child keep growing inside me.

But will it really be that simple? Orion has outmaneuvered us often enough that I can't believe it.

And even if we could be sure that a widespread massacre of every rat in existence would lead us to victory, it's not just simple but brutal—so brutal it turns my stomach.

The images from the Murk memories I witnessed flash through my mind—the violence, the bloodshed, the horror. Madoc told me he didn't want to win Orion's vicious, sadistic way… and I don't want us to win that way either. I don't want to see all the fae around me turn as vicious as the fae who savaged my parents and shoved me into a cage, as the ones who tore apart Madoc's family or the children in that orphanage long ago.

Shaking off Corwin's hand, I shove my chair back and push to my feet. Every head around the table snaps toward me.

"No," I say, as if I can make that call. Maybe if I speak as if I can, that'll be enough for them to listen to me. "I would rather *die* than get my cure like that. You think the Murk like Orion and his followers are horrible, vicious animals. What do you think *you'll* be if you massacre every fae who happens to have been born a rat shifter? Why *should* any of them trust you if you jump straight to that solution?"

"Talia," Sylas says gently, but I'm not done.

"They have some good in them," I say. "Maybe not Orion, but there are horrible Seelie and Unseelie too. Most of the Murk I talked to were angry, but they felt a lot of other things. They cared about their families and their friends. They supported each other and defended each other. They had hopes for a future where they *didn't* have to worry about the fae of the Mists descending on them with claws or talons at any moment.

"Attack Orion and anyone who insists on standing with him. Destroy their Heart. But if you're going to support killing Murk who won't ever raise so much as a finger against you, then I'd rather go back to their Refuge than stay here."

The declaration takes the last of my energy out of me. I slump back into my seat. Everyone is staring at me, Whitt's face gone sickly pale, horror trickling through my bond with Corwin.

Sylas recovers first. "I agree with Talia that we can't lower ourselves to the same baseness as the worst of the rats. We owe ourselves and our people more than that. But we obviously can't stand by and hope any of the Murk will advise us either. We should start sending out more search parties to track down the Refuge."

Laoni draws in a breath. I wince inwardly in anticipation of a caustic remark, but to my surprise, her voice comes out measured. "There are ways we could draw out the Murk who mean us ill to ensure we stay focused on destroying our primary enemies. They believe they can outsmart us—we can play into their assumptions, lay traps where we look like easy targets but can turn the tables on those who take the opportunity to attack."

Her fellow Unseelie arch-lords nod, slowly but without argument. Celia wets her lips. "Fine. For now. But we can't go easy on any intruding on our lands. We imprison and interrogate those we easily can; any who fight back will get what they deserve."

My hands clench on my lap. They still talk as if the Mists belong only to them, when obviously this is the world all the fae came from. Madoc isn't wrong that the other fae shoved the Murk out.

"What about Madoc?" I ask quietly, my chest constricting at the thought of him. "If he comes back, shouldn't we give him the chance to give his side? As far as I can tell, he hasn't violated the terms of the deal. *He* didn't attack anyone, did he?" I look at Sylas and Whitt.

"Not that anyone's reported witnessing," Whitt admits. "I lost track of him in the chaos, but I didn't see him so much as draw a weapon or speak a spell."

"Then all we know that he's done is hurry over to see what some of the warriors were doing. We can't destroy his life over that."

There's another silence. Corwin breaks it. "I'd say it depends on *how* he comes back. If he strikes out at us or joins others doing so, we'd obviously assume the alliance is over. If he makes a show of peacefulness but can't adequately explain his actions, the same. I do think he's earned the right to be heard after getting Talia back to us and then warning us of Orion's new assault on her."

The faces around the table don't exactly look happy about his proposal, but one by one, the arch-lords incline their heads. I wrap my arms around myself, wishing I felt more reassured.

I can't help suspecting that we're teetering on the edge of becoming monsters ourselves, and I'm afraid of how little it might take to push the rulers around me over that line.

16

Talia

The first of the new kind of fit hits me when I'm walking across the wintry plain between the border castle and the palace of Heart's Cadence, meaning to have a quick visit with Charles and Beth in the kitchen. I haven't spoken to them in ages. Even with everything going on around me—and inside me—I have to hold on to a few pieces of normalcy.

But I've only made it about halfway there when pain spikes between my lungs. My legs buckle beneath me, and Corwin, who was walking with me, catches me just before my knees smack into the icy terrain.

"Talia," he says, his voice tight with the strain of the agony I'm too wrapped up in to shield him from. "Focus on me. Ignore it as well as you can. I'll get you back to your room."

"Is there anything I can do?" Zelpha asks, hovering

behind him. My mates have continued to insist that at least two trusted protectors are with me any time I venture outside one of our castles.

Corwin scoops me up into his arms with a ragged breath. "We haven't found any spells that do much to dull the pain. At least I can bring her to where she'll be most comfortable."

Before he's taken two steps toward the border, though, the searing sensation that tore through my chest subsides. I gasp and tuck myself closer against him, shaken. Can it really be over already?

Corwin pauses, looking down at me, registering the change at the same time as me. "It hasn't let up anywhere near that quickly before, has it?"

I shake my head. "Maybe—maybe something we've tried has worked to weaken the curse after all?"

A flicker of hope crosses his face—and in the same instant, another vicious blade of pain slices through me, as if I'm being carved open from the inside out.

I cough and sputter, my muscles clenching up. A shudder runs through my body. Corwin hugs me close, his emotions as agonized as my body is. I know how much he wants to shield me from this pain and how deeply it wrenches at him that he can't.

"The pattern has shifted," he says to Zelpha. "Get Sylas—he should be at Hearth-by-the-Heart. Have him meet us in the border castle."

I don't see Zelpha's response, only feel the waft of air as she flaps away as a raven. Corwin extends his own wings in their larger form, the rest of him remaining a man as he soars across the frozen terrain the fastest way he's capable of.

As he lands on the doorstep of the winter entrance, the pain eases again. I don't trust the reprieve this time. I take shallow breaths, testing my lungs, still huddled in my soul-twined mate's embrace.

"You can endure this," he murmurs to me, sounding a little choked. "You're stronger than any Murk king's magic."

Maybe I am, but that doesn't mean it's any joy living through it.

Halfway down the hall, the next attack seizes me, with a slamming sensation as if not one but several knives are plunging between my ribs. I can't help crying out.

Corwin swallows thickly and hustles up the stairs toward my bedroom. The knives keep digging in until a moment before he's laying me on the bed covers.

I pant, my whole body aching in a duller but still distressing way. Every time the pain comes on me, I tense up, and the back and forth is wearing me out faster than if I were riding out a continuing wave. You'd think getting breaks would make it easier, but I can't appreciate them when I'm tangled up in the apprehension of wondering how long I'll get before it happens again.

How will I know for sure when this fit is even really over? *Will* it ever be over, or is this the new normal: switching between relief and pain over and over every couple of minutes?

Don't think like that, Corwin says through our bond, but I can tell he's worried about the exact same thing.

Sylas pushes past the door a moment later with Whitt close at his heels. "What—" he starts.

And then the pain is in me again, blaring through my awareness, drowning out every other sensation. I hug myself, pressing the side of my head into the pillow.

I can get through this. I am stronger. But oh God, I wish I didn't have to.

When I come back to myself, Corwin and Sylas are speaking in hushed, urgent voices. Corwin has walled off some of his impressions so I can't read them or hear what they're saying through his ears.

They're *arguing* about something… I can't tell what. Corwin seems worried. Sylas's jaw is tight with resolve.

Whitt catches my eye, his own expression fraught with concern. "I think we should let Talia decide," he says abruptly.

Despite the horrible state I'm in, a swell of love for him fills my chest. I even manage to smile.

"Let me decide what?" I ask in a croak.

Then I'm gone. The pain somehow spreads and shrinks at the same time—not several knives but dozens of piercing needles. My lungs are going to puncture and deflate like dying balloons.

I return to reality with tears stinging the corners of my eyes and a sob caught in my throat. Corwin sinks onto the edge of the bed next to me and swipes the moisture away. He looks at Sylas. "How can we put her through that stress when she's already suffering like this?"

Sylas frowns. "How can we not try when there's a

possibility he could help? You know what she'd say—you heard her yesterday."

It takes me a second to gather myself enough to use my voice. "Whatever it is, I—"

Another searing wave, another spell of disorientation. After that, I give up on trying to have any kind of conversation, and I think my mates do too. Corwin murmurs soft words over me, conjuring a cool tingle that distracts from the pain the tiniest bit. Whitt sits down by the head of the bed and strokes my hair.

"If I could take this on for you, mite, you know I would," he says.

Sylas paces. In one clear moment, I think he's going to leave, but he doesn't. When a break in the fits lasts long enough that I start to relax into the mattress, he's still there.

My hair is sticking to my forehead with sweat. Whitt brushes it aside too. Corwin grips my hand. We wait, all of us anticipating another round...

But it doesn't come. The minutes tick by, and the memory of the agony fades. There's nothing left but the prickle behind my breastbone.

A laugh sputters out of me. "It's over."

For now. Until the next time.

Whitt gives Sylas a pointed look, and the Seelie arch-lord gazes down at me, his mouth twisting.

"Madoc has returned," he says.

I jerk upright, and Corwin tightens his grip on my hand. I sway with momentary dizziness before refocusing on Sylas. "What? When? What's he said?"

"A few hours ago," Whitt admits. "We wanted to question him thoroughly before we proceeded any further."

Before they told me he was here, they mean. I grimace.

Before I can complain about their secrecy, Sylas goes on. "I'm not sure he meant to engage with us any more than the first time he came. August and a few of our pack-kin caught him lurking in the woods near the castle. He *says* he was waiting for the chance to speak to you directly, that he doesn't want to deal with the rest of us."

"And how can we trust him if that's how he's approaching the situation?" Corwin demands, all protective ire.

Whitt shakes his head. "You haven't seen him. He's clearly furious with us because he thinks *we* ruined the parlay."

"Or maybe he's angry because his attempt at betraying us didn't work as well as he'd hoped."

Whitt raises his eyebrows at the Unseelie man. "I'll admit that using one's actual emotions in a deception can be an excellent tactic, and putting your opponent on the defensive is one as well. But he tried to avoid speaking to us at all. And he's brought several items that show no harmful properties that he says he gathered back in the human world—remedies the Murk use for various ailments. He simply wanted to give them to Talia."

"Which doesn't mean we should necessarily let him anywhere near our mate," Sylas puts in. "But we could bring what he's offered and see whether it helps her at all."

Corwin frowns. "Before anything of his comes near her, I'd like to—"

"Stop!" I break in. My chest is wrenching in a totally different way at the thought of the treatment Madoc must have gone through in the past few hours without my knowing. "I want to see him. What can he do to me that's worse than what I'm already going through anyway? Do you think Orion needs to send someone to double-curse me?"

I narrow my eyes at all three of the men around me. "If Madoc was trying to manipulate you, he wouldn't be antagonizing you. So stop antagonizing him and each other, and let's get on with seeing what he brought."

Whitt's mouth twitches into a tight smile. "She does know her own mind," he says to Sylas.

"She does." The Seelie arch-lord turns to Corwin.

I squeeze my soul-twined mate's hand, and he sighs before pressing a kiss to my temple. "All right. I don't like it, but… it's true that I can't see what he'd gain by specifically speaking to Talia." He pauses. "I'm not sure we want him having access to this castle, though. Talia, are you well enough to come down?"

I test my feet on the floor and nod. "I'll be fine."

Sylas and Whitt go ahead to collect Madoc from wherever August is watching over him. Corwin stays with me for the trek down to the entrance. My legs do hold me just fine, but partway down the steps, a whiff of broiled fish reaches my noise from the kitchen, and my stomach starts churning. Most food hasn't bothered me so far, but every now and then some odor brings out a rush of queasiness.

"There's nothing you can do to get rid of the smell fast enough for it to help," I tell Corwin. "Let's just get out of here quickly."

The scent is thicker in the hallway below. My jaw clamps tight against my rising nausea. The effort isn't quite successful, though. I've just made it out the door, about to take my first deep breath of fresh summer air, when my gut twists and I find myself vomiting what's left of my breakfast into the grass at the base of the wall.

Footsteps come hustling over, and I look up to see my Seelie mates, Astrid, and a couple of other guards hurrying toward me with Madoc in their midst. So wonderful to have an audience for this.

I swipe at my mouth, the lingering nausea subsiding, as Corwin rubs my back and intones a quick spell to remove the mess. Refusing to let the embarrassment hold me back, I step forward to meet the coming entourage.

"Has it gotten worse?" Madoc asks the second he's close enough for me to hear him, worry clouding his eyes. It doesn't look as if the guards who caught him hurt him, thank goodness. "If it's progressed to your stomach—"

I hold up my hand to stop him. Weirdly, the sight of his crookedly handsome face soothes my spirits even more. I can tell just looking at him, at the way he's looking at me, that I was right to argue on his behalf. I have the unexpected urge to try to hug him again, to feel those well-muscled arms wrap around me like when he hid me on our way out of the Refuge, to—

I jerk my mind away from those rambling thoughts, squashing down the flash of heat that came with them, and focus on his questions. "I think that was being pregnant, not the curse. A much happier reason to be sick but not great having both in combination."

The Murk man pauses, and I realize I hadn't told him that particular piece of news. It hadn't seemed relevant.

His gaze darts to Whitt and then back to me. "I wondered, after certain questions—" He doesn't seem to know how to go on. Finally, he settles on, "I'm sorry Orion's managed to ruin even more happiness than he could have intended."

"It isn't totally ruined yet," I say. "And it's the curse that matters. I hear that you've brought back some things that might help?"

"Yes, some medicines we use and a couple of charms… None of it's specifically for a curse like this, but they're at least different from what you'll have already tried. We combine a lot of human products with our healing creations, so maybe they'll have a stronger effect on you." He hesitates again, studying me. "You're going to accept them, just like that? Not run me through another round of questions about how the parlay went to hell?"

He sounds so uncertain of my reaction that something twists in my chest. Without letting myself second-guess the impulse, I step across the short distance between us. Corwin makes a sharp noise in his throat, but Sylas motions for the guards to stay where they are.

It's probably better if I don't actually hug Madoc, considering every time I even think about it, other emotions stir that I shouldn't be feeling. But I can offer at least this much. I touch his forearm, giving it a light squeeze as I gaze up into his eyes. He stares back at me, the storminess in his gaze simmering down into something warmer, and the feelings I hadn't meant to provoke flutter inside me anyway.

I have to focus on the matter at hand. "Did you *want* the parlay to go to hell?" I ask.

Madoc frowns. "Of course not," he says, his eyes flashing as they dart toward the men around us again. "I didn't want the Murk attacking your people. But although this fact is apparently a problem for some of them, I also didn't want *them* attacking any of the Murk there."

"Which none of us did until we were attacked first," Sylas says evenly.

"What counts as an 'attack' is obviously debatable," Madoc mutters, and turns back to me. "They don't trust me, and I don't trust them, and it seems that's just how it is. So I won't arrange any more parlays. But even if they all want to be dicks about it, that doesn't mean I'm going to abandon you."

And there's the passionate defiance that allowed him to shake off his loyalty to his king on our behalf before. Always trying to do what's right for the people he cares about, even though it must be harder than ever for him to tell right now what that is.

I can't help thinking I'm lucky to have become one of those people.

I pull myself back a step, dropping my hand, before the conflicted sensations inside me rise up too far. He's an ally and maybe even a friend, but I definitely shouldn't feel any inclinations beyond that.

Even if I set aside my instinct to believe the man in front of me and look at the signs more logically, I have to agree with Whitt's assessment that Madoc doesn't appear to be trying to win any points or pull the wool over our eyes. His anger actually sounds more genuine than the restrained wariness he let show around the other fae before when he was trying to keep some kind of peace.

"That's good enough for me," I say, and glance around at my mates. "And that means it's going to be good enough for all of you too."

17

Corwin

I've always done my best to allow Talia all the freedom she could want, to show I respect her opinions and believe in her strength. It's never been quite so hard to see those intentions through as it is right now.

She's sitting in the grass next to Madoc, just a few steps from the border castle and with several fae who could leap to her defense in a split-second watching over them. Still, my hackles rise as the rat shifter offers her a small nugget of molded powder that's one of his people's "medicines." I want to leap in there right now and tear it from her hands.

But she's been firm that she trusts him at least in this, and her arguments have been sound. I can't imagine how her situation *could* get any worse than it already is. And I can't say the Murk man has ever shown the slightest hint of wanting to hurt her. If anything, it's been the opposite.

The rest of us is another story.

I tamp down on those thoughts, not letting my uneasy emotions travel through our bond. I don't want to cause her more distress, and I'm a little ashamed of how much my emotions are affecting me right now. Between all of us here, I'm supposed to be the level-headed raven, and I feel as wild as if there's a wolf underneath my skin.

"You'll want to chew it quickly," Madoc is saying. "Hopefully it won't upset your stomach."

Sylas clears his throat. "What exactly is in that thing?"

The Murk man glances up at him. "Various herbs, magic to bring out their healing properties, and stuff the humans call penicillin."

"Oh," Talia says with a soft laugh. "I had to take that once when I was a kid—when I had an ear infection." She looks at the nugget with amusement and then pops it into her mouth. Her throat bobs with her swallow. "It doesn't taste too bad. Not sure this curse works quite the same as bacteria in the ear drum, though."

Madoc gives her a crooked smile. "We don't typically use it for curses. Or for bacteria. But magically speaking, bringing out the gist of a material's properties can increase a similar effect you're going for."

"That's solid magical theory," Whitt agrees, if grudgingly.

"I guess it makes sense that your magic is much more entwined with human things than the spells the other fae use are," Talia says to Madoc. "Since you live so much closer to them. I've forgotten about a lot of what seemed so normal to me before I was brought here."

Her voice fades out, and I catch the flicker of concern in Madoc's eyes. He quickly produces another object from the inner pockets on the leather vest he arrived wearing. The item looks like a flower, silky purple petals with a small cloth bundle sewn into the center. He hands it to Talia, who brightens again.

"Very pretty," she says. "How does it work?"

"It's supposed to deflect hostile energies," Madoc says. "Not the most likely strategy to work when a lot of that energy is already in you, but again, I figured it couldn't hurt to try everything. It's got its own human component too."

He motions to the underside of the flower, and she flips it over. A giggle spills out of her. She beams at him with a rush of fondness that carries through her connection with me. Then she holds it up so we can see the symbol stitched to the base of the bundle. "It's the emblem for a squad of heroes from a TV show. I watched it all the time with Jamie. I didn't know it was still popular."

"Humans get very attached to their stories," Madoc says, smiling back at her. Then the smile tightens a bit around the edges. "As I suppose we fae do too."

I don't have to ask what sort of stories he's thinking of. Certainly we Unseelie and the Seelie have told plenty of horrifying tales about the Murk over the centuries. I haven't seen proof yet that those weren't warranted, though.

His remark reminds me of another sort of storytelling *he'll* have been doing recently. "You must have needed to give your king some kind of report when you returned to your home. He wasn't expecting you back so early, was he? What did you tell him?"

Madoc meets my gaze steadily. His wariness has eased a little with Talia's acceptance of his presence. "I had a perfectly good excuse. You don't think he'd have heard that a scuffle went down between Murk and fae of the Mists? And it wouldn't take much for him to guess *why* you might have tried to meet with Delta. He might be unhinged, but he's not an idiot. Now, if you'd managed to carry out the parlay peacefully, it could have been kept much more quiet."

"That doesn't answer the question," August says with a hint of a growl. "I'd like to know exactly what you told him too."

Madoc shifts his attention to the warrior. "I said that from what I'd gathered, the lot of you were getting desperate enough about Talia's situation to turn to Murk for help, but that being how you are, you obviously couldn't help screwing it up."

Talia frowns. "Isn't he going to realize that someone from the Murk side must already be helping us? How else would we have known to approach Delta—that she'd be a good choice to go against Orion?"

The rat shifter shrugs as if to try to hide the tension that's come into his stance at the question. "No doubt he'd already put those pieces together as soon as he heard there was some commotion with Delta's colony. It only means I have to keep being every bit as careful as I have been so far."

Talia glances around. "You don't have to worry—if he has other spies, and you're seen here with us—?"

Madoc snorts. "Even I couldn't manage to dodge all the protections around these domains, and I'm better with our concealing spells than anyone else Orion has working for him. I'd only be worried closer to the fringes."

Perhaps that's another reason he's come back to us—to keep him out of his king's sight. Although the moment that thought crosses through my head, I recognize the unfairness of it. Even if he dismisses the possibility, he knows that every moment he spends in our presence, he risks discovery.

And if his association with us is discovered, he won't be able to return home at all.

I may be too hard on him, too skeptical of his intentions. But I can't stop another rush of protectiveness from flaring inside me when his fingers brush Talia's as he hands her a small jar with a salve he's brought, or when he studies her so intently as she examines it.

It might not be all protectiveness. I can admit there's also a twinge of jealousy woven in because of the way she smiles back at him. Because of her laugh when he explains that the substance combines another human-sourced ingredient, this one a popular brand of soap.

She leans toward him just a little as she thanks him. And there's a joy humming through her at their conversation, at getting to talk with someone who understands that side of her old life in ways the rest of us never can.

"Did you ever see that commercial with the talking cat

that ends up eating it?" she asks, and Madoc chuckles at the memory.

"We're pretty sensitive to anything that involves cats," he tells her with a quirk of his eyebrow. "That one definitely stuck with me. Thankfully I don't think any cats are required for the cleansing properties to come into effect."

Talia turns away to rub some of the salve into her skin over the spot between her breasts where she feels the curse even between the bad fits, and Madoc averts his gaze for her modesty. Somehow his courtesy niggles at me more than if he leered at her.

At least then I'd have a good excuse to want to peck him to death.

Talia tucks the jar into the pouch on her belt where she's also stored the flower charm. As she turns back to face him, Madoc studies her. "Are you feeling any different at all? I know it's early."

But he can't help hoping, just like the rest of us. The recognition of that hope and how the expression on his face aligns with my own sends an odd twist of emotion through me.

Talia touches the spot through her dress and appears to concentrate for a long moment. Her mouth slants downward. I can tell that she's as much sorry to disappoint us as disappointed herself. "Not that I can notice. But maybe it'll just take some time."

Madoc ducks his head with a grimace. "It was a long shot. I just didn't want to come back empty-handed."

"It's all right. *No one's* been able to affect the curse, so you can't beat yourself up that you can't either." Talia reaches out and rests her hand gently on his forearm like she did when he asked her if she trusted his offerings at all, determined to reassure him.

Madoc swipes his other hand over his face. "I know." But his voice comes out raw, and his expression has tightened.

I wish I could appreciate how much he cares about my mate's well-being. It's getting harder to believe it's an act. Talia doesn't think so, and her concern for him jabs through me.

"If that's everything, Talia should get some rest," Sylas says. "She's had a rough morning, and it'll give more of a chance for your potential cures to work."

Talia nods reluctantly and gets up. "What about Madoc?" she asks. "Are you going to shove him back into that little cabin for the rest of the day?"

Madoc speaks up before any of us has to. "It's actually for my benefit as well, Talia. If a spy did manage to make it this far by some miracle, they're less likely to notice I'm around if I'm hidden away in there. I was prepared this time, brought a couple of books." He pats the other side of his vest and looks at the rest of us. "You'll let me know if you think of any other way I can try to help Talia?"

Just Talia. Not the war effort, not our defenses against his people, not our own curse. Only her. He couldn't have made it clearer since he returned that he's given up on the rest of us.

Can I truly blame him for that?

Talia recognizes that part of his statement too, and a pang of distress shoots through her—both for us and the alliance she'd hoped we were building with him. She believes we've let him down too.

August helps her through the doorway toward her bedroom, and the guards move to escort Madoc to the cabin. As they leave, I motion to Sylas and Whitt. "A word?"

We gather in one of the border castle's smaller sitting rooms. I wait until August rejoins us a few minutes later. The cheerful expression I've come to expect from him has been gloomy more often than not in recent days.

"I can't see that anything he's done has hurt her any, but we'll have to keep a close eye on her," he says.

"Despite my earlier hesitations, I don't think he wants to harm her," I say. "I think she's the only person in the Mists he has any interest in defending at the moment."

"I'd have to agree," Whitt says with a sigh. "Which makes me more certain that what happened in the cove was an accident. We were reaching out to Delta mainly to see if she could cure Talia. Any assistance she might have offered in a war with Orion was a secondary concern at the time. I can't see the rat wanting to jeopardize that unless he honestly believed we weren't going to stick to *our* word."

Sylas considers me. "Is that what you wanted to talk about?"

I shake my head, but I have to dredge up the words. "I've also noticed how fond of him Talia's becoming."

Whitt's eyebrows leap up. "What are you suggesting?"

I spread my hands. "She feels a connection with him, and she's grateful for the ways he's helped her. She also sympathizes with the tragedies he's faced and his devotion to his people. He's continued to prove himself a loyal ally and even friend to *her*... It's not surprising that she'd come to care about him quite a bit too, is it?"

August bares his teeth. "If that rat even tries to lay his grubby paws on her—"

"I don't think there's much chance of that," Whitt breaks in. "I've watched them together—I think he's quite charmed by her, but he holds himself back. He knows how devoted *she* is to us, I've no doubt." He pauses, meeting my gaze. "But I have seen a little of what you're talking about, now that I think about it, and obviously you have more direct insight into her emotions."

"But a rat..." August mutters.

"She managed to give me a chance even when she saw me as the enemy, even when the bond was forced on her in a way she found terrifying," I remind them, my stomach knotting. "And you all accepted my place in her life, by her side, as well. I only thought we should have the subject out in the open between us, and possibly come to some sort of tentative understanding of how we'll handle their attachment to each other if her feelings continue to develop."

Silence settles over us. Sylas gazes off toward the window and then returns his attention to me. "She won't step outside the bonds of our relationship. She only revealed the deeper affections she'd come to feel for Whitt to him after August and I had assured her that it wouldn't be a betrayal—it was the same with you. She has one of the deepest senses of loyalty I've ever seen. If we don't mention it, she never will. She'll simply put her feelings aside."

"And that's what you think we should do?" I ask. "Ignore it?"

"We can't trust him," August says. "Whether he cares about her or not, he'd like to see the rest of us dead in the ground."

The corner of Sylas's mouth crooks upward. "I'm not sure that's true, if only because he knows how much losing us would hurt Talia. But I do feel it's too early to make any calls, and as long as we don't intervene, nothing significant about the situation is going to change. We have time to see how deep *his* loyalty runs, especially once war looms. Any affection she feels for him will shatter quickly if he shows he's willing to attack the rest of our people."

He's right. Of course he's right. That's undoubtedly how it'll play out: for all his doting, push will come to shove, and he'll take up arms alongside the rest of his people. Talia will never forgive him for giving up on the hope of peace.

And then nothing that's been eating at me will matter.

"I do think there's one part of his strategy we should consider taking up ourselves," Whitt remarks with a faint grin. "Try every possible cure, no matter how unlikely? There are options we haven't pursued yet because we assumed they'd have no effect. But I'd like to show our mighty mate that we aren't giving up either. She could probably use some time away from languishing around one castle or another day in and day out."

Our problems are hardly solved, but his suggestion lightens my spirits just slightly. I offer him a smile. "What do you have in mind?"

18

Talia

"So, this spring is supposed to heal people?" I ask, peering over the bow of the carriage at the terrain ahead. Only the faintest gleam of water shows in the distance.

"Not specifically from curses," Sylas says from where he's standing next to me, guiding the vehicle. "And like much of the natural magic in this world, it isn't entirely consistent. But many fae have reported severe ailments that were washed away by a soak in the waters. We don't want to leave any stone unturned."

Because nothing my mates thought had a better chance of working has accomplished anything so far. Because despite everything they and Madoc have done for me, I woke up this morning feeling weaker than ever before.

The prickling sensation in my chest has expanded and

sharpened. It's not as unbearable as the worst fits, several more of which struck me last night in quick succession, but harsh enough that I hesitate to breathe too deeply, avoiding the jab of discomfort that'll come. My heartbeat stutters at odd moments for no clear reason. And every now and then a splinter of pain pokes down to my gut.

I feel like I have a jagged-edged creature growing inside me, getting more restless by the hour.

Corwin can tell because he can sense quite a bit of that through our bond. I don't have the energy to shield him from much. I haven't told my other mates more than the briefest of details about my worsening condition, though.

They already know the situation is dire. They're already worried enough. The fact that we're taking this trip even with war on the horizon proves it.

"Even if it doesn't help anything, a good soak is always enjoyable for its own sake," Whitt says in a more typical wry tone, though I can hear the tension creeping through underneath. "I fully intend to take advantage of it."

"We can't have Talia in the spring on her own anyway," August points out. "If a fit came over her while she was bathing, she wouldn't be able to concentrate on keeping her head out of the water."

Corwin hums in agreement, and I restrain a grimace. So many considerations I never expected them to have to make. It wasn't that long ago that I told them to stop hovering over me because being pregnant didn't make me an invalid. I *am* an invalid now, thanks to the curse.

The questions that've haunted me more and more since the curse's effect intensified gnaw at me again. What if we can't cure it? What if I only have a few weeks left? A few days?

I swallow hard. I knew I wouldn't have a full fae lifespan with my mates, but I thought I'd at least get a full human one. I meant to reach out to Jamie when I didn't have to worry as much about the tensions of the fae world harming him—but even if I can't wait that long, how can I appear in his life out of the blue if I'm just going to really die on him right after?

Corwin steps closer and brushes a comforting hand over my head, sending a rush of devotion through our bond at the same time. *We'll find a way. Whatever it takes. It won't come to that.*

He can't be sure of those words, but I shove the grim thoughts away anyway. They don't do me any good. They only add to how much awfulness the curse can make me feel.

I will not lose hope like I almost did in the cage in Orion's throne room. I will not let the Murk king win.

A stretch of dark stone comes into view up ahead. As the carriage slows, passing into that area, I can see it's not just dark but pure black. But there's something soft about the blackness that gives the impression of a thick blanket or coat of fur, not the polished chill of the obsidian stones that made up the old castle at what's now Hearth-by-the-Heart.

Just looking at the darkly opaque surface calms something deep inside me. When Whitt and August help me out of the carriage, I find the ground is lightly spongy under my feet.

"It's a type of moss," Whitt tells me, observing my curious reaction. "It grows all over the stone here except right in the spring itself—and this is the only place in the realms it grows. Some have speculated that it's what gives the water its healing properties, but no one's really sure. Taking the moss away and trying to make a cure out of it elsewhere has never worked."

There are so many mysteries in the fae world. I find that somehow reassuring—that it isn't so odd that we'd have trouble unraveling my curse, that it's just the way many things work here. And overall, this world hasn't turned out so terrible, so maybe this situation won't either.

My mates lead me to the water. At the other end of the springs, a stream spills down a shallow, slick slope where the moss-covered rocks rise a few feet in the air. Then it courses into five separate pools, the one in the middle as large as my bedroom back home and the others less than half that size.

"I just… get in?" I say.

Sylas nods. "To ensure the full effect, if you're going to get any effect at all, it's best to soak for an hour or so. But I understand it's quite pleasant. If you start to feel unwell, just tell us."

I nod and start to pull off my dress. Whitt chucks his clothes aside with no apparent concern for modesty, which doesn't surprise me, and the others follow suit more slowly.

Corwin leaves on his boxer-like undergarments and sits at the edge of the pool. "It seems wise for one of us to be observing from outside the water."

"Hmm," Whitt says. "Don't want to get your feathers wet?" He winks and jumps into the gently flowing water.

I slip in more carefully, August sliding into the water next to me and holding my arm to make sure I'm steady. The moss might only reach the edge of the pool, but the rock surface my feet come to rest on has a rippled texture that makes it easy to grip.

The water, warm enough to immediately relax my muscles but not steaming hot, glides against my skin and around my shoulders. A sigh slips out of me, and I lean back against the wall, not really feeling up to doing more than that.

Corwin eases over so I can rest my head against his knee. He glances at Whitt, who's making a slow circuit of the pool, and I catch a flicker of good humor through our connection. "What's that you're doing, then?" he asks. "The dog paddle?"

"Oh!" Whitt clutches his chest as if wounded, his eyes sparkling. "Shots fired across the bow by Lord Bird."

August laughs, and Sylas shakes his head at all of them, sinking into the water up to his chin. Then he makes a gesture beneath the surface alongside a quick movement of his lips, and a little wave rises up to splash over Whitt's head.

As a giggle tumbles out of me, the spymaster mock-glowers at his brother. "Now I'm getting ganged up on by two arch-lords. I see how it is. But you forget that it's never wise to tangle with an expert in strategy."

He hasn't even finished speaking when a wave of his own shoots out of the water. Sylas dodges it—right into the path of a sudden larger one that completely douses his dark hair.

Swiping the wet strands away from his face, Sylas chuckles. August takes the moment of his distraction to aim a well-placed swell of water at the back of his brother's head.

"Now who's getting ganged up on?" the Seelie arch-lord asks with an amused glint in his dark eye.

The three of them swim, feint, and dodge around the pool, each getting drenched by one of the others in turn. A smile stays on my lips, watching them horse around like, well, wolf pups at play. How long has it been since *they* could really relax?

August ends up ducking past me, and I can't resist taking the opportunity to splash water over his ruddy hair with my cupped hands. He swivels with a grin and gives me a quick peck with his slick lips.

And I realize that I can fully enjoy the moment. The jabs of pain inside me have retreated. The prickle is still there, but dulled to its previous intensity. I don't know if that means much of anything, but it's enough of a relief that my smile widens.

I nudge myself away from the side of the pool. "I want to float," I announce.

"And what the mite wants, she'll have," Whitt says.

He catches my shoulder, making sure I'm steady in the water as I stretch out on the surface. Rivulets stream over the mounds of my breasts, and a flicker of desire reaches me from Corwin watching, but he reins it in.

The water holds me up in its warm embrace. I drift

along, each of my Seelie mates guiding my path in turn with a tender touch to my head, my side, my hip. The sky stretches out above me, perfectly blue.

In that moment, I want to float like this forever, as if the world itself is holding me up, as if nothing could drag me down beneath the surface.

After a while I feel the urge to move again. I paddle around a bit and then come to a stop by the edge again. "I am feeling better," I tell my mates.

"That's wonderful." August swims over and tugs me into an embrace.

I nestle against him, but with the pain retreating, the feel of his naked skin against mine sets off a spark of my own desire. I tip my head, seeking a longer kiss.

August obliges with a pleased growl low in his throat.

A headier heat floods me with the meeting of our lips. My limbs slide against his, and he cups my breast beneath the water. The slow rotation of his thumb over the peak has me whimpering against him in an instant.

I can feel all my other mates' gazes on us, but they don't rush to join in. Corwin gives off a sense of caution, wanting to be sure I don't end up overwhelmed. They're going to let me take the lead.

I want this so much while I can enjoy it. I kiss August harder, arching into his touch. Another growl reverberates through his chest.

He holds me against the wall, careful not to press too tightly, and tucks his knee between my legs. The movement of it against my sex makes me gasp into his mouth. His tongue teases over mine, and he shifts the attentions of his hand to my other breast.

For a while, I just rock there, floating on pleasure as much as the buoyancy of the water, each graze of his thigh against me taking me farther from the worries of the present. Just as I'm starting to tremble with the sensations spiking toward my release, August pulls back.

"I can do better than this," he murmurs.

Hoisting me up, he sets me on the edge of the pool with my legs still splayed. Then he presses his face where his thigh was before, lapping his tongue over my opening and flicking it across the sensitive nub above.

Bliss ricochets through my body. I lean back on my hands with a cry, unable to stop myself from swaying my hips toward him, urging him on.

A dripping form crouches beside me, and Whitt's voice reaches my ear with a tickle of heated breath. "Can I help take you to even greater heights, mighty one?"

I manage a nod, punctuating it with a whimper as August eases a finger inside me. He pulses it inside me in time with the rhythmic swipes of his tongue, and Whitt trails his fingers over my damp skin. The spymaster strokes down my spine and across my belly, then up to circle my breasts.

My head tips farther back, and Whitt leans in to support it. His fingers swirl closer and closer to my pebbled nipples as August suckles me harder. Then, just as the final surge of pleasure crashes over me, Whitt squeezes the tips of my breasts.

The extra jolt of delight sends me careening even

higher. I moan, clutching his arm, my other hand grasping at August's hair.

As I come down from the high, Sylas gets out of the pool next to us. Watching the water stream over his massive, muscular form sends a renewed flare of hunger through me.

I reach for him, and he smiles, scooping me up as if I weigh nothing at all. It's like floating in the pool, this sense of being totally supported above the ground... except in Sylas's arms, I can also do *this*.

I twist against him, tucking my hand behind his neck to tangle my fingers in his hair and tugging his mouth to mine. With a groan, he claims my lips. My hip brushes the hard length of his shaft, already fully erect, and a pang forms between my legs—a longing to be filled.

But I can still feel Corwin watching all this, restraining himself. The passion inside me needs all my mates with me for it to be fully satisfied.

I beckon the Unseelie arch-lord through our bond, and he rises. "Perhaps our mate needs to see just how well we can support her," he says as he walks over to us, with an unexpectedly husky note in his voice that makes me twice as eager as before.

The raven shifter grips my thighs, and Sylas loosens his hold so that Corwin can adjust me against him, spreading my legs. He teases his fingers over my sex before positioning me over Sylas's rigid length. A strained sound of impatience escapes me, but he has to know this isn't all I need from him.

I want you in me too. If—if you want too… He's never taken that role before.

The only response I need is the rush of desire that careens into me through our connection. Corwin lowers his head to nip my shoulder as I sink down onto Sylas. He eases one hand away for just long enough to wrench down his boxers. Then he brushes his fingers over my other entrance with a soft murmuring that turns his touch silky with conjured slickness.

Sylas nuzzles my cheek and my neck, dappling my jaw and throat with tiny kisses and grazes of his fangs. His hardness seems to swell even more inside me, filling me with a giddy burn. Then Corwin is sliding into me too, inch by inch, until I'm suspended between the two of them, held up by the potent mix of love and lust *we've* conjured together.

They move together as if they've worked in unison their whole lives, as if no border or animosity has ever divided them. Corwin's enjoyment of our closeness and the carnal delight brought by the squeeze of my muscles around him flows into me in a continuing current. All I can do is ride the growing surge, propelled higher and higher between them, weightless amid the torrent of pleasure.

Heat sparks all through my torso and sizzles through my veins. *Oh, my love,* Corwin says silently, his breath ragged against my spine. *Oh, my soul.* Sylas steals another kiss, his groan carrying into it, and Corwin bites down on my shoulder.

I come so hard it's as if I'm literally flying, soaring up

into that endless blue of the sky. Quivers radiate through every nerve in my body.

The searing bliss of Corwin's release flings me even higher. I lose my breath, shuddering and then gripping Sylas even tighter as I feel him tense and jerk with his own peak.

How could anything be wrong when we can feel this way together?

Exhaustion rolls back over me as the two arch-lords lower me to the ground. I reach for Whitt and August to join me too, and my four mates sit in a ring around me, supporting me on the ground just as two of them did in the air just minutes ago.

My breath evens out, my muscles going slack. I wish I could go to sleep right here, and maybe not wake up until the nightmares of my waking hours are over.

But those horrors aren't going to leave of their own accord. After a short rest, I force myself to stir. "We should get back. Whatever the spring can do for me, it's already done, right?"

Sylas kisses my temple and meets my gaze with his mismatched eyes. "We can spare more time if you want to relax here a little longer."

Can they really spare it, though? *I* won't be able to relax if I start worrying that I'm keeping them from everything else they need to be focused on for too long.

I ease to my feet. "I can relax in the carriage. I do feel a lot better. Maybe this was what I needed all along."

The hope in those words stays with me for the first several minutes after we set off toward the Heart. I snuggle in between Whitt and August on a cushion they've set on the carriage floor and drift into a doze.

I'm half asleep when the next attack of the curse hits me, cutting through me so deeply and sharply a scream bursts from my lips.

19

Whitt

My voice spills out into the silence of my study, intoning the last few magically charged words that will bind the pieces of my spell together—and to the item I'm attaching it to. Energy tingles through me, thrumming in my throat. Then I lean back in my chair, contemplating the duskapple tart on its plain plate.

What would August have thought of my request to nab one of these if he'd known what I was going to do with it? Well, I suppose I'll find out soon enough. I'll set the process in motion, and the knowledge that it's already done should help ease any qualms he has about dishonesty.

He won't be deceiving anyone else, only making use of a pre-existing trick.

No, I don't actually feel any guilt about going ahead

with this without August's preapproval. I'm simply doing my job. What makes me hesitate is the thought of how I'm going to present it to our mate.

I know what Talia would say if I told her my full intentions. She'd refuse to have any part in my plan. The blasted rat has won her over enough that she'd put his rights over the possibility of saving her and ending this war—and he's possibly won more than I'd like of her heart as well. If Corwin is picking up on other emotions brewing inside her…

I set that thought aside and tuck the tart into a cloth pouch before looping the drawstring cord around my wrist. My mate is ill, and it's also my job to protect her. If I could go far enough to erase her screams of pain from her past as well her future, I would. Whatever anger she might feel toward me afterward will be mine to bear.

I'll bear it happily if she's well enough to lay it into me.

When I step out of the study, the hall is quiet. No screams or groans carry through the air now. After the bad series of fits on our way back from the Serene Springs, which gripped her on and off for most of the journey, she had another wrenching spell that kept her up a significant part of the night. Nothing we attempted appeared to lessen her agony at all.

By the end of it, the whites of her eyes were ruddy and her nose had started to bleed. The Murk king's destruction is seeping right through her body now.

We have to end this curse before it tears her apart completely.

Nudging open Talia's bedroom door, I find her subdued but awake, nestled against Corwin on the bed. The raven shifter nods to me in acknowledgment and kisses the top of Talia's head. She eases her arms away from him, knowing we're changing "shifts." Corwin has business to attend to in his domain, as much as I know he wants to spend every minute at our mate's side.

Technically it isn't my turn to watch over her. Sylas intended to come by in an hour or two. I'm simply getting my work done in the meantime, and I can't say I mind being in Talia's presence while I do.

As Corwin gets up, I sit down at her other side. She leans into me, a tremor running through her body against mine as if it was taking a huge amount of energy just to sit up on her own for the few moments she did. Another twist of concern winds around my gut.

We may not have much time at all. Orion wants to draw out her torment and our distress alongside hers, but he also wants to see us crushed sooner rather than later. And even if she'll survive for weeks longer, I'm afraid the curse is starting to damage her in ways we won't be able to fix even if we can free her from its continuing grasp.

I leave the pouch with the tart at the end of the bed and wrap my arms around Talia, taking all of her weight. She sags into me with a sigh that speaks of exhaustion and frustration.

"I hate feeling like this," she mutters. "So wrung out but like I can't really relax. It hurts a little bit *everywhere*."

I nuzzle her temple, my throat constricting. If my plan

works, I remind myself, she won't have to feel this way for much longer.

"We're still exploring possible cures," I say. "And searching for a way to get at the source of Orion's power. Perhaps our rat shifter friend will come through with another inspiration."

I brought up Madoc on purpose to get us started on that subject. Talia reaches toward her pillow and picks up the flower-shaped charm the Murk man brought her. I hadn't realized she was keeping it so close to her.

She traces its petals, gazing down at it as if she's hoping to find some kind of answer in its stitching. The thought of her having this present from him next to her as she sleeps twists me up inside in a totally different way. I have to hold back my fangs from emerging.

Talia glances up at me. "Is Madoc all right? You've been letting him leave the cabin now and then, haven't you? And he'll have to go back to check in with Orion again at some point."

She's worried about him even when she's in such a bad state. I swallow down the knowledge that if all goes as I intend, he'll be scampering back to his king much sooner than expected.

"As far as I know, he's faring just fine," I say. "He's a rat; he must be used to holing up in tight spaces."

Sick as she is, Talia manages to shoot me a chiding look. I run my fingers up and down her back, tamping down on my guilt. "Would you like to go have a visit with him? We could have him come over to the castle like he did before so you don't have to strain yourself much."

And then I'll offer her the tart to present to him, and of course he'll take any gift she offers without the suspicion he'd level at a similar gesture from one of us fae. When he eats it, my spell will take hold all through his body without him even noticing it. And after they've spoken, I'll take him aside and "reveal" that we've discovered the location of his Refuge. That we're going to launch an attack as soon as we've gathered our forces.

Then August and I will decide on arranging a convenient moment when he can escape. Madoc will dash right back to warn his king—and my spell will let us track him there. We'll descend on the Refuge right at his heels and destroy both his king and the false Heart that's powering all our curses.

Simple, elegant, and quick—the best sort of plan. If Madoc won't help us confront his king directly, then why shouldn't I force his hand?

Maybe he'll even thank me in the end.

Talia rubs her mouth. "I would like to spend time with him, just to give him some company. But I don't want him to feel bad when he sees me and can tell nothing he brought really helped."

Oh, my mighty, tender-hearted mate. I gently kiss the side of her head. "I think he'll be more worried if he doesn't hear from you, and that he'll appreciate spending the time with you enough to offset the rest."

Talia raises her eyebrows. "Are you starting to believe that helping me really does matter to him and that it's not all some kind of trick?"

I let out a soft laugh and answer totally honestly, "It's

not very hard to believe that, the way he's stuck his neck out for you."

The way he talks to her. The way he looks at her.

Talia tucks her hand around mine, twining our fingers. "I'm glad. It was good, seeing the two of you working together. Maybe you'll be able to come up with another plan like that. Thank you for giving him a chance. I know it isn't easy with all the history between the Seelie and the Murk."

Her gratitude sends a sharper jab of guilt right through my chest. I have to force my smile. "I'm willing to keep an open mind if it makes it easier for us to protect you and the rest of the Mists."

"Good. You know..." She pauses as if it's taking a moment for her to get her thoughts in order. "It isn't really fair that the Murk lost so much. So what if a lot of them liked to lie and trick people, and that weakened their connection to the real Heart? Why should Madoc or any of the others have had to start out already so distant from it when they hadn't done anything yet? And—*you* and the other fae of the Mists find all kinds of ways of tricking each other and giving the wrong impression by talking around the truth, but as long as you stick to the letter of the law, the Heart's given you a pass. At least... at least the Murk are upfront in their lies instead of acting like they're being truthful when they're not."

She lapses into silence again, leaving me struggling for words. She can't know what I was thinking. The unfairness she just commented on has obviously been on her mind for a while.

But I can't say she's wrong, can I? I *have* deceived my fellow fae, more times than I can count even since I've known her. I mean to do the same with Madoc just minutes from now—laying out just the right words to make him think what I want him to without actually saying anything that's strictly untrue.

Is that really so much better? Does it make me so much more deserving?

As far as the Heart is concerned, apparently so. But to Talia…

A knot forms in my stomach. She just thanked me for being someone I'm not, someone much more open and generous. And, blast it all, I want to be the man she sees me as. She's always found the goodness in me even when I had trouble believing in myself.

My other hand reaches for the pouch with the tart, but I don't mention it to her, only carry it with me as I help her downstairs to the summer-side entrance. A quick word to one of the castle guards sends him off to fetch Madoc. Talia settles into the grass, and I magically summon a few pillows from inside the castle so she can lean back against them to better preserve her strength.

I can still go through with my plan. I haven't backed out of it. I simply want to observe Madoc once more to be sure of my resolve before I make the final arrangements.

I find myself watching my mate as much as the direction where Madoc will appear. The moment he comes into view, her face brightens, her posture steadying just a little. Seeing him *reassures* her in a way I can't explain.

Or maybe I don't want to because of the jealousy that flares at the same time.

She isn't wrong about his reaction to her obviously weakened state. The pleased light that gleams in his eyes at the sight of her dims as he gets closer, his expression clouding over with concern. He sits down across from her gingerly as if he's afraid even moving near her might cause her pain.

He doesn't comment on it directly, but the first words out of his mouth are, "I've been thinking over all the healing spells I've witnessed, everything I've heard or seen about curses… and ways that maybe I could get more information out of Orion when I go back. As soon as—"

Talia holds up her hand with a gentle smile that I'd swear could melt the hardest heart. "I know. It's okay. It is what it is. I'd rather talk about something happier. Have you been enjoying the books you brought?"

The corner of Madoc's mouth quirks up at a bittersweet angle. In that moment, there isn't one part of me that can deny the devotion with which he's gazing at her.

It's a pity he isn't especially skilled in the healing arts. I have no doubt he'd stretch himself to the limits of his magic if he believed he could cure Talia on his own. He obviously has plenty of that Murk magic at his disposal, given his skill with illusions. If only it could be channeled—

An idea sparks in my head so abruptly that for a second it blots out everything else. I blink, testing the edges of the inspiration, reining in my eagerness in case I spot some flaw. But the more I prod at it, the more excitement swells inside me.

I should have considered this earlier. But I didn't—because I didn't really trust Madoc enough to open my mind that much.

It still might not work. But it feels like a much more solid possibility than our trip to the springs or Madoc's little cures.

And it doesn't require me betraying my mate's hard-won trust.

My mind keeps spinning, working through the details, as Talia and Madoc discuss his recent reads and then other favorite books, a few they're both familiar with. It's far too soon that my mate's energy begins to flag. I notice the drooping of her shoulders, and Madoc glances at me in the same instant.

He turns back to Talia, giving her the respect of addressing her rather than calling on me to make the decision. "You look like you could use some more rest. As much as I enjoy getting a break from the cabin, I'll feel better knowing you're keeping your strength up as much as you can."

Talia sighs, but she accepts his point with a dip of her head—which tells me she's faltering even more than she's letting show. The guards converge around Madoc to escort him away, and Sylas comes striding over from the castle of Hearth-by-the-Heart to meet us.

My brother gives me a quizzical glance, and I shoot him a smile that promises more explanation later. "I thought the mite could use a little fresh air and social stimulation," I say out loud.

Sylas hums to himself and gathers Talia up. I brush a kiss to her knuckles before heading after the guards.

I catch up with them at the edge of the woods. "Hold on a moment," I say, and they stop immediately. A cadre-chosen's words are worth that much.

Madoc's quizzical glance is much more suspicious than Sylas's was, but given what I intended to be saying to him when I first imagined this conversation, I suppose I can't blame him.

The smile I offer him I mean just as much as the one I gave my lord. "Our last collaboration didn't end up going so well, but maybe that's because there were too many conflicting factors in the mix," I say. "I have an idea for another way we could work together that might be just what Talia needs to set her free from your king's curse."

20

Talia

I've usually enjoyed carriage rides—the rush of the landscape sweeping by, the wash of the breeze. Today, every tiny hitch of the vehicle with the shifting currents in the air sends a splinter of pain through my ribs or my gut.

It hurts more if I'm holding myself at all upright. My mates created a sort of nest for me out of pillows on the floor of the carriage, where I can sit with my back resting against the bench by the stern, totally cushioned and out of the reach of the wind. I don't really like being down here where I can't see much except the sky and the upper branches of any trees we pass, but I like the pain even less.

I know there are two other carriages around us even though I can't see them. Sylas is directing one and Corwin the other. Each carries the skilled healers my arch-lords already assembled for my care as well as several warriors in case we need their protection. August and Whitt are in charge of the vehicle I'm in, which also holds Madoc and his now-typical contingent of four guards, as well as a couple of others who are scanning the landscape around us rather than the Murk man.

August has spent most of the ride sitting on the bench opposite me while Madoc and Whitt consult on our exact course. We're heading to the area of the fringelands that contains the portal that connects to the spot closest to the Refuge and the Murk Heart. Madoc hesitated to give full directions ahead of time, even though there are dozens of other portals in the same area and no way for us to know which is the key one without him specifying.

He was probably afraid that my mates would change their mind about their current strategy and attempt an invasion instead. I'm not sure he was wrong to worry about that. The wary alertness in August's glances around us suggest he's prepared for a battle.

But mostly he's focused on me. He's set his legs to one side of me so I can lean my head against his knee, appreciating the warmth of his body. Any time I wince, he tenses. He brought a sack full of delicacies that he put together in the kitchen before we left, but I haven't had any appetite. My stomach feels like it's stuffed full already —with needles and jagged gravel.

"We would have done this back in Hearth-by-the-Heart, but we didn't want to drain whatever power Madoc has left if it didn't work there," he says with a note of apology in his tone. "We might only get one real chance. We won't risk bringing you right through to the human world, and there our magic might not be up to the challenge anyway. But Madoc's component is the most important since he's the only one who can tackle the Murk aspects of the curse. He says he should be able to draw a little on their Heart just being close to the portal."

I nod. Most of that my mates have already explained to me in bits and pieces—or maybe more coherently, and I just haven't been able to hold my attention well enough to realize. How much is August reminding me to reassure me and how much for himself?

"Do you really think there's much chance it'll work?" I can't help asking, studying his expression. August is the most earnest of my mates; he isn't in the habit of using subterfuge. I'll get the most accurate sense of the odds from his reaction.

He smiles, and it looks genuine enough to lift my spirits despite my discomfort.

"I think it's the best chance we've gotten," he says. "We should have tried it earlier—if it didn't rely so much on Madoc's contribution… But mingling magical affinities is a longstanding if not all that common practice. There are lots of accounts of it working. We just need to get the balance right and to give him enough of a boost of energy to work through the trickier parts of his king's magic."

I thanked Whitt earlier for being willing to work together with our Murk ally, and now he's taken that alliance a step farther. I don't totally understand the magical theory of how it all works, but they're going to combine August and the other healers' medical magic with Madoc's Murk-based power to try to unravel the curse.

The way Whitt described it to me, they'll be able to construct an effect kind of like the bunch of them are actually one super powerful Murk healer.

If this strategy doesn't work, I can't imagine what would… other than managing to destroy the Murk Heart itself. Which we'll probably still have to do to end the other curses afflicting the Mists. But I know as well as my mates do that it's going to be difficult fighting Orion on his own turf. I may not have enough time left for them to save me by winning that war.

My view may be too restricted for me to see much from my nest of pillows, but I can tell we're getting close to the fringes from the rising humidity in the air, turning it hot and sticky against my skin. My head starts to burn as if the weather has provoked a fever. August murmurs a cooling spell over me that provides a little relief, and then Whitt calls him over to discuss something.

As I lean back on my cushions, gazing up at the sky that's now streaked with clouds, Madoc picks his way across the benches to join me. He moves tentatively, as if expecting to be called back by the guards at any second. Was he waiting until August left to come over to me at all? I guess it'd make sense that he wouldn't feel terribly welcome around my mates.

No one hollers at him, though. He stops for a moment when he reaches me, the wind licking through his pale hair and turning it even more tousled than usual, and then sinks down on the bench next to where I'm leaning. He's careful not to sit too close, leaving enough space between us that we don't touch.

The pensive look on his face makes me want to reach out and squeeze his hand, to reassure him that I'm happy to have his company even if the other fae are still unsure of his loyalties, but I'm afraid of the reaction that large a movement will provoke in my body. So I simply adjust my position a little so I'm angled to face him, still tucked against my pillows.

Even that small movement provokes a wince, and Madoc flinches as if he feels responsible. "It's gotten worse again, hasn't it?" he says, looking me over.

"I'm managing," I say automatically.

He gives me a tight smile. "You're good at covering it up, but I've had a lot of practice at keeping things hidden myself. I can recognize the signs. You don't have to hide it with me to spare *my* feelings."

A sigh tumbles out of me. "What if it's easier for *me* to deal with it if I'm pretending it's not so bad?"

"Then that's fair enough." Madoc pauses, his gaze lifting to the landscape around us. "Do you want to be left alone, or would talking help too?"

I'm not sure how much talking *I* want to do, but listening to him could be a welcome distraction. Not just from the pains of the curse, but from all the other worries hanging over us as well. I look up at the Murk man, thinking of the glimpses of his life I got in the Refuge, the pieces he's shared with me since, all the weight I know he's carrying.

I want to know him—know what drives the complicated but brave and devoted man I've slowly come to understand. But I don't think I can handle anything too serious right now.

"Tell me about the things that've made you happiest in your life," I say. "I want to hear about something good."

Madoc blinks as if surprised by the request or maybe by the idea that anything in his life has been all that happy. But then he settles more solidly into his seat, his heavy-lidded eyes going distant with thought.

"I told you I spent most of my childhood in an orphanage," he says. "That one was under a street that had a popular candy shop on it. Once a week, the fae running the orphanage would let us go up in the middle of the night while the shop was closed and pick one treat to eat then or save for later. I think I ended up trying just about everything that store carried, getting a little thrill out of what flavors I'd stumble on next week by week."

The curls of my mouth twitch upward. "So that's how you got your taste for human snacks."

"It must be, although they had pretty different types back then. The best night, though, was when we found the shop had held some kind of party and no one had cleaned up yet. There was part of a cake left, and streamers and fancier snacks—we romped around like it was all of our birthdays at once. It felt like some higher power must care what happened to us, if it'd give us a gift like that."

The bittersweet thread that's crept into his voice tells me he doesn't see the joyful night that way anymore, but it's clearly still a fond memory. It's hard to imagine the man next to me as an excited child, delighting in something so simple that I'd have taken for granted when I was little.

"What else?" I nudge.

He hums to himself. "The first time I drew a star chart and really saw the meaning in the patterns there—that was exciting. There was an old Murk woman who taught me a lot of the skills, and I always enjoyed going to see her. She had a voice like crisp autumn leaves. It could spark images right in your head if you listened right."

"You'll have to show me how it all works sometime."

He glances at me, startled, and then smiles. "I'd like to see what you make of it. And there's also…" He draws in a breath and hesitates.

"What?" I ask when he doesn't go on, flicking my hand to tap his lower leg.

Madoc's smile twists. "A lot of my happy memories aren't things you're likely to be happy hearing about. Meeting Orion, taking in the power of his Heart, realizing that there was a real chance the Murk could get the home we deserve. Seeing the same hope in so many others around me. Taking steps to get us closer to that goal, knowing I was helping make up for all the things so many of us have lost…" He trails off, a shadow crossing his face.

My throat tightens. "I can understand why those things made you happy. I know… I know everything you've done with Orion has been because of how much you care about the rest of the Murk. I *like* that you care so much about them and that you've worked so hard to make things better for them, not just yourself. It's only the way Orion wants you to get your home back that's a problem."

"His way used to be how *I* wanted it to happen too, so maybe you're overly generous." Madoc lets out a rough laugh, his gaze drifting away from me again. "I just was so caught up in the dream of having all the Mists for us to roam freely through, and so angry with the fae who ran us out—"

He meets my eyes again. "The anger clouded my vision, and even when I was out there watching to see how you fared, I didn't *really* see. I should have realized it wasn't right, the way he was using you. I should have warned you sooner, not dragged you off to put you under his power even more."

The anguish of his admission turns his voice even hoarser than usual. I rest my hand against his leg again, an ache closing around my heart. "It probably wouldn't have made any difference. It might even have been worse that way. I don't know if any of us would have believed how much power he's built up if I hadn't witnessed it myself. No one would have trusted you at all. And he could still have triggered the curse in me. It's not like you could have saved me from that."

"I guess not. But all the same, I'm sorry." Madoc's throat bobs. "I'm not sure you even should forgive me. I'll do whatever I can to reverse the damage I helped him do to you, today and every day after."

I don't know what to say to answer the emotion in his words, and then a sharper pain shoots down my spine. A gasp escapes me. I pull my legs closer, hugging them, bracing myself to ride out the next onslaught of agony.

It doesn't escalate just yet, though. I close my eyes, but

I feel Madoc's fingers brush over my hair in the lightest of caresses.

When I don't pull away, he repeats the gesture of comfort a little less cautiously. His touch sends a pleasant quiver through my nerves that I can't look at too closely right now. Not when another jab of pain slices through my stomach. I grit my teeth.

Then the carriage eases to a halt. Madoc stands.

August's voice reaches me as if from much farther away. "The others are going ahead to make sure the area is safe. We'll join them in a moment."

He comes over to me, but Madoc doesn't move away. I'm aware of him still standing over me as if guarding me as August crouches in front of me. "Will you need me to carry you over, Sweetness?" my mate asks with heart-breaking tenderness.

The pain has subsided a little. My thoughts have jumbled, but I know that I want to stand on my own two feet as long as I can. "I'll be okay," I murmur. "I might just need a little help getting out of the carriage."

"Of course."

While we wait to follow the others, there's a span of time where my thoughts are blurred by another pain that's not as sharp but digs in deeper, longer, with an insistent throbbing. I'm starting to think I won't be able to walk after all when Whitt calls over, "There's the signal. Let's get over there and begin."

The fae guards disembark around me with thumps of their boots hitting the ground. Madoc stays with me, steadying my balance with August as the two of them guide me out of the vehicle. As the Murk jumps down beside me, I sway and catch his arm to stop myself from falling—

And a harsh cry rings out up ahead where the fog is thicker between the trees. Footsteps thunder; bodies dart through the haze.

"Everyone, to me, *now!*" Sylas shouts from beyond my view. "We're under attack."

21

Talia

At his lord and brother's call, August jolts forward a step before he glances at me, his eyes wide, torn between staying with me and defending the rest of his people. The guards are already dashing to Sylas's aid. August's lips pull back in a snarl of frustration.

"Stay here," he orders both Madoc and me. "Keep out of sight." Then he charges into the fog with the others.

He reaches them not a moment too soon, from what I can tell. Grunts and groans and snarls are filtering through the haze—the battle already sounds desperate.

I strain my neck to see around the side of the carriage, but even that tiny motion sets off a wave of pain through my body. It condenses in the middle of my abdomen, right between my heart and my stomach, and continues to radiate in a steady, searing pulse.

"What's going on?" I ask, my voice coming out ragged.

Madoc frowns, peering into the fog. "I don't know." At a yelp and a raven-ish shriek that carries from the fray, he winces. His fingers tighten where he's still gripping my arm.

All at once, he tugs me farther around the back of the carriage, where I won't be able to see anything at all. His breath is coming fast.

Panic lances through the pain inside me. "Are they heading this way?"

"Not yet, but if they can cut through your fae to get to you, they will." His eyes dart to the trees around us, his mouth pressing flat, and my muddled mind pieces together one clear thought.

It's the Murk. My mates and their warriors have been ambushed by rat shifters. Who else *could* it be? Why would any of the fae of the Mists want to prevent me from being healed?

"They'll look for you at the carriage first," Madoc says, his expression hardening as if he's made a difficult decision. "We can't stay here—we can't take the chance."

He wraps his arm right around me, easing my own arm across his shoulders so that he can support my weight. I stumble across the ground next to him, barely able to control my steps. Every press of my feet against the forest floor sends fresh knives up through my thighs and belly.

I grit my teeth against a cry that might bring the attackers straight to us. A hiss still escapes me.

"I'm sorry," Madoc mutters. Then he scoops me right off the ground, tucking me close against his chest. His stormy scent fills my nose, matching the furor in his eyes.

He hurries several paces away from the carriage to a spot where a few trees stand close enough together to provide a decent amount of shelter. There, he lowers me so I can lean against the trunks. He pauses for a moment to touch my cheek, gazing into my eyes as if trying to read just how much distress I'm in.

"I'll get you away from here—back to your Heart," he says. "I won't let them hurt you more. I wish— That's the only thing I *can* do."

He turns and starts to intone magical words under his breath, spreading his hands over the damp earth. Pebbles and twigs jitter and dart across the ground to combine into a heap beneath his palms. More and more come, along with clumps of mud and bits of bark—a mess of debris that makes no sense to me.

Pain stabs through my gut, and I muffle another gasp. My jaw is aching from how tightly I'm clenching it. I close my eyes, trying to think myself away from the growing agony, to run somewhere inside myself where I can avoid the need to scream and sob with it.

A shudder wracks my body. I start to slump to the side, my muscles refusing to hold me up. My back scrapes across the trunk as I topple.

At the squeak that slips from my lips, Madoc whirls around. He catches me just before my head smacks into the dirt. As he eases me upright, his arms slide around me again, and for a moment he just hugs me. I tip my head against his shoulder, a whimper working its way up my throat despite my best efforts.

"I've got you," he says, his voice raw. "You'll get

through this. You're too fucking strong for Orion to get the better of you—I *know* it."

In that moment, I can't say *I* know it. I feel as if I'm already unraveling, sheared into slivers of myself as I do.

Madoc keeps me nestled against his body as he swivels back to his work. I tense and shiver with a sharper hail of pain, and he alternates between the words of magic he's chanting and murmurs of reassurance.

When the agony eases back briefly, I manage to glance over to the heap he was conjuring. Except now I can see it's not just a heap or a mess.

The pebbles and twigs and the rest have assembled into the vague shape of a boat—so narrow only one person could sit in any part, only maybe five feet long but growing as Madoc continues working his magic.

Of course. He wouldn't be able to direct the Seelie carriage or Corwin's Unseelie vehicle with his magic, so he's making one of his own. The Murk I talked to in the Refuge did say they'd found their own way of traveling quickly through the Mists.

"It'll only take another minute or two before it'll fly," Madoc says before taking up his incantation again. The strain the hasty magic is taking on him carries through his tone and the flexing of his muscles where I'm pressed against his solid frame.

He's barely added to his carriage when footsteps and shouts ring out closer behind us. I flinch in Madoc's arms instinctively before I recognize August's voice, rough with worry. "Talia! Talia, where are you?"

"We're here!" I call back, the words coming out more a

croak than anything else. But August hears me. He races over, twigs crackling in his wake.

Madoc stands to meet him, setting me on my feet but keeping me close against him for support. He's just straightened up when August reaches us, my other mates and a few of the guards right behind him.

August's eyes are wild, blood streaking past one of them from a cut on his forehead. Corwin is bleeding too, from a wound on his shoulder that I only catch the ache of now that I'm seeing it, I was so lost in my own pains. That's all I have time to take in before Whitt is springing at us, wrenching me from Madoc's grasp.

As he gathers me against him, the other men stalk toward Madoc, who backs away with his hands raised and his face paling.

"You set them up to be ready for us," Sylas growls. "And then you thought you'd steal away our mate?"

No, that isn't what happened at all. I try to speak, but as I open my mouth, the curse erupts through my torso, and all that comes out is a squeal of pain.

My mates are already lunging at Madoc. He shoots a frantic glance at me and then springs away, transforming into his rat form in midair and dashing between the trees to vanish into the haze. August moves to sprint after him, his shoulders hunching with the start of his transformation, but just then one of the Seelie carriages soars into view.

"My lord," one of the warriors on it calls out, his arm hanging limp at his side.

"We have to go," Sylas barks, and August draws up

short. The Seelie arch-lord raises his voice to echo through the hazy woods. "But the treacherous rat should know that if he shows one whisker around my domain again, he'll be torn to pieces, along with any others of his kind."

No. This isn't right. I shake my head against Whitt's chest as he hefts me into the carriage, but he doesn't understand.

"It's all right now, mite," he whispers in my ear in a soothing tone. "We've got to get you out of here before the Murk follow us. They won't venture far from the fringes." He looks past me to the arch-lords who've just climbed in, the carriage jolting forward the second they're inside. "He was fashioning a vehicle of his own, did you see?" he says to them, his tone sharpening. "Heart only knows where he was planning on taking her."

Home, I think. *He was only going to take me home where I'd be safe.* But the pain is jumbling my mind too much for me to form any kind of coherent speech. I can barely even follow what's happening around me.

The Murk attacked. My mates and the guards fended them off—but not completely. Only enough to come for me and escape? *All* of them are bleeding here and there— there's a warrior slumped in the bottom of the carriage with one of the healers murmuring hastily over her—a few snarls still echo out of the fog. Are we leaving people behind? That's not right. That's not—

The next searing blade cuts right through my chest down to my core, and a scorching blaze of agony explodes in my belly. The scream I've been bottling up for so long rips out of me. I double over in Whitt's arms, my muscles quaking, cramps burning all through my abdomen. They throb on and on and—

Whitt makes a choked sound, his arms going rigid around me. "We need the healers with Talia. *Right now.* Please…"

There's something horrifyingly desperate in his voice, but I don't really understand. Nothing's changed— nothing's *worse* than it was before, is it? He only hates seeing me in so much agony. He only—

The world tilts as gentle hands come to rest on my belly and my thighs. I become vaguely aware that something down there is… wet. The fabric of my dress, sticking damply to my skin. What—?

As my eyes pop open, the three healers who made it onto this carriage weave their voices together in a single chorus. I stare at the place where they're touching me, where the pain rakes its claws through me again—and all I can think is that I might as well already be dead, the way I look. How can they fix this?

There's blood on *me*. So much blood, spreading all through the skirt of my dress even as I watch, pooling beneath me on the cushions.

How can— No one cut *me*. Has the curse slashed through something deep inside me?

Then, as the healers' increasingly ragged voices swell around us, as August reaches to squeeze my shoulder with a shaking hand and stark horror reverberates through my bond with Corwin, understanding hits me.

I'm not dead. I'm losing the other life I was growing inside me.

No. No! I rally against the realization with everything I have in me—but almost everything in me is agony.

The curse's endless blades pierce my lungs, my heart, and then my mind, and the world around me blinks away into nothingness.

22

Sylas

I'm not sure how many hours we've all been gathered around Talia's bedside when I notice that Corwin has left us. I raise my head from where I've been gazing down at my unconscious mate and realize only my brothers remain around me.

My hand stills where I've been stroking her hair continuously, as if the gesture will eventually summon her back to us. "Where did Corwin go?"

Whitt shrugs where he's sitting at Talia's other side, caressing her hand. "I can't say I was paying that much attention to Lord Bird."

There's no hostility in the nickname, but he can't give it any humor either. I suspect he feels just as broken as I do, watching Talia lie there, unable to rouse her from this new stage of the curse. Not knowing if we've only lost the child we expected to welcome or our mate as well.

This is exactly what the Murk king wanted: all of us struggling with terror for her and a sense of impending mourning. Distracted from whatever plans he's shaping. I can't let him accomplish the rest of his evil ends, but I couldn't walk away from my mate right after the tragedy. My fellow arch-lords are capable of handling the security of the realms for a short while.

The soft, erratic patter of Talia's pulse that my wolfish ears can pick up only reassures me slightly. She's still alive for now, but the curse hasn't stopped its horrible progression. If there's more ahead while she's still living, I have no doubt it'll be even worse, as hard as that is to imagine.

August stirs where he's been massaging one of Talia's feet, looking as if he's trying to coax wellness into her with the press of his thumbs. His lips pull back with one of the fits of fierceness that come over him whenever he glances at Talia's face, probably thinking of the vermin who did this to her. He manages to retract his fangs before answering. "He didn't say where he was going, just walked out."

The knowledge sits uncomfortably with me. Corwin has been most affected out of all of us. He's barely spoken in the hours since we returned to the border castle. I haven't seen him drink so much as a sip of water, let alone eat. Once I glanced at him and my deadened eye picked up a faded image of a raven's head imposed over his own, thrown back with its beak open in a wrenching cry.

The Unseelie arch-lord holds his emotions close. He started to shut down when Talia was missing too. I don't want to leave our mate even now, but I do have other responsibilities that will protect her and her happiness as well as the rest of the fae world.

I don't think she'd want me to ignore her soul-twined mate's distress.

"I'll find him and speak to him," I say. "And we'll need to regroup and put all the energy we can into finding the Refuge and destroying the Murk's false Heart."

I don't care about Madoc's warnings about the foolhardiness of attempting to challenge Orion in his home so far from our own. That rat was as treacherous as the rest of them, leading us into an ambush so his people could overwhelm us. We barely made it out alive. Several of our warriors fell to give the rest of us a clear path back to the carriages. There were too many of the rats—we might have all fallen if we hadn't decided we needed to run for it as quickly as we did.

I hate having fled in the wake of an enemy, but I'd hate to have seen my brothers, my mate, and all the rest of my men carved up by rat claws even more.

Whitt nods. "Call for us if you need us, and we'll send word if anything changes with her."

I stalk out of the bedroom, my heart so heavy it seems to have sunk to my gut, and sniff out the raven's scent in the air. He's gone downstairs, into the winter side of the palace...

When I hear voices down the hall, I pause and walk the rest of the way on silent, stealthy feet, keeping close to the wall. Corwin is standing in the entrance room with the woman from his coterie whom Talia's become friendly with—Zelpha. It's obvious from her voice that she's upset.

"I shouldn't be the one giving those orders to the flock and everyone else," she says. "They'll want to hear it from you. They're already at a loss, knowing the state Talia's in, knowing—" She cuts herself off before her voice gets more ragged.

"I have other things to deal with," Corwin says, more sharply than I've ever heard him talk to his inner circle. "Between you, Olander, and Verik, you should be able to keep things in order for a little while. Meriol and Domhnall will be returning soon if you need extra support."

Something about his words sends a prickle of apprehension down my back, and Zelpha looks as if they've struck her the same way. She narrows her eyes. "How long exactly are you planning on being busy with 'other things'? What's going on, Corwin? I know that with Talia so—"

"We aren't talking about this," Corwin interrupts. "Please go carry out the orders you've been given."

I get the impression Zelpha might want to say more, but she shuts her mouth and turns on her heel, her expression in the glimpse I catch of it not at all happy.

Corwin shakes himself in a gesture that reminds me of a bird setting its feathers smooth, and my apprehension grows. I step out into the entrance room—and at the same moment his older coterie man, Verik, comes hustling in.

The gray-haired man bobs his head lower than usual at the sight of Corwin. "I'm sorry to interrupt you. A small party has arrived from Brambledown. Their lord's chief warrior has come down with the curse."

Corwin closes his eyes for a moment, looking as if there are a few curses *he'd* like to put into words. As I walk over to him and Verik, his stance turns even more rigid. "You'll need to inform them of my mate's current condition. Tell them we're doing everything we can to see her well again, but she's incapable of carrying out her healing ritual for the time being. And offer my deepest apologies."

Verik's mouth twists, but he bobs his head again and heads back out. Corwin lets out a long sigh and looks at me. I catch the briefest flicker of hope before he takes in my expression and it dies. He must be able to tell I haven't come with good news.

"She hasn't even woken, has she?" he says.

"No. But Whitt and August will alert us right away if she does." I glance toward the doorway. "Word hasn't spread all the way through the winter realm yet?" We've had several representatives from other domains arrive at Hearth-by-the-Heart and the summer side of the border castle already to express their condolences.

"I'd imagine most know by now that she's been faltering, but this latest— Brambledown is one of the more distant domains. It won't take long after this." He rubs his forehead. "Did you need something?"

"I was surprised that you left without speaking to any of us," I say. "And I'm more surprised to overhear that you apparently have business you're attending to that you haven't mentioned. We need to move against the Murk quickly and decisively—and that means planning our strategy together."

In that instant, there's a light in Corwin's eyes so furious and yet wounded it reminds me of a tuskcat caught in a snare. "My soul-twined mate is hovering on the verge of death after days of agony," he says in the same curt voice he used with Zelpha. "She's lost the child I'd have considered mine regardless of its exact parentage. If I need to take some time to myself, I think I'm owed it."

He spins on his heel as if he thinks that'll be the end of the discussion, and not just apprehension but alarm clangs through me with a creeping suspicion. He's only taken two steps toward the doorway before I spring into his path, blocking him.

"You can have all the moments to yourself that you need," I say in a low voice, "but I ask you for Talia's sake to tell me where you're going."

Corwin outright glares at me with a fury I've never seen cross his face before, even when he was telling off his colleagues for disrespecting Talia. "I'm doing what has to be done. Get out of my way."

He tries to step around me, but I side-step and snatch at his arm. Corwin jerks back before my fingers can catch hold and shifts in a blink, but I manage to grab one of his raven feet before he's flown high enough to escape my reach. With a furious squawk, he pecks at my hand and then shifts again, shoving me backward with the hands of his man.

I sprawl on the floor but whip around in time to knock his feet out from under him with my heel.

Sputtering, Corwin thumps on the ground and rolls over. The next second, I've pounced on him. I stare down at him in wolf form, my lips curled back. But no growl fills my throat, only a dull ache of grief.

Before he can fight me any more, I shift again so I can speak, letting my greater weight hold him in place. "You are *not* going to go off there and try to take on the blasted Murk king all by yourself."

The flicker of Corwin's gaze tells me I'm right. "Who said anything about taking on the king?" he asks haughtily, but it's too late for him to dissemble.

I glower at him. "Do you think I don't want to as well? Every time I *think* of those wretched rats I—" I cut off that sentence with a gnash of my teeth, anger surging through my chest alongside my grief. "Maybe I don't feel it quite the same way you do with your bond, but I understand enough. And I know that neither of us has a hope of destroying the threat on our own. We're going to have a hard enough time with the full force of our warriors behind us."

"But that will take time," Corwin says, giving up on any pretense. "He won't be expecting anything yet—he won't be expecting a single raven. I could get to him and slash out his throat before he even realizes he's under attack. I know where to go—approximately. I saw which portal one of the vermin we injured darted back through."

My heart leaps at the thought that we're that close to finding the Refuge, but anguish for the man beneath me washes through the rest of me. "Maybe you're right. Maybe that part would work. But killing him won't end the curse. You need to destroy this Heart he's made. You have your raven's logic—you can't tell me you honestly believe you'll be able to banish that all by yourself with all of his supporters shrieking for your blood."

Corwin grits his teeth, but then he sags against the floor, the fight going completely out of him. "I don't know. I thought… maybe if I worked the right magic to tie it to him somehow… It wasn't a solid plan. I meant to figure it out on the way there. And if it didn't work, then at least I'd send the Murk into disarray with their king's death while our larger force moved in to finish the job I started."

"And while you'd die starting it," I have to point out. "You can't for one moment believe that's what Talia would want. And if you didn't even make it to Orion, then it'd all be for nothing. Worse than nothing, because then they'll know we've located them and we'll lose any other element of surprise."

"But she— If I lose her too…"

He sounds so hopeless I pull back—warily, in case he was waiting for an opening. But Corwin just sits up, rubbing his shoulder with a vaguely abashed expression. He doesn't quite meet my eyes. "I can see my idea might have been foolhardy, but I have to do something. I can't just leave her lying there like that—who knows what she might be going through that I can't even feel—" His breath rasps with unspoken emotion.

"I understand," I say. "And we aren't letting them get away with this. Starting with the traitor who led us into that trap."

Corwin's eyes flash. "Have your colleagues already sent the proof to turn his king against him? I'd like to see how much he likes the reward he'll get in return for his *loyalty*."

I shake my head, a weightier anger settling in my gut. "Not yet. I told them to wait until I'd had a chance to think on it. And what I think is this: we use it the same way Orion has meant to use Talia against us. We prepare as quickly as we can to strike, and the moment we're ready, we send the message on. Let *him* be distracted by the double-crosser in his ranks just when we descend on him."

Corwin smiles thinly. "I dislike borrowing a rat's tactics, but I do appreciate the poetic justice—and the strength of the strategy. Perhaps it'll be what turns the tide for us."

He pushes himself to his feet and looks down the hall toward Talia's room, then toward the entrance he meant to leave through on his suicidal quest. He squares his shoulders. "They *are* going to pay," he says in a quiet voice so laced with menace I'm sure I'd never want to be on this man's bad side. "Both the king and the traitor. There could still be a chance…"

He stops, swipes his hand across his eyes, and takes a deep breath. "But you're right. It isn't much of a chance, and our mate deserves more than a half-cocked effort that might do as much damage to us as it does to them. I'd have shown our hand too early. I—I apologize for my carelessness."

I cuff him lightly on the shoulder. "I admire your dedication to our mate. Knowing you'd go to such lengths to defend her only makes me more glad to stand by your side. You ravens spend so much time focused on staying even-handed and balanced in your reactions that it's no wonder you fly right off the handle when you give your emotions free rein. Let's put all our strengths together with our colleagues' and come up with the surest way of crushing those vermin so thoroughly they never see the light of day again."

And—Heart help us all, especially Talia—let it work.

23

Talia

Everything is melting together. I'm walking across the ice fields between the Unseelie arch-lords' domains, and with one step I'm picking my way through the forests around my pack's former home of Hearthshire. A reddish haze seeps through everything, thickening and then spinning me around.

I'm lost. I need to get back to—to somewhere. But every part of me aches, and my head keeps spinning. My feet stumble under me. A fever sears through my veins.

I blink, and I'm standing in the hazy woods of the fringelands. Madoc runs up to me and throws his arms around me.

I sink into his embrace automatically, seeking the solid steadiness of his body, the stormy scent that speaks of the fire inside him.

Even though I'm already burning up, I want to absorb

that fire. I want to—I want to kiss him, tuck myself against him with no clothing between us, listen to his gently hoarse voice telling me of the grand future he wants to conjure for his people, for us…

No, that's not right. I can't—

I spin away from him, and just like that, he vanishes. I trip onto the grass outside the border castle.

This is my home. Where I live with the men I love. I shouldn't be thinking—I shouldn't be *feeling*—

But a different sort of ache has formed in my chest with Madoc's disappearance. There's something in him that calls to me, even if it shouldn't.

I just have to ignore it. Preventing this war, or at least preventing it from destroying my home—that's what matters. That and my mates—where are they?

A sob fills my throat, and I turn around only to sway and topple right onto my back. The sky spins overhead.

I've lost them all. I've lost so much. Even—

There's faint sunlight seeping past a curtain. A gentle hand drifts across my forehead, holding a soft cloth that wipes sweat away. I blink and manage to focus on the face above me, pale with overlarge eyes and framed by sleek, flaxen hair.

"Talia?" Harper says with a sharp intake of breath. Her head jerks around to look at someone else. "She's awake! At least more than before."

I wet my lips, still feeling dizzy even though I'm not moving at all. Is the bed spinning under me?

Astrid comes into view, the wizened fae warrior's face looking more worn than usual. A smile touches her lips when I meet her eyes. "There you are. You've been gone a while."

She doesn't say that they were worried I wouldn't come back, but I know they must have been. *I* was worried, somewhere deep beneath the delirium of fever dreams.

I inhale slowly, testing my lungs. I can only take in a little air before the curse starts to jab at them. The pain echoes all the way down to my feet now.

There's another burning sensation around my abdomen. My hand goes to my belly, and tears rush to my eyes with a jolt of memory. My throat chokes up so much it takes me a minute to force the words out. "The baby..."

Astrid's mouth twists, and Harper blinks hard. I already knew—lost, so much I've lost—but the grief smacks into me as if I've been hit by a car.

I squeeze my eyes shut, taking one shallow breath after another, my fingers curling toward my palms. I want to tear and rip, I want to punch and claw... I can't even say what. I just want to unleash this horrible wrenching sensation inside me on something else.

"I'll get your mates," Astrid says, with a rustle as she moves from the bed. "They wanted to know as soon as you were lucid. They stayed with you for hours, but they couldn't cure you that way."

She slips out of the room. Harper grasps my hand, squeezing it.

My mates—they must be making plans for war. The only way they can cure me with Madoc gone and every other avenue exhausted is to destroy the Murk Heart.

But even if they manage that, even if I don't lose any

of them in the attempt, it won't bring back the life we made together that had only just started to bloom.

A sob hitches out of me. The tears that collected in my eyes spill out. I turn my head to the pillow so it can soak them up, and Harper eases closer, rubbing my shoulder with her other hand.

"I'm so sorry," she says. "I know that doesn't help—I know there's nothing I can say or do that would help. But if there was, I'd do it. It isn't fair."

No, it isn't. Nothing in my life has been fair, from the moment Orion decided to plant the seed of his magic in my family line, from the moment he stole me away from my parents to unfurl that magic into something that took over my body and soul.

I had this one thing that was only mine, that wasn't touched by him at all, and he managed to rip it away from me anyway.

The next stabbing pain of the curse is almost a relief because it's a distraction from the anguish of mourning.

Harper brings a goblet of water to me, but I find I can't sit up to drink properly. I end up spilling it all over the sheets as I sip sideways while still lying down. My limbs won't cooperate with me—even the slightest movement brings a wave of fatigue and prickles of pain over me.

I'm dying. Really dying, closer than I've ever been before. The thought sinks in and just kind of settles there, as if I can't fully process it. There's been too much wrongness for me to take it all in.

There was so much more I wanted to do and see, so

much I wanted to accomplish. Who'll stand up for the humans in the fae world if I die? Who'll watch over Jamie? Will my mates take up the causes that were important to me, or will they mourn and then move on, with all the centuries they still have ahead of them?

And what about the man I'm not totally sure where I stand with? The fever weaves through my mind again, and for a second I think I see Madoc standing there at the edge of my vision. When I turn my head, he vanishes.

Sylas thought it was a ploy, bringing me to the fringes where the Murk were waiting to ambush us. Is he right, and my mind is too addled for me to see the situation as clearly as he does?

Madoc didn't feel like an enemy when he held me through my shudders of agony. He didn't sound like an enemy when he swore to bring me home.

What am I abandoning him to if I don't make it? Will Orion kill him as horribly as the Murk king once threatened to mutilate me?

I should have said something more to him before... Before everything...

My gaze latches onto Harper again, and I'm jolted by another abrupt shift in my emotions. Resolve grips me. I can't control anything about what'll happen with the men in my life when I'm gone, but she—she still has chances—

"There's a true-blooded fae you're in love with," I say, tugging at her hand. "I know you don't want to admit it, but there is."

Harper twitches with surprise and then flushes. "You

shouldn't be worrying about my romantic prospects right now. It doesn't matter anyway."

"It does," I say. "It does to me." In case I never get to talk to her again. She made one misstep with me, but otherwise she's been here for me so much, done so much for me. If I can help her in one small way before I'm gone… "Why won't you go after him? Maybe he'd want you too."

"Talia… I know he won't. It's all right."

I frown at her. "Even if you don't think there's hope, you should tell me who it is. Just to get it off your chest, to tell *someone*." A rough giggle slips from my throat. "It's not as if I'm going to have much chance to give away your secret."

Harper stiffens. "Don't talk like that," she chides me. "They're—they're going to destroy the Murk and their Heart and then you'll be fine."

My fever flares; my thoughts fragment. My eyes flutter shut for several seconds. Then I focus on her again. "We both know that might not be true. Let me do this for you. Let me listen. Maybe you'll figure some things out if you just say it out loud."

Harper bites her lip, but my insistence has obviously affected her. She looks down at her hands and back at me. "I don't need to say it out loud to know there's no point. He hasn't met his soul-twined mate yet, but I've been around him lots of times now, and it's definitely not me. And he could have so many other women—why he'd be at all interested in me…"

The way she's talking reminds me of how I once

thought about my Seelie mates, so sure they couldn't want a serious relationship with a human woman once they'd returned to their former prominent position in fae society. A twinge of suspicion runs through me alongside a fresh lance of pain.

Who would be high enough for Harper to feel so much lower than, when she's part of an arch-lord's pack?

"It's Donovan, isn't it?" I say quietly, watching her expression. I've seen her get a bit flustered in his presence before, haven't I? But I thought it was just general awkwardness, since she hasn't gotten to experience much of the fae world until recently, let alone the company of its highest rulers.

Harper's face flushes darker, and she drops it into her hands. "Don't tell anyone. He's never given any indication —I've tried to talk to him a few times, and he's very polite, but he's not particularly interested either. It's just… What would you call it? A crush. I'll get over it and find someone I'd really have a chance with."

Now that she's admitted it, I wonder why it didn't occur to me earlier. They're suited for each other as far as I can see, though of course I don't know Donovan especially well. They've both got a sort of softness to them, which hides an iron will that can come out when something or someone they care about is threatened. They're both unsure of themselves but doing their best to find their footing among people more experienced than they are.

That's not enough to make someone fall in love, but maybe Donovan just hasn't seen enough of Harper yet.

I squeeze her hand. "Yes, yes, you will." I don't know if

I should add that maybe the arch-lord will come around and start to admire her. Would that really be for the best if he's going to be distracted by a soul-twined mate later on?

But then, I don't love my chosen mates any less than I do Corwin. If I can manage that, then why couldn't a fae arch-lord?

"And who knows what will happen with Donovan?" I go on. "Things… don't always work out the way it looks like they will at first. I should know." I let out another weak laugh.

"That's right," Harper says. "We just wait and see and hope for the best."

I can tell she isn't talking about Donovan anymore. She keeps holding my hand and starts rubbing my shoulder again, and a sort of calm settles over me. My body still hurts and my heart still aches at the thought of what I've lost and how much more I might lose in the days ahead, but at the same time…

I got to have the love of four amazing men for at least a little while. I got to experience what it was like to carry a child inside me, at least the beginning of the process. Who am I to complain when there are others who've never gotten any of that at all?

I do want more. I want so much more—I want the rest of the life I thought I'd have. But I'm not going to lay that sorrow on my friends or my mates. I'm not going to make this harder for them as well as me.

If that's the last gift I can give them, reminding them of how happy they've made me rather than how sad I am to leave them, then so be it.

"Thank you," I say to Harper. It takes an effort to keep my voice audible. "For sitting with me and talking with me. You've been a great friend."

Harper turns her head away for a second to swipe at her eyes. Then she beams at me. "You've been an even better one."

The bedroom door swings open, and all four of my mates burst into the room. As they converge around the bed, Harper gives my fingers one last squeeze and then slips away with a bob of her head to her lord and his cadre.

The men seem to hesitate, braced around me, as if they're afraid they'll hurt me if they get any closer. Corwin's had his walls up against our bond this whole time, but now that he's close, a trickle of a frantic mix of relief and anxiety seeps through to me despite his best efforts.

I reach out to them, all of them, ignoring the fact that my vision has started to double, making the outlines of their forms waver and multiply. "I want you all with me. I love you so much."

"And we love you," Sylas says roughly. They move together, encircling me in a mass of warmth totally different from the burning of my fever. I nestle between them, hugging one and then another, murmuring words of affection until I can no longer string them together.

These are my men, my mates. I'm going to savour every last moment I get with them, even while I'm wishing I'd get more.

24

Madoc

I don't like the look of the Refuge when I emerge from a passage into one of the stations. All of my fellow Murk are bustling around, carrying equipment or supplies, tussling with each other in mock skirmishes that are clearly for practice rather than play.

Normally a lot of them are relaxing at any given time. The increase in activity doesn't seem like a good sign.

But maybe it should. Why should I mind if Orion is gearing up to launch his war in the next few days? Any hope of a peaceful resolution went out the window the moment the few fae of the Mists who'd agreed to collaborate with me turned on me the second something went wrong.

I was *trying* to save their mate, for fuck's sake, but apparently they'd rather I left her sitting vulnerable to attack, blithely assuming there was no way the tide could shift against them.

I shouldn't have cooperated with them in the first place. I should have learned my lesson from the disaster with Delta.

I just assumed that when it was solely to benefit Talia, they at least trusted me not to want to harm *her*. How the hell was I supposed to know that a squadron of Murk would be hanging around just in case we showed up? Do they think I somehow passed on a message in the few hours between working out the plan with Whitt and leaving?

Yes, they probably do. Maybe I emphasized my skills with illusion too much. And really, I might have been able to send a message like that if I considered all the angles well enough. I had plenty of time to observe how the Seelie guards kept watch, what would catch their notice and what was likely to slip past it.

None of that excuses them thinking the worst of me based on nothing but the fact that their attackers happened to be the same kind of fae as me, though. Why not blame Sylas and his damned cadre for the sins of Seelie like Ambrose and Aerik then?

My bad mood follows me through the station. I pause in the tunnel by the stairs to my private room, but even though I've been traveling a long time since I fled the claws and fangs aimed at me yesterday, I don't think I'll be able to relax.

Orion has probably already gotten word of my arrival.

His spies multiply by the day. He'll want me to report immediately.

Several of the Murk I pass on my way to the throne room raise their hands or tip their heads to me in respectful acknowledgment. That's reassuring. I've been watching the responses to my presence from the first sentry I sensed in the area around the entrance I used, and so far there haven't been any signs that my own people see me as the enemy. I don't think the fae of the Mists have gone as far as revealing my association with them to Orion... yet.

I've earned the respect my fellow Murk offered by standing by my king—and I nearly threw it away. My teeth grit again at the memory of the accusations Talia's mates had hurled at me. How long will I have before they try to present me as a traitor to turn everyone against me? I haven't figured out exactly how I'm going to explain away the proof they could offer. At least it'll help that Orion isn't inclined to believe any Seelie over his own proven knight.

Then I think of Talia, of how fragile she felt tucked against me while I tried to shield her from the pain inside her, and my stomach knots.

Is this what all our time together comes to? Will I be marching on her mates and the rest of the fae she considers kin in a matter of days?

Will she even be alive by then to see her hopes of peace shatter, with me at the front of the charge?

But what else am I supposed to do? Completely give up on bringing my people to the home they deserve? Talia can't force the fae of the Mists to negotiate with us. They've shown how little they're willing to give even me the benefit of the doubt. As much of a force to be reckoned with as she is, she can't change the impossible.

I just wish that turning my back on the hope of some kind of treaty didn't have to mean turning my back on her too.

Does *she* think I arranged the ambush? Will that be her last memory of me—the supposedly false comfort offered as I tried to destroy the people she loved most?

Just thinking about it makes my hands clench. I have to hold myself back from slamming a fist into the wall of the tunnel outside the throne room. Orion will definitely notice and ask about *that* fit of temper, even if he only hears about it second-hand.

I step through the broad opening and walk up to the dais. Orion is sitting in a typically casual pose on the arm of his throne, his tail flicking back and forth over to the seat, talking to a couple of my fellow knights. When he looks over at me, his yellow eyes narrow.

A prickle runs over my skin. Have the Seelie tipped him off after all? Or does he suspect something's odd for other reasons?

But he beckons me over, dismissing the others with a careless wave and standing up straighter. His movements might be nonchalant, but there's a soberness in his expression that I haven't often seen. He doesn't look exactly *sane*, but he does appear unusually focused in his fierceness.

"Here you are again, Madoc," he says. "After all those

long stints in the Mists before, I can't keep you away from the Refuge these days."

Is that why he's irritated—he feels I'm shirking my duty a little? I raise my chin, putting on the appearance of confidence though not insolence. It's a fine line between strength and rebellion in his eyes.

"I thought you'd want to hear as soon as there were any major developments," I say. "From what I understand, Talia's mates and several other fae brought her out to the fringelands to attempt some sort of cure for your curse there, and they were set on by an ambush of our people that had them running off with their tails between their legs. They've made a proclamation against the Murk, swearing to destroy any that they spot in 'their' lands. If they were getting help from a traitor among us before, that alliance has ended now."

I didn't even have to lie to say all that.

Orion hums and lets his tail loop around his wrist, tapping its tapered end with his long fingers. "They're being pushed to the brink, then, in your estimation?"

I nod. "They wouldn't have been desperate enough to bring her so close to our territory otherwise. Like I mentioned before, from what I've observed they've been trying all sorts of cures—with no success, naturally. Preventing them from going through with their most recent plan will only have unsettled them more."

My king chuckles to himself and turns so the quavering orange light of the Heart flickers over his angular face. "It *is* good that you delivered your reports in time for us to arrange that ambush. I can thank you for giving me the information I needed."

A chill wraps around my gut. What is he talking about? I couldn't have reported that the fae of the Mists would be sending a party to the fringes there, because I didn't *know* they would be the last time I spoke to him.

I manage to keep my voice even. "I'm afraid I don't follow. I wasn't aware of the ambush until after it happened."

"Of course, of course. I decided on that method after you left the last time. But you gave your account of why the Seelie went to speak with Delta, as badly as that went for all involved, and made it clear they'd realized they had no hope of saving my pet on their own. Based on those facts, it was obvious that they'd try to make use of our powers again—and where better than along the fringes, as close to our Heart as they can get." His eyes gleam with satisfaction.

I feel the exact opposite. Any enjoyment I might have gotten out of the thought of putting the fae of the Mists in their places curdles in my stomach.

They were right. Not the way they thought, not that I'd purposefully betrayed them—but I did screw them over all the same. I must have said too much, gone overboard in emphasizing one thing or another, showed too much of my hand—I didn't mean to give Orion such an accurate sense of the approach the other fae were taking…

If I'd just shut my mouth a little sooner, skewed the details a little more or left more of them out, I might be sitting next to Talia right now, seeing her free of the curse we broke her out of together.

I force a smile, because Orion is watching me, intent as ever. "I'm glad that my insight gave you that advantage."

His Heart doesn't cringe away from my lie. If anything, the orange light flares briefly brighter. Staring into it after spending time so close to the Heart of the Mists, my skin recoils from its erratic energy.

Talia's mates called it a false Heart, and they weren't wrong. It's nothing like the mass of living, harmonious power that fuels *their* lives.

It's all we've got. It's the best we can count on. And it's slowly draining away the real thing, while killing Talia at the same time.

The sudden, wild urge comes over me to shove Orion right into the center of that orange mass, to scream out words to shatter that glowing monstrosity.

I could free her that way. I'd be some kind of hero, even if no one knew but me.

But I don't actually know what words would shatter our Heart, and I doubt getting that close would even injure Orion. It's his creation, after all. I'd only be showing my hand, and he'd cut me down, and there'd be no one left to speak for reason at all.

And could I really destroy it even if I knew? At the same time, I'd be obliterating the magic my people count on, leaving us utterly vulnerable to the fae of the Mists, who are more determined than ever to exterminate us all.

There are no good options here. The best I can do is protect the people who need it most.

A sense of resignation settles over me just as Orion clears his throat. "I'm sure you've noticed that we're ramping up for our first real assault. There's just one more thorn I want to dig into their sides before we make our move. That does mean I'm sending you off again."

"Of course," I say, crossing my arms over my chest. I can't tell him that the fae of the Mists directly threatened me with death on my return to the world they consider theirs. What does it matter anyway? They'd have pounced without hesitation on any other rat who crossed their paths. Now the risks are no different for me than for anyone else.

As long as I don't walk right up to one of them and tap them on the shoulder, I've seen enough to ensure they never know I'm there.

Orion simply smirks to himself, gazing into the glow of the Heart for long enough that I start to wonder if he's forgotten the task he was about to give me. "What is it you need me to do?" I ask.

He grins wider, baring his jagged teeth. "I think it's time the fae of the Mists find out exactly what their savior's cure requires—and how far beyond their reach it is. Let them agonize over that for a day or two, and then we'll cut them down at their most shaken. Perhaps they'll even cut one or another of each other down in a vain attempt to meet the conditions."

A quiver of excitement shoots through me, though I keep my expression carefully neutral. He's going to lay out for me what would cure Talia's curse? But if it's something impossible, maybe it doesn't even matter.

"I can see to it that the word is passed on," I say. "Conjure an illusion of a Murk for them to catch, perhaps, who'll gasp it out in his supposedly dying breath. What should I tell them?"

Orion brings his hands together, his fingers tapping against each other in an unsteady cadence that echoes the Heart's dissonant pulsing. "As soon as possible, have them hear that the only way to heal the girl is for one who loves her to drench her with their life's blood by their own hand. Voluntarily, of course."

I blink, not sure I heard him right. Tendrils of tension begin to wind around my chest. "By their own hand," I repeat. "They'd need to do it themselves."

"Exactly." Orion turns his grin on me. "Perfect, isn't it? Her supposed mates will be falling all over themselves to make the sacrifice to save her, but even if they do care about her enough to qualify, their ridiculous Heart won't let them go through with it. It should cause plenty of chaos as they try, though."

It is perfect, in a horrifically sickening way. I swallow hard, suddenly feeling miles distant from this room and the man in front of me. My voice comes out, still steady, but I hear it as if from far away. "Is that really the cure?"

Orion cackles. "Why not? Every curse requires one. The trick is to place it out of reach. I was very pleased with that particular brainstorm." He motions toward the doorway. "Go on, then. We have blood to spill and heads to roll. I've waited long enough."

He's waited. As if this war is all about fulfilling his thirst for blood and chaos.

But then, to him it is, isn't it? Talia saw that within just a few days in his company. I've known it deep down all along, even if I drowned out the observation, telling myself it didn't matter as long as the rest of the Murk get what we're owed in the end.

Is this really what I owe them, though? A lifetime under a vicious king turned even more brutal in his victory? Do I doubt that he'll aim his sadistic desires at the rest of us even more once he no longer has plans of war to occupy him?

I dip my head and stride out of the room toward the nearest entrance. My pulse thumps heavy through my veins. The queasiness that came over me when Orion first announced the cure is spreading, deepening, with every step I take.

Is it so impossible?

Could I even get the chance to find out? If the fae around her get the slightest wind of my presence, they'll be chopping *my* head off...

I have my orders and my loyalties and my conscience. In this moment, they're all leading me down the same dank tunnel toward the outside world. I'll follow them as far as I can, and hope that when I reach the point where they diverge, I know for sure where I stand.

And if I have a chance to save everyone who matters— then I'll take it. I'll take it without a second's regret.

25

Talia

$\mathcal{I}$ think it's the click of the door that rouses me from my daze. What I've been doing for the past day can't really be called sleeping. Not that I've really been awake either. I seem to fade in and out of semi-alertness, never totally present nor totally gone.

Either I've adjusted to the pain so much that I'm not noticing it, or my body has gone numb in its increasingly weakened state. There's just a dull throbbing all through my torso and limbs, with an occasional sharper jab or twisting. My breath has stayed shallow, my skin hot with the fever that washes through me in waves, seeming to drain more energy out of me each time.

One or another of my men has been with me each time I've been aware enough to notice—until now. Whoever was watching over me last must have stepped away while I dozed again. They're making their plans, gathering an army of fae in the arch-lords' domains—I've caught flashes of the preparations through Corwin's eyes in moments where the wall he's holding up slips.

I don't know how soon they intend to march on the Refuge now that they've narrowed down its location, but there's a rising urgency in the air that I can sense even from here. I suspect it's only a matter of hours now.

I don't know if I'm going to make it long enough to see them return. I don't know if they *will* return. I tried to tell Sylas the last time he was here, with stumbling words and my hand clamped around his wrist, that they shouldn't rush in for me. That they should wait until they're fully prepared. I'd rather have them with me when I die than die alone, knowing they might die too because they ignored the danger in their attempt to save me.

He told me not to worry, that they'll be ready for whatever comes. That they will all come see me before they leave, and that they intend to see me well when they return. That I'm never alone, because their hearts are always with me.

So why is my heart aching?

I've had trouble stringing more than a few words together in the past few hours, though. What voice I have comes out ragged. I don't know what arguments I can make that they'd listen to.

I'm not sure *I'd* listen if our positions were reversed.

I wet my lips. My stomach pinches with a trace of hunger that's quickly swallowed by a swell of nausea. My body sinks even deeper into the bed as my muscles give up more strength.

And then a soft point of pressure touches my wrist.

I twitch, not capable of a full flinch in my current state. Slowly, I manage to tilt my head to peer down at my arm where it's lying on top of the covers. We've kept them half over me, half off, draped across my abdomen, for some kind of balance between the fever's flares of heat and the occasional chills.

There's nothing on the bed beside me. I blink a few times in case my vision is faltering, but while the details are a bit fuzzy, I'm definitely not seeing anything except my arm and the deep blue bedspread. Maybe it was just a tic of my nerves.

But then, even as I watch, I feel it again. A more deliberate nudge, still soft, with a tickling sensation and then a larger patch of gentle pressure, as if a furry body the length of my forearm has rested against it.

My pulse hiccups, and even though I still can't see anything at all, a picture forms in my mind's eye—a pointed nose, quivering whiskers, and the long, sleek shape of a rat's body, crouched beside my arm.

Madoc's voice comes back to me from weeks ago as he guided me through the paths away from the Refuge. *My illusions can stop them from seeing and hearing us, but it won't let them walk right through us.*

He's here, hidden from my sight but not my sense of touch with his magic. It has to be him, right? What other Murk knows the fae of the Mists and the working of illusions well enough to have managed to sneak right into the border castle undetected?

What other would come to me so tentatively, waiting to see how I'll respond?

A lump fills my throat. He came back, even after—even after everything. He must know how the other fae would react if they knew. He probably has no idea how *I'll* react. But if I had even the slightest doubt about whether he intended our foray to the fringes to go wrong, his presence here right now would dispel it.

He could be out there spying on the war preparations—or sabotaging them. Instead, he's come to me, offering whatever gesture of comfort he can.

I turn my hand, tracing the shape of him. The bumps of his shoulders and the curve of his haunches stay perfectly still as my fingers glide over his fur. I tuck my hand next to him, stroking my thumb over his side, hoping he understands what I'm trying to show him—that I'm glad he's here, that I'm not angry with him or scared of him.

He leans his head against my fingers with another tickle of his whiskers, and I manage to find my voice. "Thank you," I whisper roughly. "I know it was a big risk... coming to me. I won't... I won't let..."

My vocal cords tremor, and I lose my momentum. Madoc presses his nose against my hand as if to say it's all right. Then he moves away from me. A jolt of loss hits me in the moment before I understand why.

Abruptly, he's sitting on the edge of the bed as a man, gazing down at me. His blond hair lies in disarray, his gray eyes not so much stormy as overcast with pain. His mouth tightens. "He should never have brought you this low," he murmurs. "This isn't how you're meant to be at all."

I swallow hard, loosening my throat. "I—I'm sorry."

Madoc's gaze turns into a stare. "What the hell do *you* have to be sorry for?"

All the hopeful futures I imagined flit through my head. "I wanted… to help bring the Murk home… to make the other fae see… to help you…" My voice wavers, and my thoughts scatter. It's so hard to focus.

Madoc's jaw flexes as he clenches it. "Even now, when you're— I'm not sure we deserve you." He shakes his head and closes his eyes for a second before meeting my gaze again. His voice comes out even more ragged than mine. "You're a light that could brighten even the Murk. And you'll have that chance, if you still want to take it when all this is over. You'll have your mates and your child and—"

A sob lurches out of me. "No child."

Madoc goes rigid. "What?"

I squeeze my eyes shut against the renewed surge of grief. "I got… so sick… It's gone."

The Murk man hisses through his teeth and swears under his breath. "I'm so sorry. If I'd known—if I'd found out sooner—*damn* him." He pushes to his feet. "I have to be fast. I wish I could do more, but I can give you this. And may my people deserve you after all."

As my eyelids flutter open again, Madoc draws a small, thin knife from his pocket. I only have a second to register it, to wonder what in the world he's talking about, when the door bangs open and a blur of furious Seelie hurtles straight at the rat shifter.

"Get your filthy paws away from her," August snarls, slamming Madoc to the ground.

Astrid and a couple of the castle guards race in after him. The knife goes skittering across the floor; Astrid snatches it up and reduces it to a blob of metal with a hastily snapped true name. August raises his hand, claws flashing from his fingertips, to slash at the man pinned beneath him, and my heart nearly bursts with panic.

The words wrench out of me. "No! Don't hurt him!"

August's arm is already swinging, but at my voice, he catches it with a jerk. His claws must still slice Madoc's skin, because I hear a pained noise from beyond my view, but it isn't the fatal blow my mate meant it to be.

"I was only trying to—" Madoc sputters, but August moves to clamp his hand over the rat shifter's mouth. My mate peers over the side of the bed at me, his eyes wild with a mix of fury and bewilderment.

"He was going to *kill* you," he says. "He snuck in here —the knife— We can't give him another chance. I'll tear out his throat right now."

I know how the situation must look, especially when August blames Madoc for the ambush as well. But not one particle of my body can believe that Madoc meant to use that knife on me, not in any way that would harm me.

Why would he have been talking about the chances I'd have, about getting to be with my mates and my child, if he meant to end my life right now? Why would he have offered any comfort at all instead of stabbing the blade into me the first moment I was alone?

I don't totally understand what he was going to do,

but I know it's not that. I know I don't want him dead because he risked everything to help me.

"He wasn't— You can't—"

But my words won't come together quickly enough, and August is tensing to deliver another blow. He isn't listening to me.

Horror sears all through my body, and with a gasp, I launch myself forward. I fling myself upright and toward the edge of the bed, toward August, with a surge of effort that tears at my lungs and floods me with agony. But I manage to sit up, swaying and dizzy but holding off a collapse.

August's head jerks toward me. Astrid rushes to my side, but when she tries to help me lie back down, I shake my head as firmly as I can. My breath comes out in broken pants.

"*No*," I say, holding August's golden gaze, not daring to break that connection to even glance at Madoc beneath him. I summon every shred of strength left in me from every dark crevice in my being, propelling it all up my throat to move my tongue. "He hasn't betrayed us—he never did. He's been trying to help all along. He came back—he came back even knowing you'd react like this—"

"Trying to finish what he started," August says with a growl, but he hasn't moved to strike Madoc again, not yet. I have his attention now. I have this one chance, maybe my last chance, to set one more thing right before I'm gone.

My fingers clench at the sheet. "What he started was a bond between the fae of the Mists and the Murk. A way to stop the worst of the fighting, a way to— You have to let him— You don't trust him, so trust me. I've seen him; I know him. Whatever he was going to do here, it was to save us, not to hurt us. Give him a chance to talk. *Listen* to him. Believe what he says. Please. For me. Believe *me*."

As those last words fall from my lips, a deeper tremor shakes my body. All the breath goes out of me. I try to clutch at the covers, but my fingers won't move.

I've used up all the energy I had left, and now my limbs are crumpling, my spine sagging.

Astrid inhales sharply and leaps to slow my fall. My head sinks into the pillow, the room spins, and then my mind goes totally blank.

26

August

All the color drains from Talia's face as she collapses on the bed. My muscles pang with the urge to spring to her side, but that would mean releasing the villain beneath me, the rat that stood over her failing body with a knife in his hand—

Astrid is closer anyway. She slips her arms around my mate just in time to guide her more gently onto her side. Talia's eyes roll back, and her limbs go slack. Her eyelids twitch and close.

My heart stops. "Is she—"

"She's still alive," Astrid says quickly, leaning over Talia. "But her pulse is very weak." She glances at me with worried eyes. I've rarely seen the seasoned warrior show fear.

The man beneath me tenses and flexes his muscles, but I've pinned him too firmly for him to have any hope of escape. I hold my clawed hand up, imagining how easily I could slice through his jugular. How satisfying it'd be to watch this treacherous creature's life spill out of him. Even now, he glowers at me, not even pretending to make a show of peace.

But Talia's words linger in my head. The words she pushed herself so hard to speak. He was worth that much to her, worth expending the little strength she had left to defend him…

The guards gather closer around me, ready to assist. I close my eyes, struggling between anger and reason. I want so badly to destroy the man who represents everything that's hurt the woman I love…

I know my mate, though. Talia is sweetness personified, kind-hearted and compassionate, but she isn't *stupid*. She's never softened to the fae who've mistreated her—if anything, she's gotten more confident in standing up to the scornful arch-lords and the enemies of her past.

She wouldn't forgive Madoc—no, talk as if there was nothing to forgive him for in the first place—unless she understood something I didn't.

She asked me to listen to him. Heart help me, she *begged* me to trust her. What kind of mate would I be to her if I refused what might be the last request she ever makes of me?

I drag in a breath and glare down at the rat again. I wish we'd kept that iron-core collar Celia used on Corwin all those months ago. If Madoc still has the use of his magic, how can I be sure he won't shift and flee our grasp?

I'd rather have brought him before my brothers and

Corwin for them to interrogate him. Warring with words is more their area than mine. But if I don't have the choice, I'll question him myself, right here, with my claws inches from his throat and my fangs ready to chomp on a fleeing rat.

His only way out would be the door. I jerk my head toward the others. "Shut the door and guard it. Don't stray from it until I give the command. Two of you, let out your wolves. Stay ready in case he tries to dash for it."

One of the guards gapes at me. "You're not going to kill him?"

I give him a stern look. "I'm going to find out if there's anything useful he can tell us before I kill him. It doesn't work so well the other way around. If there are more rats already on the way—or already here—we need to know."

That isn't the main reason I'm sparing him for the next few minutes, and maybe they realize that, but it's an explanation the warriors can accept. They step back in formation by the door, two standing directly in front of it and the other two dropping onto all fours to flank them, their wolfish eyes gleaming.

Astrid remains on the bed next to Talia. She murmurs a few words I recognize as an invigorating spell, designed to encourage the flow of blood and the rhythm of the lungs. I can't tell whether it helps.

Time is ticking away from us. I keep my legs planted over Madoc's, my forearm locking his crossed wrists to his chest, but ease my hand down just enough to rest my claws against his neck instead of covering his mouth. "She asked me to listen," I say with an edge of a snarl. "I can't promise how *long* I'll listen for. So talk fast."

The rat shifter swallows audibly and opens his mouth, but Astrid speaks before he can, her tone urgent. "August, she's fading. I don't know—nothing I'm doing is keeping her with us."

My lips pull back from my teeth as my gaze snaps back to Madoc. "You *did* hurt her—you did something to her without even needing that knife—"

"I was trying to save her!" he rasps out, twitching under me again in a futile effort to shake me off. "For fuck's sake—I know how to cure the curse."

The blood roaring in my ears seems to still. He—what? "You found out—" I start, but the details of how it happened don't matter. All that matters is— "*How?* What do we have to do?"

Madoc grimaces. "I have to show you. You need to let me get closer to her."

I bare my fangs again with a rush of suspicion. "I'm not letting you get anywhere near her ever again. Just tell me what she needs."

"That won't do any good," the rat shifter snaps. "You can't do it. None of you can do it. Are you going to let me save her, or are you going to watch her die because you're too much of a stubborn prick to give me the chance? Why the hell would I have come all the way back here to kill her when she's already dying, you idiot?"

He might have a point, but his insults aren't exactly increasing my faith in his good intentions. "Why in the lands should I trust you if you won't tell me what this cure *is*?"

Talia shivers on the bed. A series of spasms run through her limbs. I can sense without even looking right at her that the last sparks of life are spilling out of her.

Astrid tugs the covers back from my mate's body. She presses her hands to Talia's legs, her stomach, her chest, and then her head, gasping desperate words, but I can tell nothing's bringing Talia back.

Madoc's eyes widen at the sounds from above. "You won't believe me," he says, struggling again. "Or you will, and you'll do something stupid. There isn't time to argue about it. I don't even know if I believe I can do it, but I'm the only one who can. Let me try, please!"

A groan of frustration catches at the base of my throat. He sounds like he means it, but he's a master of illusions. What do I know about deciphering lies? This is Whitt's domain.

But I was by far the closest when the spell we set all through the castle to alert us to Murk presence sounded the alarm. The others will be coming, but I don't know if they'll be here fast enough.

A thin whine carries from Talia's parted lips, and Madoc winces, his expression taut with apparent agony. "I'll—I'll give you my true name," he spits out. "You can *order* me not to hurt her. Just hurry up and let me get to her."

I can't help staring at him for a second as his offer sinks in. Our true names are something tied to our souls. The Murk might have lost their ability to wield magic when they shunned the Heart of the Mists—until they made that false Heart of their own—but that hasn't changed anyone's ability to wield magic on them. He's offering up utter control over his mind and body.

Talia shudders again, and I make my decision. "Tell me then," I growl, leaning close.

Madoc drops his voice for my ears only, the softest of whispers. "*May-dim-goss.*"

The tingle that races through my mind with the syllables speaks to the power in those syllables. He isn't lying about this. "*May-dim-goss,*" I repeat under my breath, and add, louder, with magic crackling through my voice, "You will not take any action that would harm Talia."

"I won't," Madoc agrees, with a wince as my intent latches onto his mind.

"You won't attempt to harm any of the rest of us either," I add, willing the strands of the true name's control to lace even tighter between us.

"Of course not. I just want to save her life. Now let me up!"

As I pull back, footsteps thump in the hall outside. Madoc scrambles up, spinning toward Talia.

"Wait!" I say, panic shooting through me, and he stops in his tracks with a hiss of frustration. His true name's power holds him in place.

At Sylas's command from outside, the guards move from the doorway. He, Whitt, and Corwin burst into the room, their expressions fierce and frantic.

Whitt glances from me to Madoc and then Talia and sputters, "Heart save us, what are you—"

Sylas is already lunging forward. I throw out my arm, only managing to hold him back because he catches himself at the gesture.

"He says he knows how to cure the curse," I babble. "He's given me his true name—I made him swear not to hurt her or us. But I—" I swivel back toward the rat. "Before you do it, tell us what the cure is."

My use of his true name is still fresh enough that I drag the answer out of him even as I can see the defiance in his stance. "Someone who loves her needs to offer up his life's blood by his own hand and cover her in it."

I feel my brothers and Corwin freeze as I do, horror rippling through me from head to toe. My first instinct is to throw myself at the bed where Astrid is still murmuring frantic spell words over Talia's failing body, to cut myself open from chin to gut if that's what it'd take. But even as my legs itch to propel me forward, I know I can't.

The Heart won't let me make that sacrifice. The men behind me know that as well as I do.

I turn toward Sylas, my heart thumping painfully fast. "If you did it—I'd offer myself—"

Madoc cuts me off with a short, humorless laugh. "That's what Orion wanted. That's what he imagined when he cast the curse—all of you falling over yourselves to prove your devotion in a way your Heart will never let you, maybe even slaughtering each other—but that won't work. You don't think he thought of that? *By your own hand*, I said. You have to do it yourself, and you can't. So that leaves me."

It takes a moment for those last words to sink in, and by then he's already leapt onto the bed. Corwin lets out a sound of warning, I spring forward—

And Madoc slashes the narrow claw he's extended from his fingertip right across his throat, as deep as it'll go.

Blood sprays from the mortal wound, raining down over Talia and the bed around her. In an instant, red stains every inch of her uncovered skin, soaking into her hair, her nightgown, and the sheets she's lying on.

Madoc's dying body crumples over her, more and more of the scarlet fluid gushing out. Astrid flinches backward and then reaches for him, stopping with her hands hovering over his shoulders, her own face splashed red. Her gaze darts to us. She doesn't know whether it's safe to move him.

I don't know either.

How—why— *He* couldn't possibly—

The blood coating Talia's skin starts to fade. It's seeping into her, I realize with a rush of horrified fascination. Her body seems to be absorbing the ruddy liquid everywhere it touched her directly.

In a matter of seconds, every speck of it has vanished from her flesh, leaving only her clothes and her hair drenched with the stuff. I take a cautious step to the side of the bed.

Then Talia's chest heaves with a rush of breath deeper than any I've heard her take in days.

27

Talia

$\mathcal{A}$ sickly meaty scent fills my nose. My lips part, and I instinctively suck in the air—tainted with that sour smell but welcome all the same. I drink in more and more of it until my lungs are full.

For the first time in days there's no pain, no stabbing or throbbing or even that faint prickle that's been with me so long. The relief hits me so hard my eyes pop open.

I'm lying on my bed in my bedroom still. I have a vague memory of long hours spent here, growing weaker, but none of that exhaustion grips me now.

My mates are standing around me, August helping Astrid move a heavy weight off of my body. Corwin leans close by my head. *My soul,* he murmurs through our bond, awed and yet anguished for reasons I can't totally decipher.

Sylas's dark eye gleams as he comes up beside my soul-twined mate. "How are you feeling?" he asks, strangely careful with the words.

The sensations coming back to my body in the absence of the weakness and agony are so overwhelming it's taking me a moment to catch up. "I'm… wet," I say, abruptly aware of the dampness sticking my nightgown to my skin. "What—what happened?"

Even as I ask, I push myself to sit up. Corwin jerks forward as if to stop me, but the movement comes so easily, without the slightest hint of the strain from the last few days, that a laugh tumbles from my mouth.

Then I see the carnage on the bed around me, and the sound dies in my throat. My jaw snaps shut.

The entire middle of my vast bed is drenched with red, all around me and on me—my clothes, my hair slipping wetly across my shoulders. With *blood*. That's what the horrible smell is.

And—the weight August and Astrid moved away from me—they're just easing a limp body off the bed and onto the floor. My gaze snags on the rumpled blond hair, then the gaping gash on the man's pale neck, and a cry bursts out of me.

"What—what did you *do* to him? He—"

"He did it to himself," Whitt breaks in, his voice tight and unreadable. "He did it to bring you back to us."

I push my hands back over my dripping hair, wincing at the feel of it. My mind scrambles to process my last fragmented memories.

I was in such a daze with the pain and the fever—I'm

not totally sure what was a dream and what was real. But I remember Madoc being here, first as a furry body tucked against my hand and then as a man sitting on the edge of the bed. I remember him talking, and August rushing in…

I shake my head as if I can argue the sight in front of me away. "I don't understand. You have to—you have to save him! Isn't there some magic you can do to heal him, or…?"

The solemn expressions on all my mates' faces make my voice falter and my stomach clench up. A different sort of pain radiates through my chest to squeeze around my heart.

No.

"It seems he finally found out the cure for your curse from his king," Sylas says quietly. "One that was meant to be impossible, to confound and torment us even more. Orion obviously never considered—" He pauses. "You needed to be covered in the life's blood of someone who loved you, who gave it themselves."

His words sink in bit by bit. My thoughts dart first to Corwin's mother, to her frantic, futile attempts to end her own life so she can follow her husband into death. My throat closes up. "None of you could have—the Heart wouldn't let—" The rest clicks in my mind with a jolt of understanding. "Then *he*—"

I can't say the words out loud. Madoc loved me. He loved me enough to give his own life to save me. Maybe he did it for his people as well, for the faith he had that I might prevent a bloodier war, but I have to assume the cure wouldn't have worked if he hadn't loved me for my own sake too.

My heart squeezes tighter. Tears prick at my eyes. "It isn't right," I say raggedly. "Isn't there anything you can do —any chance—?"

August straightens up from where he's been crouched on the floor where he and Astrid laid Madoc. I can no longer see the Murk man who's become so entwined in my emotions—and me in his, apparently—but the image of his lifeless body lingers in the back of my head.

August is frowning. "He's already gone. No one can bring someone back when the spark has already left them."

My hands grip the sheets with a sudden flare of hope. "But it *hasn't* left him, has it? You do the funeral ceremony for the Seelie who've fallen—the energy that makes their soul-stone is still in them. Something's left. If you could—"

Sylas reaches to grasp my hand. "That part is already disconnected from the body by then. No one's ever been able to reattach it. Resurrection isn't a power the Heart grants us, and likely for good reason."

He's trying to talk me down, to make me see it's impossible, but instead my mind latches on to the one piece of his statement that shows me a way forward.

The men around me are some of the most powerful fae in this world, but their magic has a source, something that fuels every shred of their power and all life in both the realms. Something that outshines all of them.

Corwin rubs my shoulder. "We should get you cleaned up, and—"

"No," I interrupt, propelled by a clang of desperate hope. I push myself to the edge of the bed, ignoring the clinging of my blood-drenched nightgown to my limbs.

Sylas and Corwin move to stop me, but I shove their hands away, my gaze darting to Madoc's sprawled body. The drained pallor of his face and the gouge through his neck make my stomach turn and only strengthen my determination.

"Bring him to the Heart," I insist, pointing at him as I get to my feet. My legs hold me without a hint of shakiness. *He* did that for me; he gave me back the life Orion almost stole from me, and I can't sit back while there's still even the slightest chance of repaying him for that sacrifice. "Carry him down there—now. Please, hurry."

My mates stare at me. "Talia," August says gently, "I don't think—"

"You don't *know*," I cut in, my voice rising. "You didn't think I could use true names or have a soul-twined bond before it turned out I could either. There's a chance. We have to try. After everything he did for me, I can't just leave him. *Please.*"

When they don't move immediately, I push past Sylas and Whitt toward Madoc's body. Whitt catches my arm. I whirl toward him, but before I can tell him off and yank myself away, he gives me a quick squeeze and moves to join me. "All right. If you feel there's a way, then we'll try. We owe him that much."

He and August heft Madoc between them, Astrid darting in to fold the Murk man's arms across his chest so they don't dangle. August supports the Murk man's head with his shoulder, but the lifeless loll of it against my mate's broad frame makes my stomach churn harder.

"Hurry," I say again, yanking the door wider open.

A few guards are standing in the hall. The ones who came with August when he first charged to my defense, I guess. They stare at me in my bloody nightgown and then at my mates emerging carrying Madoc's body. I must look like a horror, but I'm not going to waste precious minutes prettying myself up just for appearance's sake. I have no idea if this will work at all, but everything in me tells me that with each passing second, the chance is farther out of reach.

"Clear the area around the Heart," Sylas orders the guards. "Keep everyone away until I give another order."

The guards wrench their gazes to him with bobs of acknowledgment and then hustle down the hall ahead of us. August and Whitt heft Madoc along as quickly as they can, the rest of us keeping pace.

Corwin stays close by my side. "You're completely well? You don't feel any lingering effects at all?"

I have no inner walls up—he should be able to sense the painless strength flowing through me nearly as well as I can. But maybe after everything he's watched me go through, he needs that extra reassurance.

"Nothing hurts," I tell him. "I'm totally fine. Better than I felt half the time even before—"

Even before the curse. Especially right before it struck, when I was tired and sometimes dizzy or queasy from the pregnancy.

My hand drops to my belly with a fresh jab of loss. For a second, my legs wobble. Corwin grips my shoulder. "If it's too much—you haven't really had time to mourn—"

I grit my teeth and shake my head, forcing myself onward. I won't lose even more than I already have. The baby inside me had barely started to grow. The man I'm trying to save was a fully formed person with a tangled past and dreams for the future—so many dreams...

Now that I'm free of Orion's curse, there'll be many more chances to see a baby born into my new family with my mates. There'll never be another Madoc if I can't find a way to bring him back right now.

We march out on the summer side of the border and hurry toward the glowing mass of the Heart. Its energy pulses over me with the rhythm that's like an actual heartbeat. A silent plea starts to reverberate through me before we even reach it.

Please. Please. Please.

Whitt and August hesitate partway across the field around the Heart. I motion them onward. "Right up to it. Lie him down on the grass as close as you can get."

Without argument, they walk the last several paces to the edge of the border. Following them, the glow becomes so bright it stings my eyes. They set Madoc down and back up a couple of steps, giving me room to kneel beside him.

It's almost like when I found him lounging on the grass not far from here days ago, soaking up the Heart's energy the only way he could. Except then his body was full of life, and now it sags into the grass.

Blood from his wound has smeared across his shirt. I don't shy away from it, resting my hands on his chest. I stare into the pulsing light of the Heart with eyes narrowed to cut down on the glare and switch to begging out loud.

"Please. You have so much power in you. You gave me the ability to use true names even though I'm only a human, even though I was being used as a weapon against the fae of the Mists. You shone brighter for me at my mating ceremony. Can you shine for him too? He doesn't deserve to die. He did everything he could to help me—to help all of us. He wanted *peace*. Isn't that what you want too?"

The Heart simply keeps up its steady, indomitable thrum. The energy tingles into my skin, raising the hairs on my arms, but Madoc doesn't so much as twitch.

I wet my lips, searching for the right words. "He was the first Murk to find a way to work with the fae of the Mists in centuries. That should count for something. He ended my curse—his help might be the key to ending the other curses on this world. Please bring him back, so he can have a chance to do all the good he could have done. So he doesn't have to lose everything just so I could live. *Please*."

I put all the force I can into that last word. My throat feels raw.

But nothing changes. The Heart beats on, with no more sign that it's heard me than it's ever given before. No sign that it makes any difference to it that I'm begging it on my knees in a nightgown drenched in this man's blood, wrenched back from the edge of death by his sacrifice.

A surge of anger fills me, so swift and sudden it overwhelms everything else.

I push myself to my feet, my hands clenching. I must look absurd in my gruesome clothes and blood-stained hair, but I don't give a damn. I just want the impenetrable mass of magic in front of me to *listen*. The words spill out faster and harsher than even I was prepared for.

"How the hell can you call yourself a Heart? Don't you care about anything? You cared enough to take away the Murk's magic over something as small as a lie here and there. *That* was important enough to punish them and their children and their children's children, but everything Madoc has done isn't enough to make him worth saving? Maybe we should all turn to the Heart that the Murk made if you're so vindictive."

A hand comes to rest on my back. "Talia," Sylas says softly, and I can feel Corwin monitoring me closely through our bond, grieving with me but anxious for me at the same time.

"No," I say to them, and turn back to the Heart. "It should hear this. Everyone around here is always talking about 'the Heart' this and 'the Heart' that as if it's such a wonderful thing, but it's been horrible to some of its people too." I jab my finger at it. "The Murk *are* your people; *you* gave them whatever magic they started with and made them fae, and then you took it away, and somehow it's *their* fault they got bitter and resentful? I don't think it's that simple."

I drop my hand to motion to Madoc. "This man rose above all that resentment. He saw that things could be better, that his people might be able to live happier lives without having to ruin anyone else's. All he wanted was a home for himself and the fae like him. You promised them that when you brought them into existence, and it's about time you did something to help them get it. If you could believe in me, then there's no reason at all you can't believe in him too."

My anger starts to deflate. I swallow hard, staring into the glow again. "He believed in you," I add, my voice rough now. "Didn't you see him coming out here just to be near you? He believed in *you*. He wanted to come back to you. You know he did. That should count for something."

I sink back to the grass next to Madoc, my head drooping. I lean over him, letting my face come to rest against his motionless chest. My eyes squeeze shut against a renewed burn of tears.

It wasn't good enough. I couldn't figure out the right words, the right angle—I couldn't call on all that power. How could I have thought I would? I must look so pathetic, even deranged...

But I'd do it again. I'd do it over and over if I thought there was any chance it'd work.

That thought has only just crossed my mind when a sharper glow flares through my eyelids. I jerk upright into a wave of light that's washing over the field and all of us in it. For a few seconds, my vision is only white.

The Heart's glow contracts in on itself again. I blink

away the blotchy afterimages left in my vision—and hear a faint rasp below me.

My gaze snaps to Madoc. To the slight hitch of his chest as if with a breath. To his neck—

The gash in his throat is gone. The pale skin has sealed over as if it was never torn. His eyes have closed and his lips parted.

When I hover my hand over his mouth, a wisp of an exhalation grazes my hand.

My own heart thumps so hard with joy I think it might burst out of my chest. I grip Madoc's hand and tip my face toward the Heart of the Mists, the tears that prick at my eyes now only grateful. "Thank you."

My mates gather closer around us. Whitt lets out a low, awed whistle. "You do know how to get things done, don't you, mighty one?"

Pride flows from Corwin into me, although with a twinge of hesitation.

When I glance at him, puzzled, he crouches down next to me. For a moment, we both consider the still-unconscious Murk man, watching the rise and fall of his miraculous breaths.

"You spoke well for him," my soul-twined mate says. "For all of the Murk, but especially him."

"I had to," I say automatically.

"I know. Because you love him too."

I twist toward him, my gut lurching. The truth of his words rings through me, but at the same time, I can't bear that he—that any of my men—would think I'd betray them. "I love *you*. All of you. I—anything else I feel doesn't change that at all. You're my mates, and I'd never let anything threaten our bond."

"We know you wouldn't, Sweetness," August says, resting his hand on the top of my head.

Corwin nods. "I don't bring it up as an accusation. I —" His mouth twists, and he inhales deeply before going on. "Three rabid wolf shifters once agreed to share their beloved with a chilly raven. How can I accept that kind of generosity and not extend it in return when it's so earned?"

I blink at him, hardly daring to breathe myself. "What are you saying?"

His affection streams through our connection as he smiles back at me, enveloping me with tender, accepting warmth. "He's proven his love for you. I can feel how much he matters to you. If there's room for five in your heart, I won't ask you to hold back."

He glances at my Seelie mates, and I follow his gaze, not knowing what to say.

Whitt lets out a chuckle and shakes his head, his expression uncertain but his eyes gleaming when they meet mine. "A rat shifter. I wouldn't have thought. But then, there was once a stuffy Unseelie who managed to welcome not one but three feral wolves as his soul-twined mate's paramours, so I'd be an awful hypocrite if I balked, wouldn't I?"

Corwin's lips twitch into a wider smile. I catch Sylas's gaze next. His mismatched eyes contemplate me for a long moment.

"I think we all owe Madoc an apology," he says. "We thought the worst of him so many times when you saw the truth. I've never denied you the right to follow your heart, my love, and I'm not going to start now. We can make it work."

August brushes aside my damp hair and kisses my temple. "He was willing to die to protect you. I wouldn't argue with that kind of devotion."

I thought… I thought I had to carve out that part of my emotions and set it aside. But they see—they understand—

I can't kid myself that it's going to be easy. The wariness and the knee-jerk distrust aren't going to completely vanish in an instant. But they're willing to embrace Madoc's role in my life—to welcome him into the makeshift family we've been forming.

A smile splits my face, so wide my cheeks ache with it. "I love you," I say again, choked up, to all of them.

28

Talia

The next time I walk into my bedroom, it's clear that a lot of magic has been worked there. No trace of blood remains on the sheets or in the air. The only sign of how much has changed is how normal I feel—and the presence of the man lying on one side of the expansive bed.

Madoc is still unconscious but breathing more steadily than when I left him in my mates' care to get myself cleaned off. They agreed that my room was a reasonable place to let him rest and recover from the ordeal his body has been through.

With his blood-splashed shirt removed, the daylight streaming through the window catches on the toned planes of his bare chest, highlighting the stark lines of the scars that mottle his skin. I feel a little strange seeing him partly undressed, but then, I saw him in nothing but boxers when we showered in the Refuge, so maybe he wouldn't mind.

I've spent a lot of time lying in this bed in the past several days, but after my stand-off with the Heart and going out to offer tears to the winter fae who were waiting for me, one of them nearly totally frozen, I could use a little rest myself. My mates are conferring with the other arch-lords about how to best proceed with the conflict with the Murk now that destroying their Heart isn't quite so urgent. I won't be needed anywhere else for at least a little while.

And I'd like to be with Madoc when he wakes up.

I climb onto the bed and lie down on the other side, leaving enough space between us that I could only just graze his shoulder with my fingertips if I stretched my arm out straight. For a few minutes, I watch the rise and fall of the Murk man's chest, take in the softening of his face in a deeper state of relaxation than I've ever witnessed before. How will he feel about what I've done?

I don't really know, but I can't regret my decision to do whatever I could to save him.

After a little while, I drift off into a more peaceful doze than I've gotten to experience since the curse dug its claws into me. I'm drifting in a serene, dreamless current when the movement of the body next to me jerks me back into full awareness.

Madoc is blinking, his arms flexing at his sides. He stares at the ceiling and then raises his hands to stare at them too. His expression shows total bewilderment.

I sit up, tucking my legs close beneath the simple dress

I put on after I got cleaned up. The Murk man's gaze snaps to me. He looks dazed, as if he wasn't totally woken up yet. Maybe he isn't sure that he really has.

"It worked," I say, figuring that's what he'd want to know first. "Your cure. As far as I can tell, the curse is gone. I can't feel its effects at all."

Madoc blinks at me, his eyes slowly clearing, a crease forming in his brow. He sits up too—quickly at first and then slowing, wobbling and catching his balance when he must realize he isn't totally recovered. He pushes himself the rest of the way up carefully and touches his neck, the place where the flesh was slashed through. Not even a tiny scar remains.

"Then how— I was supposed to *die* for the cure to work," he says, and I'm weirdly relieved to hear that the Heart's touch hasn't smoothed out the familiar hoarseness in his voice. "'The life's blood,' he said, and—it should have…"

He looks at me, a clashing interplay of emotions crossing his face, as if he's relieved and unsettled, pleased and concerned, all at the same time.

"It did," I say. "Kill you. But I—I wasn't willing to accept that ending." My mouth twists into an awkward smile. "I asked my mates to bring you in front of the Heart, and I pleaded with it to heal you. And then I yelled at it for a while too. I'm not totally sure which part worked. Maybe it was both together. But one way or another, it did listen in the end, which is what matters."

Madoc's eyes widen even more. "The Heart—" His gaze jerks to the window, and his hand flies to the spot on his chest over his own heart. He breathes in and out, and every other emotion on his face falls away in the wake of a rush of awe. "I can *feel* it. Inside. The magic, the energy—I could—"

He halts abruptly and murmurs what sounds like a true name. A gleaming metal ball the size of a marble forms on his palm. He studies it for a long moment and then meets my eyes again, something startled but elated shining in his gray ones. "You brought me back to it. You—"

His voice falters. He seems to focus onward, his gaze going distant. His throat bobs. "I can't feel Orion's Heart at all now. My connection must have severed when I died, and the Heart of the Mists filled it in."

I don't know if I should apologize for that. "I didn't know how it would happen," I say quietly. "I didn't know if it would work at all. I just couldn't give up after... after everything."

A moment of silence stretches between us. Madoc looks down at his hands and then back at me. His jaw works. "You know, don't you? They told you the conditions of the cure, why the rest of them couldn't have — Why it had to be me."

He sounds oddly nervous, as if he's braced for some kind of rejection. As if he thinks I'd have brought him back from the dead mainly to tell him he didn't stand a chance of winning my heart.

Even if my mates hadn't given their blessing, even if I'd been going to bury these feelings down and accept that I was lucky enough as it was, I think I'd have told him. He'd have deserved to know even then.

"They did," I say. "But it still means a lot—even if you were the only one who *could* do it, you didn't have to. You could have let me go."

"No," Madoc says immediately, "I couldn't have."

The corner of my mouth curls upward, an ache of affection forming at the base of my throat. "I still have to thank you. There aren't enough words to thank you. And in case it wasn't obvious from the fact that I scolded the Heart of the Mists into bringing you back to life, I love you too."

Apparently it wasn't obvious after all. Madoc stares at me even harder for a beat. His voice comes out ragged, strained yet full of so much longing it tugs at my heart. "Talia…" He shakes himself. "I know how you feel about your mates—I wasn't expecting anything. I mean, I expected to die." He laughs roughly. "And that's fine. Even that would have been enough."

I reach across the covers and wrap my fingers around his hand. "I think you and my mates have a lot of talking to do to understand each other better. But they recognize the sacrifice you made—they respect it. There won't be any more questions about your loyalty. And they've managed to accept each other's place in my life. They're willing to accept you too. I didn't even have to *ask*. They took it upon themselves to inform me that you were welcome into the family."

My lips twitch with a wider smile, but Madoc seems lost for words. He opens his mouth and closes it again, his brow furrowing. His gaze searches mine. "You're saying…"

"I'm saying this castle has plenty of space, and everyone's agreed there's room for one more mate in it." I hesitate, my stomach abruptly sinking. "I mean, if *you'd* want that. I know it's not what most of the fae would typically hope for—to be sharing their mate. I know everything has been complicated, and you haven't gotten a great welcome here to begin with. If you couldn't see yourself in that kind of arrangement, of course I'd understa—"

Madoc's fingers tighten around mine, and he hefts himself closer to me, close enough to bring his other hand to the side of my face and rest his forehead against mine. "Talia," he breathes, "I'd take any amount of you over none at all. I'm only having trouble wrapping my head around the fact that you'd want *me*."

Oh. I raise my hand to his cheek and trail my fingers along it to his jaw and then down his neck, feeling the thump of his pulse. His chest hitches at the contact. All at once I want to touch that too, the taut ridges of muscle all the way down to the waist of his jeans.

"You're brave and generous and one of the most honorable of the fae I've ever met," I tell him. "Even when it's hard. Even when it means going against things you've always believed. You have the same kind of dreams I do, and I've seen how far you'll go to see them through—for everyone who matters to you, not just yourself. So don't sell yourself short."

He swallows audibly and nuzzles my forehead. "And

you're my bright one, my light in the darkness," he says, barely more than a whisper, and then his head is dipping and mine is rising, and somewhere in the middle our lips collide.

The kiss feels like being caught in a thunderstorm, electric and wild, a flood of heat washing over my skin. Madoc makes a noise low in his throat and pulls me closer. I wrap my arm around his neck and tease my fingers into his hair, my other hand tracing down his naked chest the way I imagined a few minutes ago. My fingertips skip over the tiny indents and ridges where the scars cross his otherwise smooth skin, but I don't shy away from them. They're a testament to the trials this man has been through to make it to this moment with me.

More desire than I realized I was holding in rushes up through me, filling me to the brim. We kiss and kiss again, until I can't tell where each ends and the next begins. Hard, soft, urgent, and lingering, flowing into each other one after another.

It isn't long before I'm breathless, clinging to him, wanting more. Wanting to get as close as I can to this man who literally split himself open for me and yet somehow still can't see himself as a hero.

Madoc pulls back, but not far. A noise of protest forms in the back of my mouth, but the hunger in his eyes stops me from voicing it. He's not done. He just rests his hands on the skirt of my dress in question. "I want to see you."

I nod and lift my arms and my hips. With a ragged inhalation, Madoc lifts the smooth fabric up over my head and sets it aside. His gaze roves over me, nothing but adoration in it, and any self-consciousness I might have felt flees.

"So beautiful," he murmurs. "My fierce little fighter. *Mine.*" He lingers on the word as if testing it out, and a smile tugs at his lips.

Holding my gaze, he brings his hand to my breast, cupping it and then slowly sweeping his thumb across the peak. At the jolt of pleasure, my nipple pebbles instantly. He swivels his thumb over it again, sending more sparks shooting through me until a gasp slips out of me and my head tips back, my body swaying into the caress.

He growls and tips me back on the bed, kissing the crook of my jaw and then down my neck with gentle nibbles here and there. "You have no idea how many times I imagined doing this. It's like a miracle getting to touch you for real. It's a miracle I'm here at all." A chuckle tumbles from his mouth with a wash of breath. "The one woman who could boss around the Heart of the Mists."

I make an impatient sound, my fingers curling into his hair, and he drops his head lower to suck my unattended nipple into the heat of his mouth. At the flick of his tongue, I whimper, my fingers digging tighter. I trail my other hand over his shoulder and arm, caressing every inch of skin I can reach as he worships mine.

He dips lower, kissing his way down my sternum and across my abdomen. When he reaches the spot just below my belly button, he pauses and presses his most tender kiss yet there. He glances up at me, sorrow momentarily overcoming the desire in his expression.

"There will be more," he says, as if he can conjure the

future he's talking about into being like a spell. "A wolf and a raven both. I know the Heart will shine on you."

A pang fills my chest at both my loss and the way he's left himself out, even now. I stroke my fingers down the side of his face. "One of each then. A wolf, a raven, and a rat."

His stormy eyes flare, and all at once he's rising back over me, claiming my mouth so passionately that every nerve in my body quivers with delight. His fingers hook around my panties, and I grope at his jeans. The knot of longing swelling in my core turns desperate with the need to be fulfilled.

As Madoc kicks off his jeans and boxers, a tremor runs through his arms where they're supporting his weight. He did die just a few hours ago—he isn't quite back to his usual strength. But he simply sinks onto his side and rolls me toward him, enveloping me in his embrace and capturing my lips with another kiss.

I reach between us and wrap my fingers around his shaft. It presses rigidly into my palm, so hard the sensation is giddying.

Madoc groans and kisses me harder, guiding my thigh up over his at the same time to spread me open. I tuck myself closer to him with a whimper when he grazes the head of his erection over my opening.

"So many things I want to do with you when I have all my strength back," he mutters. "But this is more than enough for now."

I arch toward him, and he sinks into me, slow and steady. Another gasp ripples up my throat. He grasps my hip, angling me to receive his next thrust with an even headier burst of bliss. His other hand closes over my breast. His mouth drinks in my whimpers and moans.

And something else, like a silky finger, traces over my bowed back, across my bottom, and down the back of my thigh.

My muscles twitch in surprise, and Madoc pauses. His tail sweeps up to stroke across my upper arm like a fifth limb. "I can stay totally human-like," he says, watching my expression, "if you'd prefer it that way. There's just… more I can do with more of me to work with."

A sly gleam comes into his eyes, but I can recognize the wariness there too. The fear of rejection he's still grappling with—and why not, after how the fae I've allied myself with have treated him because of what he is?

I rest my hand against his cheek, gazing back at him. "I want to enjoy every part of you."

That's clearly the right answer, because Madoc dives in for another kiss. His fingers massage my hip in time with the building rhythm of his thrusts inside me, and his tail drifts down my back again.

When it dips, carefully, to tease across my other opening, the tingling pleasure brings a fresh gasp to my lips. I kiss him harder, in case there's any doubt about me enjoying *that*, and he starts to stroke up and down across that sensitive area in time with the rocking of his hips.

Bliss is radiating through every bit of my body now. It builds in an expanding rush. I'm awash with the giddy burn between my legs, the shivers of delight as Madoc fondles my breast, the deepening tingles with each caress of his tail, and his tongue twining with mine to draw out a moan.

When I start to tremble, he picks up the pace just a little, just enough to send me spiraling right over the edge.

I cry out and clutch onto him as if I'll soar away completely if I don't hold on. Madoc groans and buries himself even deeper inside me, shuddering with his own release. He kisses me and kisses me again, murmuring gentle sounds that aren't quite words, hugging me close against him.

I hug him back, the joyful ache inside me spreading until it fills me completely, as if I'd been missing something up until this moment and now I've finally found that lost piece.

29

Talia

I wish that we could lie amid the sheets and cuddle and continue exploring each other's bodies for hours more, then welcome my other mates into the bed and see what kind of unity we could start to build between us all there. But there's still a war looming over us. My interlude with Madoc was only a brief escape, a luxury I start to feel guilty about after we've sprawled a little longer in the bed.

"Are you feeling well enough to get up and walk around?" I ask, kissing Madoc's cheek. "We should see where my mates are with their plans—and they'll want to speak with you." Corwin has kept himself at a distance so their discussions didn't intrude on my rest... and everything else... but I know he's aware that the Murk man woke up.

Madoc lets out a tense guffaw. "Somehow I don't think

it's the walking that's going to be the biggest challenge." But when he gazes into my eyes, his expression softens. "There is a lot we need to discuss, and not just about you."

I reach out to my soul-twined mate enough for him to recognize my intent. *We're just finishing up a talk with the other arch-lords*, he says through our bond as I ease back into my clothes. *We'll meet you downstairs in a few minutes.*

Madoc, of course, doesn't have any shirt at all, so I dig one out of the closet in Whitt's bedroom, since he's the best match for the rat shifter's build. Madoc eyes the silky collared tunic skeptically but accepts it, probably preferring to feel a little over-dressed than to have this conversation with the other men while half-naked.

I feel it when Corwin enters the castle alongside the others, his mood apprehensive and yet hopeful. With equal wariness, Madoc follows me downstairs to the sitting room where my mates have gathered. A nervous twinge races through my own gut.

My mates accepted the role Madoc could play in *my* life, but how easy is it going to be for him to fit in here among the fae of the Mists overall? In the rush of relief and released emotion, we haven't even talked about how he'd like the future to look.

Is he going to stay here with us? *Could* he even go back to so much as visit his people if he wanted to?

How long will it take for Orion to realize what's happened and send out a call for his no-longer-loyal knight's death? How will the other arch-lords react to Madoc's continued presence among us?

What if I've saved him only to lose him all over again?

As we step into the sitting room, I force myself to shove those worries to the side. We have to deal with one thing at a time. None of the rest matters if even my mates balk now that the Murk man is standing in front of them again.

Madoc stops just inside the doorway, and I halt alongside him. My other men have dispersed through the room. Whitt is leaning against the arm of a nearby sofa, his eyebrows arching slightly when he catches sight of Madoc's borrowed shirt. Corwin sits at the other end of that sofa near him. Sylas has been pacing by the window, but he stops and turns toward us at our entrance. And August is standing behind one of the armchairs, his elbows braced against the top of its upholstered frame.

The apprehension I sensed from Corwin permeates the entire room. No one speaks, the four pairs of eyes settling on Madoc, no doubt noting how close we're standing to each other and the new familiarity in that closeness.

I can't bear to let the silence stretch for long. I made my choices, I feel what I feel, and now I have to own all of it.

I reach up to touch Madoc's cheek. When he leans his head toward me, I bob up to give him a soft kiss. His posture goes rigid, but he kisses me back, his hand rising to my shoulder. I remember the day when I went to hug him and how he tensed up then.

It really wasn't a rejection of me. He must have been as nervous of the reactions my gesture would provoke as he is now.

A flicker of possessive resistance carries through my

connection with Corwin, but I can't say it's any worse than similar feelings he had toward my Seelie men. And this moment isn't just about Madoc. It's about all of them.

I go to Whitt next, trailing my fingers along his neck and seeking his kiss. His lips twitch with one of his sly smiles, and he indulges me with a pleased hum.

From him I step toward Corwin, bending over him on the sofa and brushing my lips to his from above. My soul-twined mate sets a steadying hand on my waist, tender fondness rushing from him into me. *You don't have to prove anything.*

I just thought I should set the right tone for this conversation from the start.

When I ease back from him, there's a faint gleam of amusement in his eyes. *I suppose there's something to be said for that strategy.*

Having watched my progression through the room, Sylas moves forward to meet me next to the sofa. As he claims my mouth, he strokes his hand over my hair, his massive presence sheltering me as he always has.

August has straightened up by the chair. His mouth twists with a bittersweet expression before he gives me a quick kiss and wraps me in a hug. The tension in the flex of his muscles around me tells me he's still not quite over the horror of my own near death.

Madoc has tracked my circuit of the room without comment or complaint, but he still looks a little uncertain as I return to him. I tuck my hand around his, feeling he needs the extra support.

I meant to say something, but before I can decide on

what, August strides forward. He stops a few paces from Madoc and clears his throat.

"I'm sorry," he says. "I thought the worst of you more than once—I almost stopped you from saving her." The anguish of that knowledge rings through his voice.

Madoc relaxes just a tad beside me. One corner of his mouth ticks upward. "To be fair, I was standing over her with a knife. I can understand that it didn't make the most innocent-looking picture."

"Talia knew you weren't going to hurt her," August goes on. "I trust her judgment, and I should have trusted her more about you."

Sylas nods. "I believe we all should have. It was an immense sacrifice, what you offered—one none of us could have made, as much as we might have wished to. Even with Talia's efforts to bring you back… I assume you won't be able to return to your home and your king now."

Madoc's jaw tightens. "No. As soon as Orion hears that Talia's curse has been cured—if he even needs to hear it, if he didn't sense it through his magic the moment it happened—he'll realize what happened, and I won't be remotely welcome there if I want to keep this second chance at staying alive."

He pauses and then inhales sharply. "I should tell you —the ambush in the fringelands—it was partly my fault. Accidentally, but all the same… I said too much to Orion in an earlier report, enough for him to guess that you'd take the tactic of coming to a portal close to his Heart and to prepare for your arrival. If I'd known—you can be sure I'd never have led Talia into that trap."

"The rest of us, though…" Whitt says in a dry tone, and holds up his hands when Madoc's and my eyes jerk to him. "A joke! There's been distrust and animosity on both sides, and I don't think it helps anything to keep score. The question is where we go from here."

He glances at Corwin, who pushes himself to the edge of his seat with increased alertness.

"The ambush did serve us well in one way," the Unseelie arch-lord says. "You brought us to an area with a portal that leads to your Refuge's true location. I was able to spot which portal one of our attackers traveled through. Even without your guidance, we could march on the Refuge now. But… we'd stand a better chance of surviving that battle *with* your guidance. And of saving those of the Murk who'd be willing to survive alongside us and forge some kind of peace."

"*You're* willing to believe that the Murk could live in the Mists with you peacefully?" Madoc asks in a challenging tone.

Corwin stares right back at him, unshaken. "I think you've provided ample proof that we've let prejudice sour relations between our peoples beyond the point of reason. Unless *you* don't believe it's possible, I'm willing to give a chance to anyone who wants it."

Madoc's gaze shifts from him to Sylas. "And what about your other rulers? How are they going to feel about bargaining with the rats?"

"That's something we've already been discussing with them, in light of recent events," Sylas says. "I won't lie and say there isn't hesitation—I'd imagine we're all going to find adjusting our attitudes difficult, on both sides—but we can find a way through. It'll be easier if you'll come and speak with them. Perhaps with Talia by your side as she is now." He shoots me one of his small, soft smiles that never fails to make my heart flutter.

Madoc stirs on his feet uneasily. I squeeze his hand. "The Heart itself accepted you and decided you were worthy of taking as its own," I remind him. "They'll have a hard time arguing with that."

He looks down at me and lets out a short chuckle. "And even the Heart didn't dare argue with you." The affection that gleams in his eyes provokes another flutter.

Then he looks toward the window. "I—there's a lot I need to think through. I want this conflict settled with as few people dying as possible, and I want a home here for the Murk without persecution or being relegated to the fringes… and I need to be sure *all* of your people are on board with that idea and not looking for a chance to strike us when we let our guards down. But I can see there's a chance, and that's enough to make it worth trying. If I could take a moment—I'd like to go out to the Heart. I think I owe it plenty of gratitude too."

Sylas inclines his head. "You've been through a lot and had your life completely upended. I can't demand that you know exactly what to make of your new circumstances in an instant."

For the first time, I feel Madoc totally relax, as if he's finally letting go of the anticipation of a potential attack. "Thank you," he says quietly but earnestly.

We all walk with him to the entrance and out into the

summer air. Madoc's pace quickens when the Heart is in sight and then slows as he comes right up to its immense, pulsing glow. He looks up at it with its pure light washing over his body, as if searching for answers in its thrumming energy the way I did once.

I'm not sure if he finds any, but after a few minutes, he closes his eyes. A soft smile curves his lips.

An ache forms in my chest, knowing how much he's missed this connection and how long it's been since he last got the chance to truly experience it. Now he's reveling in it in a way he never had the chance to before.

We've all lost a lot—him, me, my mates… Everyone. But we've gained things too. We've found trust and understanding, friendship and love.

Will it be enough to overcome Orion's sadistic madness? None of us can really know. But Madoc is right. There's a chance, and that's all we need.

Madoc is just stepping back from the bright center of the Heart when a wolf comes sprinting across the field toward us. As the six of us turn to face him, a raven dives through the border haze at the same moment.

Both messengers transform almost simultaneously, the wolf looking to the Sylas and the raven to Corwin, their faces wearing matching expressions of panic. My body tenses before they even speak.

The wolf sputters his words out first. "My lord—the Murk have come. They're invading the Mists."

ABOUT THE AUTHOR

Eva Chase lives in Canada with her family. She loves stories both swoony and supernatural, and strong women and the men who appreciate them. Along with the Bound to the Fae series, she is the author of the Flirting with Monsters series, the Cursed Studies trilogy, the Royals of Villain Academy series, the Moriarty's Men series, the Looking Glass Curse trilogy, the Their Dark Valkyrie series, the Witch's Consorts series, the Dragon Shifter's Mates series, the Demons of Fame Romance series, the Legends Reborn trilogy, and the Alpha Project Psychic Romance series.

Connect with Eva online:
www.evachase.com
eva@evachase.com